TRIAL & RETRIBUTION III

LYNDA LA PLANTE was born in Liverpool. She trained for the stage at RADA, and work with the National Theatre and RSC led to a career as a television actress. She turned to writing – and made her breakthrough with the phenomenally successful TV series *Widows*.

Her six subsequent novels, *The Legacy*, *Bella Mafia*, *Entwined*, *Cold Shoulder*, *Cold Blood* and *Cold Heart* were all international bestsellers and her original script for the much acclaimed *Prime Suspect* won a BAFTA, British Broadcasting award, Royal Television Society Writers award and the 1993 Edgar Allan Poe Writers award.

Lynda La Plante also received the Contribution to the Media award by Women in Film, a BAFTA and Emmy for the drama serial *Prime Suspect 3*, and most recently she has been made an honorary fellow of the British Film Institute.

LYNDA LA PLANTE

TRIAL &
RETRIBUTION
III

PAN BOOKS

First published 1999 by Pan Books
an imprint of Macmillan Publishers Ltd
25 Eccleston Place, London SW1W 9NF
Basingstoke and Oxford
Associated companies throughout the world
www.macmillan.co.uk

ISBN 0 330 39250 6

Copyright © Lynda La Plante 1999

The right of Lynda La Plante to be identified as the
author of this work has been asserted by her in accordance
with the Copyright, Designs and Patents Act 1988.

All rights reserved. No part of this publication may be
reproduced, stored in or introduced into a retrieval system, or
transmitted, in any form, or by any means (electronic, mechanical,
photocopying, recording or otherwise) without the prior written
permission of the publisher. Any person who does any unauthorized
act in relation to this publication may be liable to criminal
prosecution and civil claims for damages.

1 3 5 7 9 8 6 4 2

A CIP catalogue record for this book is available from
the British Library.

Typeset by SetSystems Ltd, Saffron Walden, Essex
Printed and bound in Great Britain by
Mackays of Chatham plc, Chatham, Kent

This book is sold subject to the condition that it shall not,
by way of trade or otherwise, be lent, re-sold, hired out,
or otherwise circulated without the publisher's prior consent
in any form of binding or cover other than that in which
it is published and without a similar condition including this
condition being imposed on the subsequent purchaser.

This book is dedicated to someone I respect and admire. Someone who has guided me through many trials and retributions. Stephen Ross is not only a trusted advisor but a true and stalwart friend.

ACKNOWLEDGEMENTS

THERE isn't an actor in *Trial and Retribution III* who didn't give a performance of the highest quality. I am especially indebted to the leading artists whose talent and friendship I value greatly. Thank you David Hayman, Kate Buffery, Simon Callow, David Fleeshman, and to the guest stars Richard E. Grant, Anthony Higgins, and Frances Tomelty, for their talent, professional contribution and dedication to the series, which made it a very special show to work on.

Special thanks to our team of advisors: Jackie Malton, Dr Liz Wilson at the Forensic Science Laboratory, Dr Ian Hill at Guy's Hospital.

To the talented and dedicated crew led by director Jo Johnson, and supported by the peerless skills of executive producer Peter Richardson. To Susie Tullett and Georgina Weatherill and all at JAC.

To Nick Elliott, Jenny Reeks and David Liddiment at the ITV Network Centre for making it all possible.

Sincere thanks to David Martin-Sperry for all his hard work and his awesome legal mind.

Thanks to my literary agent Gill Coleridge, and to Ian Chapman, Suzanne Baboneau, and Philippa McEwan at Macmillan.

Thanks to Stephen Ross and Andrew Bennet-Smith, George Brooks, Julie Phelps, and all at Ross, Bennet-Smith.

Many thanks to Sue Rodgers and Duncan Heath at ICM, my agents and friends.

Special thanks to Julia Palca, Mark Devereux and Anita Cushion at Olswang for all their advice and hard work.

I would like to take this opportunity to thank a special group of people, the La Plante Productions team, led by associate producer and chief executive of LPP, the indomitable Liz Thorburn, Alice Asquith, researcher, and Nikki Smith, script editor.

I would like to sincerely thank the following for all their generosity and assistance:

Jean Wit of the Manic Depression Fellowship, Peter Grand and the members of the Orpington Manic Depression Fellowship group, Kate Woodward and Mike Cobb at Central Area Metropolitan Police Press Office, Sue Warr and Inspector Stephen Skinner at Kilburn ID Suite, Detective Superintendent Richard Bell and Detective Sergeant Duncan Hamon at Nightingale Lane Police Station, Marc Berners at Essex Police, Liz Justice, Professor Brice Pitt at Hammersmith Hospital, Inspector Paul Holmes of the Clubs and Vice Unit at Charing Cross Police Station, Maureen Evans at the Old Bailey, Peter Farr at the Lord Chancellor's Department Press Office, PC John Gay and Sergeant Aidan Gillett of the Metropolitan Police dive team.

I would like to give my sincere thanks to the talented writer Robin Blake for his care and skill in adapting the film of *Trial and Retribution III*.

CHAPTER 1

TUESDAY, 6 APRIL

CASSIE BOOTH loved her paper round. Most of the kids she knew, the ones of her own age, had already given up the chore, passing the torch gratefully on to the next generation, the twelve- and thirteen-year-olds. Getting up at half-past six was no joke in your mid-teens. You need your sleep, what with hormones and GCSEs, and anyway the couple of quid you got from old Mrs Singh, or young Mr Patel, wouldn't buy so much as a new lipstick or a Cinzano mixer and ten ciggies. But Cassie wasn't a typical fifteen-year-old. She hardly ever smoked or drank and she actually enjoyed the early-morning air on her flawless, make-up-free face as she cycled around the neighbourhood, her canvas delivery bag stuffed full. She was reckoned to be good at it, too. One thing she had learned was that people were highly particular about which papers and magazines they received. She knew how vital it was for the *Mail* not to be mistaken for the *Express* or the *Times* for the *Guardian*. As for the part-works, well, deliver the wrong one and see what you got from the householder next day. Once Cassie had mixed up Mr Beasley's *Horrors of the Third Reich* with Mrs Greenway's *Complete Embroidery Made Easy*. She'd never done it again.

1

This morning Cassie whistled as her bike flew between the neat houses of Primrose Road SW18, with their privet hedges, carefully crimped lawns and diamond-pattern leaded casements. Her blonde hair waved behind her in a pony-tail as she sprang from her bike, jammed the folded account of the latest disasters, wars, mayhem and murder (one *Telegraph*, one *Mail*) on to a brass letter-slot, vaulted onto the saddle and freewheeled back to the road. At the corner of her eye she noticed a maroon car drawing up on the other side. She knew next to nothing about cars and couldn't have told you it was a Ford Mondeo (which it was) even if she had paid it any particular attention. She just made sure it had stopped moving before she guided the bike out through the gate and on to the road.

Mrs Greenway was her next port of call, six houses along. Apart from *Complete Embroidery*, which came on Thursdays, this little pensioner took only the *Express* and Cassie checked with her left hand that it was ready in her bag for a quick delivery.

Four yards before Mrs Greenway's gate, Cassie braked hard and came to a halt at the gate itself. She left the bike and darted up the short path with the paper, oblivious of the maroon Mondeo as it pulled gently back into the road and idled along behind her, the engine subdued and almost stalling.

Still wearing her dressing-gown and slippers, and shuffling cautiously down the stairs, gripping the banister rail in her left hand, Mrs Greenway had heard the squeak of the cycle's brakes outside the gate. That papergirl was punctual, you could say that for her. Seven fifteen, give or take a minute or two. If the old lady hurried herself, she could reach the front door before Cassie pushed the paper through. Pretty, fresh little thing she was, always smiling. It did Mrs Greenway good in the morning just to exchange a greeting.

She opened the door just as Cassie was about to post the furled tabloid.

'Hello, Mrs G.,' said Cassie gaily.

'Hello, dearie. Lovely morning.'

'Isn't it? See you tomorrow.'

And then she was gone, back down the path and through the gate flanked by its hedges.

The old woman paused in the doorway. She would have to stoop to pick up the milk which she knew must already be standing beside the step. With her rheumatism (not to mention her eyesight) this could be tricky, so she waited a moment, scanning the newspaper headline: NATO JETS BLAST BELGRADE. She tut-tutted silently to herself. Old enough to remember the Luftwaffe's nocturnal visits to London, she knew about bombing and didn't consider this Serbian affair to be a war proper. It was just murder, really. The fact that the other side were murderers, too, made no difference. She just wished someone would give her the facts in words that were easy to understand. She would have liked to know what it was all about.

Mrs Greenway could have told you what she did know, however. People downgraded murder these days. They thought it didn't matter. That was a fact.

She bent at last to retrieve the bottle of milk. As she did so, she heard an abrupt screech of rubber: not the girl's bike this time but the harsher, angrier rasp of a car's tyres. A moment later, as she straightened up with the bottle firmly grasped in her wrinkled hand, there came a shuffling sound and the clunk of a car door. Mrs Greenway's head turned this way and that, scanning the area in front of her house – the path, the hedge. Suddenly there was the car itself, in the centre of her vision, gliding past the gate. It was dark red – maroon, if you like. The light was reflecting off the side window but she could make out the head of the driver, half-turned towards her and apparently paying attention to the rear-view mirror. Picking her way carefully, she made her way down the path towards the gate.

She found the bike lying on its side on the flagstones, the wheels spinning slowly and ticking as they turned. Peering up and down the street, she could find no sign of the pretty papergirl. Just the back end of the maroon car as it negotiated the corner at the end of Primrose Road.

At two thirty-three on that same Tuesday, after making a series of calls at the instigation of Detective Sergeant Pete Barrow, Detective Constable Ian Dawes hung up the phone.

'We've contacted all the local hospitals and TSG have completed house-to-house inquiries,' he told Barrow. They were sitting at their work stations in the CID office of Southfields police station (though it prefers to be known nowadays as a Crime Management Unit), where the initial missing-person report had come through at seven thirty. All morning long the inquiry had built up an impressive momentum, news of it spreading throughout the station until even the canteen staff were speculating. A pretty young schoolgirl had disappeared in the middle of her paper round. So what did it amount to? Abduction? Elopement? Or just a runner?

Barrow, a powerful, handsome, thirtyish man, was shuffling through a sheaf of witness statements. A cup of coffee stood cooling beside it. He had been on duty just half an hour but he knew already he had a long shift ahead of him.

'Has her mother got any thoughts on where she might have gone or who she might be with?'

'No,' said Dawes. 'And she's frantic. We've talked to the newsagent. None of the other delivery kids saw her after she picked up her papers at seven a.m. Pilling and Wilson are over at the school now, talking to her friends.'

Barrow squared off the bundle of statements on his desk and studied the incident report which lay on top of them.

'She's what, fifteen? Ask about boyfriends?'

'Yeah. No boyfriends.'

Barrow sighed and shook his head. Dawes leaned over and tapped his index finger on a name on the form.

'Last sighting by Mrs Greenway, who says she saw a maroon car. She thinks it could be a Sierra or a Mondeo. Said she'd seen it a few times before but didn't see the number plate.'

'Did she get a look at the driver?'

Dawes nodded.

'Not great, but enough to give a rough description.'

Barrow sighed again, picked up and drained his coffee and heaved himself to his feet.

'They're widening the house-to-house to include the surrounding streets. But I think I'd better go and see the mother.'

5

He unhooked the immaculate Italian suit jacket from the back of his chair and slipped it on. Then he straightened his vividly patterned silk tie.

'I'll take Holgate on this one. Can you check on the database for maroon Mondeos and Sierras? It looks very much like Mondeo Man's our chief suspect.'

Dawes reached for the pile of papers. He was disappointed but he saw the reason for taking Detective Constable Holgate on the Booth interview. As a woman she was reckoned to be more full of human kindness than a mere bloke.

'OK,' he said. 'But it could have been a Sierra, remember?'

Mrs Booth, a small, neat, petite type who lived in a respectable block of flats, gave Barrow and Holgate a look of desperate, yearning intensity when she opened the door in answer to their ring.

'Mrs Booth? I'm Detective Sergeant Barrow and this is Detective Constable Holgate.'

The distraught mother, her eyes rimmed with red, leaned forward slightly, looking along the landing left and right. Then she stood back to let the police officers into her narrow hall.

'Have you found her? You *must* have found her by now!' she said. Her voice had the vibrato of imminent tears. Barrow shook his head slowly.

'I'm sorry, Mrs Booth. There's nothing so far. But it's early days.'

He took out his notebook.

'We'd just like to take you back over a few things and

6

mention a few more matters that have come to light. All right?'

They were ushered into the living-room and ritualistically offered tea, which they refused. Holgate noticed the good but hardly top-notch furniture, the careful housekeeping, the collection of thriving cacti. It was not an affluent household but the family had been making ends meet.

Mrs Booth reached for a tissue from the box on the coffee-table and dabbed her eyes.

'I feel so helpless,' she said. 'I wish there was something I could do . . .'

Holgate sat down on the settee and gestured towards the spare place beside her.

'Mrs Booth, I'm sure you'd feel better sitting down. We've been doing everything we can, top priority. We've called Territorial Support Group in – that's a big squad of reinforcement officers if you like – and they've been making house-to-house inquiries in the area where Cassie was last seen. There are just a few points we'd like to ask you about in case they jog any thoughts that might help us.'

Barrow cleared his throat and sat down in the easy chair. He did not sit back but perched on the rim of the seat, his arms resting across his knees.

'Does Cassie ever talk about her paper round? Has she for instance ever mentioned that someone might be following her or watching her at all?'

Mrs Booth shook her head.

'No, nothing like that. She isn't like that at all, really.'

'You mean,' said Holgate, 'that she doesn't confide in you much, doesn't talk about what she does?'

7

The mother shook her head.

'No, not that. She's my only child, we have a very close relationship. I mean she doesn't imagine things like strange men following her. She's very down-to-earth.'

Barrow paused. Mrs Booth had not quite grasped what he'd been saying, but he let it go.

'Do you know anyone with a darkish red or maroon vehicle? A saloon car, Sierra or Mondeo perhaps?'

'No. I was asked that before, but no. I can't think of anyone.'

'Do you know if Cassie was having any trouble at school?'

'No. She's a very happy girl.'

'Can I ask if you're married?'

For a fraction of a second Mrs Booth did not react to the question, as if her attention had wandered and she hadn't heard it. But then she answered firmly enough.

'Divorced. Five years. He lives in Manchester.'

'Might Cassie have gone to see him?'

'No. She had no reason to. He was due to come down for a weekend in a couple of weeks' time. Anyway I've already spoken to him.'

'You have a good relationship with your ex-husband, then?'

Mrs Booth frowned as if considering.

'Yes. He's remarried, but . . . yes. And if Cassie had wanted to see him she'd have told me.'

Her voice broke and she raised the handkerchief to her nose and mouth. She began to weep quietly.

'She . . . she is such a *good* girl. Really. Never any trouble about boys or . . . or anything really. She is a great support to me you know – a mother on her own and all that. She has a head on her shoulders, they all say that.'

Holgate put a steadying hand on the arm of the woman, who blew her nose and, shuddering, began to pull herself together again. Barrow looked at Holgate questioningly, raising his eyebrows.

'May we please have a look in Cassie's room, Mrs Booth?' Holgate said. 'There might be something there that will help us.'

They were led into a small room which seemed normal in every respect. Posters of the Spice Girls and Johnny Depp dominated the walls, a rack of CDs and a cheap sound system stood on the windowsill, with a few books and magazines. One noticeable thing: scattered around – on the bed, chair and other available surfaces – was an impressive collection of little beanbag animals: frogs, dogs, a donkey and a zebra, a camel, a bear and a brace of kangaroos.

On an impulse Holgate crossed to the table beside the bed and examined everything on it. She was thinking that as a teenager herself she'd kept a journal, full of enthusiasms and not a few embarrassing secrets. She'd write it up every night before sleep. Such a thing might well provide a key to this mystery. She turned back to Mrs Booth, who was hovering in the doorway.

'Do you know if she kept a diary at all?'

Mrs Booth's answer sounded almost eager, as if Holgate's question had provided a small wisp of hope.

'Yes. Yes, I think she does. Now where would she have kept it? . . . I know!'

She bustled over to where Holgate was standing and opened the drawer let into the bedside table. She drew out a small diary. It wouldn't have room for long soulful entries, like the one Holgate had had as a girl. But it might well provide evidence of some kind.

Barrow, who had been looking in the wardrobe, joined them, taking the diary and flicking through it. There were entries, some of them very brief, for most days.

'Thank you, Mrs Booth. May we take this? You'll get it back in due course. All right?'

And he slipped it into his jacket pocket.

Chapter 2

A T SEVEN fifty-five in the morning, Detective Inspector Pat North, tall, slim and fair-haired, sat fuming in her car as Capital Radio's Flying Eye told her about the traffic congestion on the north-bound carriageway of Putney Bridge. This wasn't news to North, since she was currently half-way across the bridge and had been stationary for at least ten minutes. Moreover, there was a pile of paperwork on her desk at Embankment police station which she had hoped to clear before the ten o'clock inspectors' meeting, to be attended by the Assistant Commissioner himself. They were to be briefed on new security protocols arising from the war in the Balkans. North honestly couldn't see how the military situation would impinge on her life very significantly. Her speciality nowadays was Vice, and she hadn't noticed that the bombing of Serbia had led to an upsurge in prostitution, pornography and lewd behaviour in Metropolitan London.

The morning so far had been a strange mixture of tenderness and tension. She and Walker had been camping in the flat for five days, their furniture still not all moved in. Walker had brought her tea at six thirty, sitting on the side of the new bed and kissing her gently.

Then he'd started hunting frantically round the bedroom for his lost tie. She knew for a fact he'd been awake at least ninety minutes already. She had felt him rolling out of bed and heard him thumping around the sitting-room of the flat.

Michael Walker was a Detective Superintendent in the Metropolitan Police's Area Major Investigation Pool, London's murder squad, or AMIP as it is generally known. But with the loose ends of his latest investigation almost tied up, he was beginning to behave like a dog that has licked its bone clean and is on the lookout for another. Not that the man was very different when he did have a fresh case to chew on. If their recently instigated domestic arrangement was going to work out, North would have to get used to Walker's chronic insomnia and his interminable, restless jitters. This morning, while she tried to get back to sleep, he'd paced around the flat, boiled the kettle, surfed TV channels, boiled the kettle again, showered, dressed and boiled the kettle a third time. That was Mike Walker: insomniac, workaholic, impossible bundle of impatience – and the guy she was in love with.

Pat had never seriously considered what it would be like sharing her life with someone else in the job. For five years she'd lived with Graham, a gentle, uncomplicated chartered surveyor. When that broke up she'd gone out with a few guys from the job, mostly because they'd asked. Nothing had amounted to a real relationship, however, not even her on-and-off thing with Jeff Batchley, the extremely fanciable CID Inspector she'd first met during last year's Damon Morton inquiry. That had been mostly a matter of lust – a fling. What was going on in her life now was something a good deal more complicated, though no less irrational. She had worked with Walker on two murder inquiries in two years. He had impressed her from the start with his intelligence and utter dedication. At times he'd tried to dominate and intimidate her but North had always stood up to him. Finally, on the morning after they'd both joined a night of celebrations for the final conviction of the multiple murderer Damon Morton, Walker had let his vulnerability show through. Waking up on the sofa of her tiny flat, he'd told her in stumbling, inarticulate terms about his childhood in the slums of Glasgow, his feelings of guilt about the failure of his marriage to Lynn and about fathering two kids he loved but hardly ever saw. Finally he let North put her arms around him. It was then that he'd told her how much he seemed to think about her and how he thought maybe he was in love with her.

So now she was making a home with him. She had worked out that this would have significant pluses. They both knew the job and were realistic about its extraordinary demands. Neither would harbour cosy expectations about home life. On the other hand, North and Walker worked equally mad hours. To try to knit their lives together into a loving domestic relationship was not just a challenge – it was dicing with disaster.

The traffic started moving again at last. For another five minutes they crawled until, at last, North reached the north bank of the Thames. She immediately darted down a side street, skirted the Hurlingham Club and took her favourite rat run to Chelsea Harbour and the Embankment. In the end she made it to the office by ten past nine, by which time she was contemplating her in-tray, stacked even higher than she'd anticipated –

letters, faxes and e-mail printouts, as well as messages sent up from the desk.

'God – what's all this? You had a look, Jack?'

Detective Constable Jack Hutchens was a strong, handsome officer in his late twenties. He had a reputation around the station as a young Lothario, with a habit of frankly eyeing up any attractive female who appeared within range. North, certainly attractive enough but his senior by almost ten years, was out of his range and he knew it. But he maintained an easy, not-quite-flirting relationship with her nevertheless. Now he came over with two frothy white cappuccinos in styrofoam cups. He handed one over.

'You read my mind, I'm gasping,' she said gratefully. 'Took me over an hour to get here.'

Hutchens nodded at the stack of paper. He said, 'Half of those are from that nutter. If he's not phoning in, he's writing. Now he says he's going to contact his local MP.'

He was referring to a member of the public who had been bombarding them with complaints for the past fortnight. She put him down as one of those curtain-twitching paranoiacs who thought the police were a branch of the mental health service.

'I thought he already had. Who did we put on it?'

Hutchens thumbed over his shoulder towards the empty desk in the corner, used by Police Constable John Jones.

'Jones. And he says what's his name—'

'Warrington, Stephen Warrington,' supplied North, picking up the topmost letter, which was all about a house near Mr Warrington's which, according to his allegation, was a working brothel.

14

'That's him. Off his head, according to Jones.'

He looked over the Inspector's shoulder at the neatly handwritten page she was studying.

'It's a group of nurses living there,' he explained. 'So they're bound to come in and out at odd hours. And if they pull the odd bloke, it's their business, isn't it?'

'Well, he's now written to South Area Commander.'

North turned over and grimaced, scanning the second, stapled-on page.

'Nice of him to send us a photocopy. Exactly how many nurses are living at the house?'

'Two or three. It's not a brothel, Pat! The guy's a nutter.'

'Well, maybe, but it's quite an upmarket street. We looked at a flat round there.'

She looked at Hutchens and instantly knew it had been a mistake to refer to her new relationship. His eyebrows had arched in amusement but now he showed her the palms of his hands.

'What you looking at me like that for?' he asked. 'I never said a word.'

'You didn't have to,' said North grimly. 'This whole place thrives on gossip.'

She replaced Warrington's letter decisively and opened a transparent briefing file marked 'Kosovo Conflict – Contingent Security Arrangements'.

'OK, let's get the day started, shall we? Oh, hello, sir.'

Chief Superintendent Frank Bradley, North's boss in Vice, had tapped on the door and was peering in from the corridor.

'Pat,' he asked, 'have you had any contact with a

Stephen Warrington? He's a persistent complainer – convinced his neighbours are running a brothel.'

North seized a heap of papers from the pile in front of her and dropped it again.

'You've got to be joking! We need a special filing cabinet just for him.'

Bradley opened the door fully and walked in. Tall and lean, in his mid-forties, he was looking as brisk and energetic as ever.

'Well, it's no joke, I assure you. South Area Commander's been on the phone about him. I think he needs a visit from a senior Vice Officer. To put his mind at rest.'

North spread her hands in a gesture of incomprehension.

'I don't believe this. It's a house full of *nurses*! We've already checked it out.'

Bradley smiled emolliently.

'As a favour to me, Pat. Do it again – personally.'

He spun on his heel and marched out. Pat made a face at his departing back and murmured to Hutchens.

'What's the betting this Warrington belongs to the same Masonic lodge as the Commander?'

She didn't murmur softly enough. Bradley stopped and turned. He had a broad grin on his face.

'Close,' he said. 'His father-in-law does.'

North laughed, picked up the Kosovo file and pushed herself out of her chair.

'All right, sir – I'll go round there this afternoon.'

In Southfields the night had passed, yielding not a word of Cassie Booth. Detective Sergeant Barrow was at his desk early next morning ready to direct another day's work for the Territorial Support Group. It was a hell of a time for his Inspector to be away on a course but Barrow was an ambitious officer, planning to put in for promotion later in the year and confident he could handle the pressure of a high-profile case. If they didn't get a break in the next couple of hours they'd have to instigate a search of local parks and waste-ground. He'd be needing a register of empty proper-ties, too. There was also the question of how to handle the media. He'd been mulling over the possibility of the Booth family going on television, to appeal for witnesses and sightings. He would talk to the press office about it.

Bringing him a cup of coffee, Gwen Holgate noticed that Barrow was thumbing through the missing girl's pink-covered diary.

'Not looking good, is it?' murmured Barrow, nodding his thanks for the coffee. 'Anything come up from the house-to-house?'

'No,' said the Detective Constable. 'We've listed the addresses she delivered to, so we know her route. She disappeared at approximately seven fifteen.' She nodded at the diary in his hand. 'Anything in that?'

Barrow snapped it shut and passed it to her.

'Nothing obvious. She's definitely a high-risk missing person and judging from the evidence so far it looks like she was abducted.'

Holgate shook her head sadly as she turned the pages of Cassie's little book, a neatly kept catalogue of netball fixtures, homework, parties, visits to the cinema, school gossip.

'She was a good kid. We've not heard a bad word

said about her. She wouldn't have got into a stranger's car voluntarily.'

Barrow pulled his keyboard and mouse into position and clicked open a new window on the screen.

'Yeah, well, we don't know who the driver was yet, do we?'

'What d'you mean?'

Barrow shrugged.

'She might have known him. A relative, family friend, whatever.'

But Gwen didn't think so.

'No go. They've all been contacted. And the father's arriving today.'

Barrow opened a document listing internal area phone numbers.

'OK,' he said. 'Let's speak to the area press officer and see if the parents want to do an appeal.'

Stephen Warrington lived in Barnes, a district south of the Thames which is bounded on three sides by that deep, sensuous curve of the river between Fulham and Chiswick. The street, called The Gables, was indeed upmarket – one of those areas where inner London approached closest to the more suburban aspirations of social order and community discipline.

'Very nice,' commented North, looking up and down the road. The Victorian Gothic and neo-Tudor houses were stepped back from the road behind low, redbrick walls and freshly leafed chestnut trees. 'What number are we looking for again?'

'Eighteen,' said Hutchens, as they slid past a parked Ferrari. The grille of a Bentley could be seen inside one of the driveways. This was opulent territory and, remembering North's claim to have viewed properties locally, Hutchens said in an innocuous tone, 'I didn't think they *had* flats round here.'

Hutchens was fishing for information about her private life and North knew it.

'It wasn't in this road, nosy.'

'So where did you end up buying?'

'We didn't.'

She offered Hutchens no further details. Instead, leaning forward to look beyond him, North checked the house they were passing. It was number twenty. She drove on to the next, which was eighteen. It was a substantial Victorian property in its own grounds and approached along a short gravel drive.

'My, my!' exclaimed North. 'Mr Warrington must have a nice income, wouldn't you say?'

'Yes, lucky sod.'

They drove through a pair of open white gates and pulled up opposite a large double front door, whose stained glass was distantly influenced by the pre-Raphaelites. A tall, impeccably dressed man in his mid-forties opened the door and favoured them with a hospitable smile.

'Hello, hello. Do come in, please. I am Stephen Warrington.'

His words were measured, his voice assured. North would have said he was money and a public school in the background. She returned the smile but in a brisker, more businesslike fashion.

'I'm Detective Inspector Pat North and this is Detective Constable Jack Hutchens. We're attached to the Vice Unit at Embankment police station.'

'Of course, of course.'

He showed them into a large, airy drawing-room in which a grand piano, its lid cantilevered open and with sheet music ready on the stand, took pride of place. From somewhere deeper within the house they could hear the rattle of a kitchen drawer, the bang of a cupboard.

'Coffee? Tea?' asked Warrington, pleasantly. He was rubbing his palms together like a head waiter.

'Oh, coffee would be very nice, thank you,' said North.

Their host disappeared into the inner recesses of his home and soon the rattle of crockery could be heard. Meanwhile Hutchens prowled around the piano. First he checked out the sheet music – it was by Schumann and Mendelssohn, names which meant next to nothing to him – and then the collection of silver-framed family photographs. One showed Warrington himself standing with an older man at what might have been a royal garden party. There were two young girls in stiffly posed school portraits and beside these a stylish blonde woman who was evidently their mother.

'Wife's very attractive,' Hutchens commented in a voice not quite low enough for his superior officer's liking. She came close to him and whispered.

'Just remember, this is a damage-control exercise, Jack. *Humour* him a bit.'

She nodded towards the images of the children and said, in a slightly louder voice, 'Those must be his daughters.'

There was a sound by the door and they turned simultaneously.

'Correct!' said Warrington. 'My darling daughters. And actually *they* are the reason I'm so concerned about number twenty-one opposite. The eldest of the girls is Charlotte. She's fourteen. Lucy's only eleven.'

He was carrying a tray with a coffee-pot, cups and a plate of biscuits, which he deposited on a low table in front of the large, comfortable settee. He gestured for the two police officers to sit, flashing his teeth at them in another, not entirely natural, smile.

'Do you take it black or white, er, Pat?'

As he poured he apologized for the absence of Susan, his wife, who he told them was out arranging flowers at the parish church. It was an art she was good at, apparently.

'She could make her living by flower arranging – if she wished . . .' he said, gesturing proudly towards the corner, where a large, complicated array of blooms and ferns exploded from a vase that had been placed on a mahogany stand.

After offering the biscuits, Warrington took his own coffee and settled himself with a sigh in a deep armchair.

'I have my own company, as a matter of fact. I import fine wines. In fact . . .'

Suddenly he had put down his untouched coffee, uncrossed his long legs and stood up again.

'If you'd care to try a very special Merlot . . . It's actually Chilean, but I think you'll find it's not too bad at all.'

North had just taken a swallow of coffee. It was real, not instant. She held up her hand.

'No, thank you. I would really like to discuss the reason we're here.'

21

Warrington was on the move again, striding over towards the piano, fingering the photographs which stood upon it.

'Absolutely, Inspector. You see, with two daughters at such a very vulnerable age one feels very . . . I suppose you know a young girl is missing as we speak over in Southfields.'

North shook her head.

'No, Mr Warrington, I didn't know that,' she told him. 'But about your complaint, we've made inquiries—'

'Which were obviously not good enough.'

Warrington swept back to his seat. This time he did not relax, but sat upright, bristling agitatedly.

'These women are very devious, you know. By sending out some fresh-faced copper—'

'Mr Warrington,' said North, anxious to prevent this criticism of an officer going any further. 'PC Jones was very diligent. He also contacted the landlord of the house in question, that is, number, er . . .'

'Twenty-one,' broke in Warrington, triumphantly in possession of the facts. 'And that man can't be trusted. He's a bloody Iranian and considering what's been going on in his own benighted country, I don't think he should be allowed into this one, let alone owning a property like that.'

Warrington was talking so fast he was almost gabbling. North looked momentarily towards Hutchens, who was fixedly studying the coffee-pot. He seemed to be holding back a wave of laughter that threatened to wash over him at any moment. She stuck doggedly to her brief: patience – damage limitation – public relations.

'The property is legally rented to a number of nurses, Mr Warrington, so I don't think—'

'They may have *told* you that. But I do assure you, the number of men going in and out of that house at all times of the day and night is extraordinary.'

'But you must consider that the employment of these women is shift work.'

Warrington, however, was not to be deflected from his theme.

'Detective Inspector, I'm *telling* you: what goes on in that house has nothing whatsoever to do with a hospital. They are quite blatantly taking in clients – "johns" I believe is your terminology.'

North placed her half-finished cup on the table and stood up.

'Mr Warrington, I think—'

But the righteous complainant once again forestalled her. He was striding across the room towards an antique desk, where he slid open a drawer and whipped out a pocket notebook. He brandished it.

'I have listed the times and dates on which I have seen men going into the house for sex. Here.'

Defiantly Warrington proffered the notebook and North took it. She had no choice but to turn the pages, which she found crammed with instances, each one meticulously dated and timed, of single men entering the premises of number twenty-one. Against several entries there was also a departure time given – on average about forty-five minutes after they had arrived. Warrington had been thorough, you had to say that for him.

'I'm very impressed with your public-spiritedness, Mr

23

Warrington. I'm sure that if more people paid such attention to what's going on around them, London would be an even safer city to live in than it is already.'

Her host beamed with pleasure and nodded his head vigorously.

'Exactly! I'm so glad someone *finally* understands.'

There was something conspiratorial about the man's expression now. Hutchens was excluded: he, Warrington, had brought Inspector North on side and now he would get what he wanted – he would be taken seriously.

North closed the notebook.

'This obviously distresses you, so I think—'

'Yes, yes, as I've said. I have two young daughters and my poor wife's scared to walk out of the house at night in case she's accosted. One poor missing child should be a warning, yes?'

'Well, we'll go over and take a look, Mr Warrington. I can't promise anything, but the least we can do is check it out.'

After he'd shown them out, a thin smile of satisfaction playing on his face, Stephen Warrington whisked the coffee-tray back into the kitchen. Susan Warrington was there with her rubber gloves, meticulously wiping down the surfaces.

'Well, they finally saw what I was driving at,' he proclaimed. 'It was the evidence in my notebook that swung it.'

Susan Warrington looked at her husband with the expression of one who had heard more than enough on the subject of number twenty-one.

'Stop getting so wound up about this, Stephen!' she

said. 'Anyway, I'm staying out of it. Don't look to me for collaboration, or whatever it's called.'

Warrington had by now dumped the tray and was retreating back into the hall. He stopped in the doorway.

'Corroboration, Susan, that's what it's called. And I don't need it – from you or indeed anybody. The police are not stupid. They'll certainly see that I'm right and take the appropriate action, because something must be done.'

And with impatient strides he returned to the sitting-room, snatched up a pair of binoculars from the windowsill and ran up the stairs. From the window in their bedroom, between the trees and parked vehicles, he had quite a good view of the front of number twenty-one.

'*Is* there a girl missing in Southfields?' asked North as she drove back into the road.

'Don't know,' said Hutchens. 'But either way, he's a fruit and nut case.'

Number twenty-one was unlike all the other houses in The Gables. Once as elegant as the Warrington house, the property was now palpably run-down. It was obviously years since the place had enjoyed the attentions of a gardener: the gate hung drunkenly askew from its hinge, the driveway was pot-holed and overgrown, and a pair of terminally rusty bicycles leaned abandoned against the side of the house. In several places the brickwork was stained by dribbling water and limescale where the guttering had blocked and fractured. The slates on the roof were mossy and loose and weeds sprouted here and there from the gable end. The painted window-frames were in an advanced state of peeling and much of their underlying wood lay exposed to the elements.

'Maybe he has a point, though,' commented North. 'Look at this place! Let's see if anyone's at home.'

Hutchens rang the door-bell, which resounded loudly in the hall, and they waited. The door was eventually opened by a young woman, wearing pyjamas under a man's dressing-gown, who told them her name was Emily. Her hair was tangled and squashed flat on one side: clearly it had only just left the pillow.

'I don't believe this!' she exclaimed. 'We had a policeman here last week asking questions.'

In the shambles of the kitchen she rummaged about for the means to make herself a cup of coffee. Meanwhile North and Hutchens gazed around them. In their considerable experience the place was typical of houses shared by single people in their twenties. A washing-machine stood open, vomiting out wet clothes. An ironing-board was piled with crumpled underwear. Boots and shoes were heaped higgledy-piggledy in the corners. In the sink, crockery lay half submerged in scummy water.

'So how many of you live here?' asked North.

Emily heaped coffee powder into one chipped mug and poured the boiling water on top.

'It sort of depends,' she said. 'Judy and Alex rent it officially, but they let out some of the rooms.'

Her hand went quickly to her mouth.

'Oops – probably shouldn't have told you that. Oh well – there's never more than four of us, anyway.'

'So you pay – Judy and Alex, was it?'

'Judy and Alex Watson, yes.'

'You pay them rent?'

Now Emily was rolling a cigarette. She licked neatly along the gummed edge before shaking her head.

'Not *rent* rent! We just contribute towards bills and stuff. That's not illegal. You see two of us aren't qualified yet and what with the pathetically little money we earn . . . you know!'

North smiled encouragingly. 'What does Judy do?'

'She's a nursing sister. Alex, her husband, is a mechanic.'

'Well, a neighbour, Mr Warrington, has lodged a complaint—'

'Him! He's weird,' interrupted the girl. 'A few weeks back, Judy went up to the loony and told him to leave us alone. She said she'd get the police on to him.'

North thought of the binoculars, the notebook.

'Why? What was he doing?'

Emily, leaning back against the worktop, pulled a face.

'Somebody had pushed a dog turd through the letterbox. At least, we presumed it was a dog's. He's such a freak – maybe it was his! It was gross!'

Thinking of the fastidious Mr Warrington, North could hardly suppress a smile. She made her face serious again.

'Well, Mr Warrington believes this place is being used as a brothel. Is it?'

The nurse pushed herself away from the kitchen unit angrily. Her eyes flashed as she looked from North to Hutchens and back again.

'My God, not *that* again! I really resent having to

27

respond to that. I'm not a prostitute and nor is anyone in the house. Now I'd like you to please leave so I can get some sleep. I'm on night duty.'

North looked at Hutchens as she rose. His face had adopted an expression of concern. Oh God, the soft kid fancies her! she thought. She was less amused by the Detective Constable's next move, which was to pat young Emily on the shoulder and say, 'I'm sorry, love. Sorry we had to ask you.'

In return, Emily looked at him and smiled shyly.

North waited until they were in the car, buckling on their safety belts, before she issued a sharp piece of advice to the young man.

'Don't you ever do that again!'

Hutchens's mouth fell open.

'What? What did I do?'

'Apologize for me doing my job.'

The young man adopted a wounded look.

'Come on, Pat! She was obviously not a tart.'

North started the car with a savage twist of the key.

'And anyway,' she added, 'it's illegal what they're doing. The landlord could evict them all for sub-letting.'

Hutchens closed his eyes and pressed back against the head-rest.

'Oh, for Christ's sake! Rich bastards pulling strings – they make me puke.'

They were back in the road when North noticed Warrington standing in front of his driveway, waiting for them. She slowed to a stop and lowered her window.

'Well?' asked the aggrieved householder, peering down at the two officers. North gave it to him straight.

'I'm completely satisfied that there's nothing improper going on.'

Warrington clicked his tongue, his face twisting with exasperation.

'I'll have to get you proof then.'

'There really will be no need for that, Mr Warrington. As far as the police are concerned, this is the end of the matter.'

She shoved the car into gear and gunned the engine.

'Thanks for the coffee,' she said, and accelerated away. In her wing-mirror she saw Warrington move out into the road behind them, his fists clenched convulsively by his sides.

CHAPTER 3

WEDNESDAY, 7 APRIL, EVENING

DETECTIVE SERGEANT BARROW had spent what he felt to be a frustrating day directing the search for Cassie Booth. Now it was quarter-past seven in the evening, a full twelve hours since she had delivered Mrs Greenway's paper before disappearing into thin air, and he was no nearer to finding out what had happened to her.

The identity of the maroon car was the most urgent question he faced. An application to the Driver and Vehicle Licensing Centre in Swansea had yielded a list of possible Sierras and Mondeos registered in south-west London. There were plenty of them, and checks would probably not be completed until the following day. Meanwhile, wasteground, parks and empty properties had been combed, a computer search of the few names that had come up in the house-to-house had been run, suspicious prints on the girl's bicycle had been looked for and a minute search of the ground had been carried out in front of Mrs Greenway's gate. None of these measures had yielded any result: all that remained was the possibility that something might turn up unexpectedly. Barrow knew this almost amounted to an admission of defeat for a policeman. But that is exactly what often happened.

And at seven twenty-three it did.

Holgate came tearing up to the Crime Management Unit waving a slip of paper from the switchboard. She had clearly sprinted up the stairs.

'Call came in, traced to a phone box in Putney. Male caller.'

Breathing deeply, she handed the slip in triumph to the Detective Sergeant. 'Said we should search a boathouse for Cassie Booth.'

Barrow pushed his chair back and stared at her.

'Boathouse? Where? Putney?'

'Must be near where the call came from. Almost under Putney Bridge. There's several of them down there, mostly rented. Very select clientele.'

Barrow stood up and picked up his coat.

'OK, I'd better get down there, hadn't I?'

'What about me?'

Barrow shook his head.

'No, I'll take Myles and Dawes and a couple of others from uniform. You stay here. Better call the local Putney nick and tell them what we're doing. And get me a tape of this geezer on the phone. More important than anything else: if he calls again, I want you to talk to him personally.'

In the garage of the house previously shared by the Walkers – now solely the home of Lynn and the two children – a load of Walker's stuff had been piled and, for the last eight months or more, he had been nagged to remove it. This Friday morning, then, with nothing much happening at the office, he had picked up a hire van. After loading up with North's possessions from a storage place near Paddington, then emptying the few possessions of his own that had accumulated in the grubby little flat he'd been renting in Kensal Green, he had driven out to Grays, Essex, his former home, to extract the final remnants of his marriage.

He had been received with an odd mixture of mournfulness and hostility. In certain moods Lynn still wanted to believe she could touch Walker, and even control him. As he bustled around, opening up the van and the garage doors, lining up the boxes he'd brought for the packing, she hung around making remarks about the old days when their relationship had had vitality and even passion.

'Remember when we bought that table lamp? God, it seems an age ago.'

'That's what it is. We weren't even married then.'

Lynn was leaning against the side of the house, smoking. 'We had some good times, Mike. You've got to admit it.'

The van had been backed on to the apron of concrete driveway for easier loading. Walker lifted a box containing his collection of LPs – Nazareth, the Average White Band, Alex Harvey, Stone the Crows, all the good old Glasgow bands – and slid it on to the tailgate.

'Oh yeah, I'll admit it,' he said, giving the records a shove so that they slid further into the van. 'But none of them were recently – *you've* got to admit that.'

He felt it was profoundly true, whether or not Lynn chose to agree with him. The best of times for them had been that golden, dreamy, everything-is-possible phase before the wedding, before the first flat they'd shared, before the babies – and before love gave way to that bitter struggle for psychological supremacy and the moral high ground which was Walker's most powerful recollection of their married life together.

Twisting her face, Lynn blew out the smoke as if it had suddenly tasted bitter.

'You're such a selfish bastard, Michael Walker. You couldn't share your life with a bowl of fruit, never mind a woman.' She laughed cynically. 'The only romance in your life is your bloody job. This new, er, *friend* of yours – she knows that, does she? If not, she's bloody soon going to find out.'

Moving past her to lift a box of books and magazines, Walker raised his finger and stabbed the air.

'Shut it, all right? I didn't come here to talk about her.'

Sullenly, Lynn dropped the cigarette butt and ground it out with her foot. Then she straightened and marched towards the open front door of the house.

'Don't worry, Mike,' she said. 'That is the last thing I'd *ever* want to do.'

And she walked inside, kicking the door shut behind her with her heel.

He didn't mention this conversation when, as soon as he was driving away, he called North on his mobile.

'I'll be there by five. Meet you at the flat.'

'What for?' She sounded exasperated.

'Help me unload. What's the matter? Can't you make it?'

'I'm having a weird day, that's all, but it should be all right. I'll be there at five.'

Traversing London from east to west was slow and tedious and it was not until quarter-past five that Walker finally pulled up at the forecourt entrance of a low-rise block in Barnes. North was waiting. She had changed from her office clothing – the killer suit, as Walker had called it – into jeans and a bomber jacket. Now she was looking on with amusement as he made a hash of manoeuvring the hire van backwards through the narrow gateway.

'Plenty of room,' she shouted. 'Come on, keep coming!'

But Walker decided the angle was too acute and, seizing the stick, he riddled the gears to find first. The engine screamed, the vehicle juddered and stalled. North appeared at the driver's window, her face wreathed in a teasing smile.

'I can't see a bloody thing!' growled Walker.

'Let me. You're hopeless.'

'At giving directions *you're* bloody hopeless. I'll direct, you drive.'

Within a minute North had negotiated the van into the forecourt and Walker had yanked the rear doors open.

'God', he said, shaking his head as he contemplated the closely packed load of cardboard cartons and black plastic bags. 'I'll give myself a hernia shifting that lot.'

North appeared behind him and tapped his shoulder.

'Come on then. Let's get on with it.'

They began to heave the things from the van into the lift, and then from the lift into the flat. It was a single-bedroomed first- and second-floor maisonette, not as spacious as they would have liked but smart enough, with freshly installed bathroom and kitchen fittings. They would have to redecorate, though: new wallpaper and paint would give the proper start to their new life.

As they worked, North told him about her visit to the persistent complainer's house, just a few streets away. Walker still said nothing about his own encounter with Lynn.

'So what's he like, this guy?' he asked, ripping open a cardboard box and peering inside.

'Ugh. Just the kind I can't abide – sort of crafty and superior. Fellow comes over all officer-class one moment and expects a pat on the head for his good citizenship the next. He made my skin crawl. Lives round the corner from that flat we looked at renting – the one with the balcony overlooking the big garden.'

Walker grunted. He wasn't sure if this particular box had come from Grays, Kensal Green or Paddington and couldn't see what it contained.

'Is this stuff yours?' he asked.

She pulled aside the cardboard flaps and saw a dismantled brass wall light, a few paperback books and the contents of a kitchen drawer.

'No, yours. And why did you want to keep *that*?'

She nodded towards a horseshoe-shaped formica-topped coffee table standing incongruously among the crates and cartons. It was pure 1950s, with legs ending in feet like four snooker balls. Walker laughed.

'Lynn didn't want it.'

'I'm not surprised.'

With mock pride, Walker rapped the tabletop with his knuckles.

'One of these was on the *Antiques Roadshow*, I'll have you know. It's true – twenty years and it'll be a collector's item.'

'Oh yes? And meantime, what are we going to do with it?'

At last all the boxes and bin-bags were heaped inside the flat.

'That's everything,' said North with a sigh. 'Bar the unpacking, we're in.'

It was in its way a decisive moment and Walker had noticed the sigh.

'No second thoughts?'

North gestured at the enclosing walls. She was smiling.

'Fine time to ask.'

Walker took her hand.

'Look, why don't we leave the unpacking and get something to eat?'

North suddenly felt luxuriously hungry. She squeezed his fingers.

'Good idea!'

But Walker looked intently into her eyes. Was all this a good idea, too? God, he hoped so!

'You're not having second thoughts, are you? I mean, well, I'm a little older than you, and—'

North butted in with a laugh.

'And a lot shorter! Now, pizza or Chinese? You get it, I want a bath.'

The boathouses near Putney Bridge were of white-painted wood with felt roofs and concrete foundations. With the tide rising, water lapped at the stanchions which supported them on the riverside, driven into the sloping bank of Thames mud, and, in the dark, Barrow got his boots wet surveying the row of riverside doors through which the boats came and went. His torch beam showed that every one was locked and undisturbed. He moved back to landward and found that the doors on that side were equally undisturbed.

He told Myles to lever the first of them open, and it gave way easily when the Constable's enforcer was applied.

Barrow led the way inside, flashing his torch around. The sloping floor was a slipway leading down to the water's edge. On the land side it levelled off and there were dusty shelves and cobwebbed cupboards containing a variety of boating and fishing tackle. A glass-fibre sailing dinghy, with its aluminium mast lying unstepped along its length, rested slightly askew on the rough screeded floor. But there was nothing that could be remotely connected with the missing girl.

'Right, come on! Let's get the next one open,' said Barrow softly. He didn't know why he'd whispered. But these dark, musty, hollow boatsheds had a spooky and disturbing atmosphere.

It was in the third of the sheds that Myles shone his torch into an old, rotten, wooden-built rowing boat and whistled softly.

'Sir!' he said hoarsely. 'Sir, over here.'

Barrow turned from the contents of an abandoned fridge that stood in the corner and joined the constable. Myles had lifted the rowing boat's bottom boards and played his torch beam over the damp compartment beneath. It contained a single white training shoe and a red bomber jacket. The jacket was light red in colour but even by the torchlight the officers could see it was stained and encrusted with something darker. Barrow crouched down, flashing his torch around.

'Is there a body?' he asked, urgently. 'Can you see a body? Can *anyone* see a body?'

*

The foil containers, overflowing with egg foo yong, chow mein and spring rolls, lay on the table between them. Walker had opened a bottle of wine. He looked across at North in her clean clothes, her hair still damp from the bath. She looked young, fresh, untouched by the sordidness of everyday police work, the shit that was kicked at them every day, the fraying contact with violence and vice. He poured. The wine gurgled into the glasses.

Walker raised the stem glass and waited for her to do likewise. Then he reached across and tipped the side of his glass against hers.

'To us,' he said.

'To us,' she replied.

They both felt it was almost a solemn ritual – a declaration of intent and an exchange of vows. They said nothing more as they looked into each other's eyes and drank.

CHAPTER 4

OVER THE next five days exhaustive forensic tests were carried out on the young girl's blood-stained jacket and shoes, revealed by Detective Constable Dawes's torchlight at the Putney boathouse. The missing girl's mother had confirmed that in make and appearance they were like Cassie's but, with her daughter's whereabouts still unknown, the first priority was to establish that identification beyond doubt. The second consideration for the Southfields police was to be good and ready if and when AMIP was called in. The station Superintendent had decided this would be done only when a link between Cassie and the boathouse clothes was proven – a question which, he felt, must be settled one way or another by today, Monday. The police were under ever-increasing pressure to respond super-sensitively to the families of crime victims and, while Cassie's mother and father were held in suspense by not knowing what had happened to their daughter, and hadn't let out so much as a whisper of discontent about the inquiry, they should not have to endure a slow-moving investigation.

Early on Monday morning the complete forensic results duly arrived at Southfields police station and

Barrow called a meeting in the CID office. A dozen officers were present. All of them, including Holgate, Dawes and Myles, had been with the inquiry from the start.

'OK, listen up,' said Barrow, waving a stapled report in the air. 'I've got important information.'

The room fell silent as Barrow went on.

'DNA tests have proved that the blood on the jacket found at the boathouse is Cassie Booth's.'

There was a ripple of comment as the meeting reacted to the news. Everyone knew the implication: the discovery of blood-stained clothes made murder a likely conclusion. Horrific, of course, as every officer would agree. But, at the same time, murder was murder: a high-profile, make-or-break crime. There was going to be hard work for them and high drama in their midst. The spotlight would be on the team. Excitement was palpably in the air.

Barrow waved for them to shut up before he would continue.

'Before we hand over to AMIP, can I just confirm with you that we have got the following ready for them?'

He flipped over the top few pages of his report, running through the checklist of actions which he'd mentally compiled over a smoke in the station car park a few minutes earlier.

'The details of Cassie's last meal from her mother – plus, when it was eaten?'

He looked quizzically at Myles, who nodded.

'Her blood group and dental chart?'

'Got them,' said Dawes, holding up a memorandum.

'Control fibres from her bedroom for possible later comparison?'

'Yes,' called Gwen Holgate raising her hand.

'Her fingerprints?'

Holgate confirmed that she had these also. They had found a perfect set on Cassie's school lunchbox, packed by her on that fateful morning before beginning her paper round.

'Identification of all the clothing she was last wearing, including labels.'

'Sorted,' said Myles.

Barrow nodded in such a way as to include everyone in the room.

'Good,' he said. 'AMIP are on their way and an Incident Room is to be set up immediately. Yes, Ian?'

Detective Constable Dawes cleared his throat.

'Will AMIP be wanting any of us, Guv?'

'You fancy cutting your teeth on a murder inquiry, do you, son?'

'Well, yes, Guv, as a matter of fact I do. I mean, if I can.'

Barrow surveyed the whole group. He knew they'd all be eager to work alongside AMIP.

'We'll have to wait for the Senior Investigating Officer to arrive, find out exactly what their requirements are. They'll probably ask for one or two local uniform, but don't call us, all right?'

In her first week of cohabiting with Walker, Pat North had taken in more alcohol than in the whole of the previous month, although it had been nothing to Walker's own punishing intake. And yesterday, as they had shifted furniture and heaved packing chests, she had discovered that Sundays – to be more specific, any

41

Sundays on which he had no particular office work to do – were the most punishing of all. Consequently, she came into Embankment police station on this Monday morning with a throbbing head and leaden eyelids to go with the aching back from lifting boxes and furniture. Her first action was to shake a couple of vitamin C tablets from the tube in her bag into a glass of water, as she resolved to stick to fruit juice for the rest of the week.

'Got a cold?' asked Hutchens.

'No, just exhausted.'

'Uh-huh. How did the move go?'

North gulped the fizzing liquid.

'Everything's in. But we've still got boxes everywhere.'

'Well, talking of boxes . . .'

Hutchens was grinning broadly as he waved at a young uniformed constable who bent to pick up a small wooden crate parked near the door. He brought it over to North's work-station.

'Look what just arrived,' crowed Hutchens, waving at the box. 'For you!'

The constable placed his burden on a chair. The stencilling on the side told them that it contained twelve bottles of Louis Jadot Beaune, 1996. Stapled to it was an envelope with North's name on it, written with a fountain-pen in a neat hand. North had seen that handwriting before and she knew exactly whose it was. She shut her eyes wearily as Hutchens ripped open the message and extracted a card. He read its message out in a reedy, high-falutin voice.

'*With sincere gratitude for your assistance, Stephen Warrington*. Oh, and there's a p.s. *I hope you will enjoy this very fine wine and know that it will improve with age.'*

'Just send it back,' said North sharply.

Hutchens looked puzzled. He turned the card as if the other side contained the clue to North's temperamental behaviour.

'You serious?' he asked. 'This looks like vintage stuff!'

'I've got a headache. Send it back.'

She waved her hand, her eyes still shut. Hutchens looked between her and the case of wine, then rolled his eyes in understanding.

'Oh! Celebrating something last night, were you?'

North opened her eyes and they were blazing.

'Get it OUT of here!'

Walker had been on his way into the office at AMIP South Area headquarters when his mobile phone bleeped. He ignored standing instructions to pull over when using it and switched on the unit as he drove. After a three-minute conversation Walker did pull over, but only to wait for the smallest gap in the traffic, through which to change direction in a screeching U-turn, causing consternation to drivers coming both ways. He didn't care. With a contented smile on his face, he was on his way to Southfields to take charge of the inquiry into the disappearance of a fifteen-year-old papergirl.

The Superintendent at Southfields had authorized the conversion of an allocated space into an Incident Room and by mid-morning the AMIP team was up and rolling. After a meeting with the Super, Walker put his head in, finding Barrow in the thick of the arrangements. Walker had worked with Barrow before and knew what an effective officer he was. Particularly pleasing was the man's pleasantly surprised expression on catching sight of Walker.

'You on this?' Barrow asked. He paused in the middle of shifting a desk into a new position. 'That's great! Who's on your team?'

Barrow took Walker's hand, a firm, confident shake, but the vigorous movement jarred Walker's back, which was no less stiff than North's this morning. He winced.

'You all right?' asked Barrow.

'Fine. Just a pulled muscle, or something, in my back.'

A uniformed Constable was walking past, staring curiously at the unknown Detective Superintendent in their midst. Walker waved to him. 'Get me some coffee, would you?'

The young officer stopped in his tracks, his mouth falling slightly open, as if mouthing, 'Me?' Walker nodded imperiously at him.

'Black!' he said sharply.

Barrow had given the desk a final nudge to get it into its final position and he now stood watching the Constable's retreating back.

'Is it true?' he suddenly asked. 'That Pat and you are . . . you know.'

Walker looked upwards, as if appealing to some higher authority.

'God, you can't even pass water round here without everyone knowing. We're living together. I'm getting a divorce. I *don't* want any wisecracks.'

Barrow looked down at his shoes, but he was smiling.

'I just heard a rumour, that's all. She's working in Vice over at Embankment now, isn't she?'

'Yes.'

Walker pulled off his coat and dropped it on the desk that Barrow had been relocating. Then, spotting a large board on which photographs of the missing girl had been displayed, he moved across to it.

'So now *you* have the facts, can you give me some on this . . .'

He tapped the most prominent picture, a standard school photograph. 'What's her name?'

'Cassie. Cassie Booth.'

As he surveyed the board, Walker was patting his pockets. He pulled out a packet of Marlboro, selected a cigarette and ripped off the filter tip. By now Barrow was standing beside him.

'Er, Guv?'

'What?' asked Walker impatiently.

'Up there.'

Barrow indicated a large sign right over their heads. It read, *This is a NO SMOKING OFFICE. Your courtesy is appreciated.*

Walker looked at the sign as if his icy stare alone could make it disappear. A chain-smoker, he jammed his cigarette back into its packet.

'I keep forgetting we live under orders from the Moral Majority.'

'There's a smoking-room down the corridor,' explained Barrow, apologetically. 'But it's more of a cupboard, dead manky too. Most of us use the car park.'

'Thanks for the advice,' was Walker's bitter rejoinder.

*

From her desk at Embankment, North had thought it politic to phone Warrington herself.

'I'm just phoning to say that I'm arranging to return the case of wine which you so kindly—'

'Oh, but Inspector North, you must accept it! I mean, it's a classic.'

'Be that as it may, Mr Warrington, we are not allowed to accept gifts.'

'Well, I can't see how it can be misconstrued,' he protested, his voice rising to a higher pitch. 'This is simply a tribute from a grateful—'

'Mr Warrington,' said North sharply. 'I cannot accept the wine, I am sorry. I really don't want you to feel insulted but we operate under strict guidelines, you must appreciate that.'

'I see,' said an apparently crestfallen Warrington. 'Well, of course I do understand. But I would like to see you anyway. I have something you should see. I can't discuss it over the phone but if you would like to come and see me, I assure you it would be worth your while.'

To pay another visit to the Warrington household was the very last thing Pat North wanted. But she was involved in this at the specific request of the Area Commander himself. And, she thought, she could at least make sure the wine was returned at the same time.

'All right – I'll call this afternoon; about two thirty suit you?'

'Good,' he said, his voice now exuding relief and gratification. 'I shall look forward to it. Goodbye.'

What was his game? thought North, replacing the handset. There was always something forced and unnatural about him, as if he was hiding something. But what exactly? Did he fancy her? Was he trying it on? He might be doing no more than trying to buttress his own pathetically neurotic personality. People did this, she knew. Hobnobbing with authority figures such as the police got them a sense of self-worth.

She shrugged. She was an experienced police officer. What problem could there possibly be? But this was positively the last time she'd be going there, of that she was determined.

By lunchtime the last of Walker's team were in place – twenty detectives from South Area as well as half a dozen civilian administrators. They had gathered in the Incident Room with Barrow, Dawes and Holgate, the three local officers most closely involved with the original missing-person inquiry. At this preliminary session all the available information was to be aired. Perched on the edge of his desk, with the team ranged in a semicircle around him, Walker went carefully over the known facts about events on the morning Cassie Booth had disappeared. Then he moved on to the one solid piece of evidence at their disposal.

'The boathouse,' he announced, waving his fingers at the board on which the photographer's shots, taken at Putney Bridge, had been mounted. 'It's owned by a Mr Karl Wilding. What we got on him?'

Barrow raised a hand. He had been asked to stay with the inquiry and was eager to make an early impression.

'He lives in Putney and runs a small computer software company. Semi-retired, not short of cash. Left for France on the morning Cassie Booth went missing, but not until about eleven a.m. He's expected back today.'

'And who else has access to the boathouse?'

Walker had directed his question with peculiar intensity back at Barrow, who could feel Walker's eyes boring into him. The man was compelling without being exactly frightening – a natural interrogator.

'Wilding's wife seemed to think there's only one set of keys. Wilding has them with him,' said Barrow.

Walker slapped his thigh.

'Right! The blood-stained jacket and trainers were found in Wilding's boathouse, which was padlocked shut. If he was the only one with a set of keys, that's enough to nick him on. So I want him arrested as soon as the plane lands. We also need to check the availability of the eyewitness who saw the maroon car, and put her on standby for an ID parade.'

'Guv,' said Barrow. 'She's really elderly and her description of the driver was pretty vague.'

'I don't care,' said Walker, glancing at his watch. He thought a trawl for new witnesses would also be a profitable course of action: leafleting, more house-to-house, the media. Walker knew it was essential, especially in these first hours, to keep the pressure well up.

'We'll go for a letter-drop and another witness search. We've got two crime scenes now, the boathouse and the abduction site.'

He pointed at Barrow.

'Get on to the search coordinator immediately and find out if the dive team have come up with anything at all from the Thames.'

The Detective Sergeant reacted with a repressed look of slightly miffed surprise.

'You got a problem with that, Detective Sergeant?'

Walker named Barrow's rank deliberately, as if putting him on notice that his seniority in the force was on the line.

'No, Guv,' said Barrow, now writhing in his seat. 'But we've done a house-to-house . . .'

'No matter,' asserted Walker, looking now away from Barrow's face towards each of the other faces in turn. 'We go again. We also need to identify any shop or business premises close to either location that might have CCTV recordings and get hold of the tapes for the relevant day. *And* we need to talk to any tradespeople who may have been in either locality at the time.'

Barrow was nodding. He knew about this stuff.

'We're on to it,' he said.

Walker sprang forward to his feet and reached for the raincoat that he seemed to take everywhere. 'I want this on *Crimewatch*. It could really help us. So . . .'

He pointed a finger at Barrow, squinting along it like a gun as he headed for the door.

'Set it up, OK?'

Seconds later the door was swinging behind him. Barrow sighed.

'He's determined to get on that programme. Talk about an ego!'

Holgate raised her eyebrows sardonically. Barrow was one to talk about ego!

'I've noticed yours growing,' she observed. 'You know he's asked me and Dawes to stay on this too?'

Barrow dropped his voice, not to be heard by the others. He smiled mock-lecherously.

'Really? Well, I'd watch out. He's just moved in with the last female officer he requested to stay on his team.'

'Who's that then?'

'Pat North. Tall DI in Vice. They're calling them Little 'n' Large.'

Detective Constable Ross mentally pricked his ears at this. Gossip, he thought. The Met's favourite recreation!

CHAPTER 5

WITH HER left arm hooked awkwardly around the case of Beaune, North used her free hand to ring the bell of the Warrington house. Stephen Warrington opened the door, his face a mask of relief.

'Ah, Pat! You came, and so punctually!'

It did not escape her attention that the use of her Christian name, not only now but on the first occasion they'd met, was a clever piece of social manipulation. It put her in a quandary. If she called him Stephen, that would tend to legitimize the unwelcome idea that they were friends. If, on the other hand, she used *Mr* Warrington, she put herself in a position inferior to him, like a bank clerk or the domestic help. Avoiding the dilemma, North merely smiled as sweetly and briefly as possible. She handed over the wine. Allowing a momentarily troubled look to cloud his face, he grasped it, took a step back and nodded ceremoniously to let her enter.

'Would you be so *very* kind as to shut the door for me? Let's go through to the drawing-room.'

Preceding North, he carried the wine into the spacious, elegant room, placed it on the floor, then opened the desk drawer from which he had previously produced his book of surveillance notes. He drew out a manila envelope.

'I, er, have gathered some more evidence of the goings-on at number twenty-one.'

He handed her the envelope and she took a look. It contained photographs of the front porch and door of the neighbouring house with which he was obsessed. He had evidently used a special telephoto lens. Some of the pictures were taken in full daylight, but others were night shots, with all available light artificially intensified.

'It's an excellent camera – with night vision,' Warrington told her, as he gestured for her to sit on the ample, damasked sofa. Twitchy and bothersome as ever, he hovered beside her as she began thumbing through the images. They were remarkably similar, showing different men standing in front of the door, their fingers on the bell. But she had hardly begun looking through the prints when he reached over and brusquely pulled one from her grasp. He flipped it over to reveal hand-written notes on the reverse.

'As you can see, I've given each man a number, noted the date and the arrival and departure times. It's busier than Clapham Junction over there.'

A more relaxed man would have been pleased with the simile and laughed, or at least smiled at his little joke. But Warrington's eyes were deadly serious, his mouth solemnly set, his eyes glittering fanatically. North noticed how they flicked up and down and from side to side, as if afraid to miss anything that might happen in his field of vision. He returned the photograph to her and wandered across to the window. He paused to shift fractionally the position of the photographs on the piano. He twitched the full-length curtains to make their drapes fall more symmetrically and straightened a landscape watercolour on the wall. North continued to look through the photographs, turning each of them over to study the back. They were arranged in strict chronological order.

'I was sorry you were unable to accept my gift,' said Warrington. 'I hope it didn't compromise you in any way.'

He spun around, struck by a new idea.

'What if I arranged a special price for wine when your station has a function?'

The man was relentless.

'No. No, thank you. There's really no need.'

She had stopped at one particular photograph and was studying it carefully. Then she suddenly slipped the prints back into their envelope.

'Would you allow me to keep these, Mr Warrington?'

'Of course. I can always make further copies.'

Warrington was noticeably not as suave as he had been. His teeth were worrying at a hangnail on his ring finger.

'Actually, ah, there was another, very pressing reason why I asked you to pop by.'

He crossed to the closed door and opened it a fraction, seeming to take care that he did so silently. He paused, satisfied himself there was no one listening, then shut the door again without a sound. She noticed his head flick upwards and the neck twist momentarily in a tic of nervousness.

'I could think of no one to discuss this very unpleasant situation with but *you*, Pat.'

Again his use of her first name grated. She tucked the photographs into her shoulder-bag, slung it and stood up.

'*Mr* Warrington, I really have done everything in my—'

'I was *arrested* a few days ago. I've been terrified of my wife finding out.'

His interruption was as intense as it was sudden. North was momentarily nonplussed.

'I'm sorry?' she said, trying to grasp the sequence of his thought. First he'd been trying to get his neighbours arrested; next he'd been arrested himself. What *had* been going on? Warrington took a single lurching step towards his visitor, his face drawn with obvious distress.

'I was driving to one of my buyers in Oxshott and, well, there's no other way to put this, but I was held up in traffic and I was caught short. I looked around for a possible convenience but, well . . .'

He shrugged, his eyes wide.

'I wasn't even sure where I was. I'd turned off the main road. Anyway, I know I shouldn't have done it, but I went into some bushes to relieve myself . . .'

North sat down again, warily keeping her eyes on Warrington. He ran his fingers gropingly through his hair, then tried to loosen his tie. But the more he worried at it the tighter it became.

'The next moment, I was zipping up my flies when this woman starts screaming at me. *Screaming.* I was just returning to my car. I honestly had not the faintest notion that I was close to a school.'

He shook his head in disbelief.

'So now there's this appalling situation in which I've been arrested and could be charged with indecent exposure! Three schoolgirls, whom I didn't even see, claimed that I'd . . . that I . . . Oh God!'

He covered his face with his cupped hands and

dropped into a chair opposite North. He was shaking his head as he spoke.

'You cannot imagine what this has been doing to me. I can't sleep. It's a nightmare, a total nightmare. As if – Dear God! As if I would do such a thing! I'm a happily married *man*, for heaven's sake! I have two daughters.'

He dropped his hands and stared at North aghast. Over his eyes, a watery film of tears had welled up. Struggling to get into his pocket, his hand at last found a pristine cotton handkerchief, folded four times. He wiped the eyes and blew his nose noisily.

'I obviously have an excellent solicitor, but . . . Will you help me, Pat? Talk to the police at Oxshott. Explain to them that you know me.'

North shook her head and stood up again.

'Mr Warrington, you know I can't do that. It's outside my—'

'But you *know* me! Know what kind of a person I am. Couldn't you go to the school, talk to that teacher who screamed at me? She's called Zelda Fitzwilliams. She . . . I mean, you could . . .'

And he was openly sobbing now, dabbing the handkerchief into his face.

'I don't know what I'm going to do. I'm *completely* innocent.'

As soon as she got back to Embankment, North asked to see Chief Superintendent Bradley. He shook his head sadly as she unfolded the tale of Warrington and his complicated relations with the law.

'I don't know if he's really a flasher, sir. But he's

55

some kind of an obsessive all right. Latches on to things and bloody well won't let go. He's a pain in the neck and a bit weird – and absolutely set on the idea that there's a brothel across the road. He's got the place under surveillance, even taken photographs of everyone going in and out of the house.'

'Well,' said Bradley smiling ruefully, 'I'm sorry I laid this on you.'

North returned the smile, but with a hint of strain.

'Still, I'd like to be a fly on the wall at Oxshott nick. Get the real facts. D'you know who'd be in charge of the case there?'

Bradley shook his head.

'No. But with the Met's current tenure policy, it's quite likely to be some rookie detective who's been on traffic for the last ten years. Anyway, just forget this, Pat. And thanks but more important things to do, eh?'

One of those more important things was to have a word with Hutchens. She found him in the office, sipping from a can of Coke as he idly edited a report on his computer screen.

'I heard about Warrington's indecent exposure charge,' he said with a snigger. 'Told you he was a fruit and nut, didn't I? I wouldn't mind calling my mate over at Oxshott, just to get the lowdown.'

North settled in her desk and carefully placed her shoulder-bag in front of her.

'Well, Hutchens, I've got some lowdown on *you*.'

The Detective Constable looked up, surprised.

'What?'

North was only half-suppressing a smile.

'Me?' he asked. 'What have I done?'

North reached into the bag and pulled out the bundle

of photographs taken by Warrington. She selected one and tossed it across to Hutchens.

'Explain *that*, Detective Constable.'

He looked at the snapshot. It was the porch of 21 The Gables but, instead of there being just a man on the doorstep, there were two figures. One was the nubile student nurse, Emily. The other, unmistakably, was DC Jack Hutchens.

The featured subject of the photograph shifted embarrassed in his seat.

'Look, I'd just come off duty and I was driving past the hospital. She was at the bus stop . . .'

'And?'

He shrugged as if he'd been a helpless victim of circumstances.

'I offered her a lift.'

'What, you mean "Going my way?" sort of thing?'

'Yes, that sort of thing.'

'You don't live anywhere near her. In fact, you go in completely the opposite direction, don't you?'

Hutchens looked miserably at the print in his hands as she pressed relentlessly on. After his insubordinate ad lib to Nurse Emily when they'd been leaving the house the previous week, North wasn't going to let him off the hook so lightly.

'And the *time*, as you can clearly see printed on the back of the photograph, was seven o'clock when you went in and . . .'

She had another photograph out of the pack now. It showed Hutchens alone, leaving the premises. She checked the reverse.

'Oh! Well, well. You were in the house two hours. Just got talking, did you?'

'Yeah, something like that,' mumbled Hutchens.

North clicked her tongue.

'Well, I certainly hope she didn't charge you for . . . you know.'

Hutchens looked up, grinning and shaking his head.

'Course not. And anyway I haven't had it yet!'

His blush had already begun to fade as he said, in all apparent innocence, 'By the way, I think you know my mate at Oxshott.'

'Oh yeah? Who's that?'

Hutchens sat upright and looked at her straight in the face. He was noticeably smirking now. Anything you can do . . .

'Jeff Batchley,' he said. 'We play rugby together. You want me to call him about Warrington? Get the lowdown?'

Batchley? In Oxshott? Despite herself, North found it was her turn to look flustered. She leaned over and snatched Warrington's photograph from Hutchens's fingers, replacing it in the envelope with the others.

'No,' she said. 'No need. Just leave it, will you?'

Hutchens relented. He held up his hands, palms outwards.

'OK, OK! Thought you wanted to know the SP.'

'Right now, the less I have to do with Mr Stephen Warrington the better I'll feel about it. That clear?'

'Yes, Guv,' said Hutchens with relief. North was clearly teasing but he was glad the subject of Nurse Emily was closed now. He had a date with her the following night.

CHAPTER 6

WITH DETECTIVE Constable Gwen Holgate beside him, Walker parked his car outside the Booth house in Beadon Lane, Southfields, shortly after three. He took a last drag on his cigarette and dropped it out of the window.

'Right,' he told Holgate, 'you know what we're here for. We need more background. Anything on the victim that might push things forward.'

Holgate looked at him hesitantly.

'She's still only a missing person, Guv.'

Walker shook his head impatiently, elbowing open the car door.

'There was blood on her clothes. *That* makes her a victim. Come on.'

They asked to have a proper look at Cassie's bedroom. Sitting there with Holgate beside her on the teenager's bed, with its brightly coloured quilt and soft toys, Mrs Booth was tense and weepy, although Walker could see that in normal times she would be an intelligent and capable woman. Today she was finding it hard to look on the bright side. Blowing her nose in a Kleenex, she shook her head woefully.

'You don't believe Cassie's still alive, do you?'

Once again the tears flowed, as they had been doing on and off for the last six days. When she spoke, Mrs Booth's voice wavered and broke repeatedly on the rock of her anxiety and grief.

'I want her back so . . . so much! I can't think who . . . I mean I can't think of any *reason* why someone would hurt her.'

'Can't' was right, thought Walker, remembering Amy, his own little princess. We can imagine all sorts of reasons why young girls get hurt. Sex, selfishness, cruelty – in his line of work he'd seen them all. But how *can* a parent think of such things in relation to their own children? Such things were literally unthinkable.

He turned from the window.

'Do you know if Cassie ever went to the boathouse in Putney where her clothes were found?'

The distraught woman shook her head.

'Or knew anyone she might have visited in that area, in Putney?'

'No. No, I've said this! In fact, she was only just learning to swim. She was scared of water. She wouldn't have gone there.'

'OK,' said Walker, continuing in a soft, persuasive voice quite alien to his normal rapid-fire discourse. 'And she's never complained about anyone following her?'

'No.'

Walker noticed, arranged along a painted shelf, the line of beanbag animals, stuffed with tiny granules which you could feel when you pinched them. There were farmyard creatures, jungle and grassland animals, amphibians. He pointed at them.

'My daughter has a couple of these. But this is quite a collection.'

Mrs Booth looked up at the shelf.

'Oh, yes, those. She spends all her paper-round money on those.'

'I know,' said Walker. 'She mentions them in her diary, too.'

He picked up a beanbag lion.

'This must be the one she got from her uncle – the lion, yes?'

It was a squat, pudgy figure with dark beady eyes and a spray of mane around its neck. Mrs Booth looked at it, surprised.

'Uncle?' she said. 'She hasn't got any uncles.'

Walker frowned.

'Oh? I could have sworn she mentions one – an "Uncle W" or something – in her diary.'

Mrs Booth hunched her shoulders and looked at the floor.

'It must be a nickname for a friend. It's certainly not a real uncle.'

Walker caught Holgate's eye. A teenager's 'uncle' whom the mother didn't know about was certainly a person worth investigating.

He glanced around again. Standing on top of the chest of drawers was a framed photograph of Cassie, just head, shoulders and a toothy smile. Walker picked it up and studied it. An open, loving, guileless face. Something inside him clenched. Some scum took this person and hurt her, maybe tortured, maybe killed her! This was what it was about – what he, Walker, was *for*. To get the less-than-animal who did this and make him face it, make him pay in the currency of shame and public ignominy. 'Uncle W'? It made sense to look into this. A certain type of pervert always dressed himself in the guise of a kindly uncle.

Mr Karl Wilding, the owner of Boathouse 14, the waterside shed beneath Putney Bridge where Cassie Booth's belongings had turned up, was affronted when he came through international arrivals. He had collected his bag and cleared customs without hindrance. Then there had been these police officers inviting him to accompany them in connection with the disappearance of a teenage girl in London. He hadn't even *been* in London, as he kept on saying to the police. All right, so they'd found some clothes of hers in his boathouse. Well, he didn't go there that often – couldn't remember the last time, as a matter of fact. Used to own a smart river cruiser from the best boatyard on the river, but he'd got rid of that. This girl was probably a runaway who strayed in there for shelter, like a lost cat.

They took Wilding to Southfields police station and installed him with all courtesy in an interview room. The show of concern and politeness did not pacify him. He was fuming with pent-up rage and frustration – 'not a happy man', as Barrow had told Walker when the Detective Superintendent and Holgate had got back from the Booth visit.

'Are you treating me as some kind of a suspect?' he demanded to know as soon as Walker had entered the room and identified himself to the video camera. 'And what's *that*?'

He jabbed a finger in the direction of the video equipment.

'All interviews of this kind are routinely videoed, Mr Wilding,' said Walker smoothly. 'It's for everybody's benefit. Avoids any later doubts about what happened, OK?'

'Well, my time is valuable, Detective Superintendent. Can we get on with this?'

Walker sat down beside Barrow.

'All right. Do you own a maroon car, family saloon, say a Mondeo or Sierra?'

'No.'

'Could you, then, tell me your movements on the morning of Tuesday, the sixth of April?'

'I caught a plane to Paris.'

'So I understand. May I ask the purpose of the trip?'

'Mainly business in the Paris area, but I managed to get away over the weekend. Went south for a bit of skiing.'

Walker looked appraisingly at his interviewee. The skiing fitted all right. He was a tall, stylish, fifty-something businessman in a handmade suit and with expensive, highly polished shoes. His speaking voice was upper-crust to match and the gold-rimmed glasses and greying, if expensively cut, hair did not detract from the overall impression of an athletic and vigorous man. The deep tan was certainly genuine. But underneath . . . what?

'So before that – I mean on that Tuesday, before you caught the plane – what were you doing?'

'Packing, bit of paperwork, nothing special.'

'And your wife will verify this?'

'Of course. I was at home until at least eleven a.m. Then I left for the airport.'

For a moment, Wilding was intent on inspecting his fingernails. They were impeccable. Meanwhile Walker kept his gaze fixed on the man's eyes which suddenly, behind the wire-rims, started darting about. There was something predatory about the movement. As a teen-ager, Walker had kept a ferret for a while. He'd won it in a Glasgow street-corner card game, never liked it, and got rid of it after a few weeks. But that was what Wilding's eyes were right now – like a caged ferret's. Perhaps it was just a fancy, though, because now he was looking at Walker steadily again, meeting him half-way, human to human.

'I'm obviously deeply sorry that this girl has gone missing,' Wilding said. 'But at the same time, there was no need to make a public display as I stepped off the bloody aeroplane.'

Orf the bloody aeroplane, he'd said. *Orf*, like royalty. There was something about it which set Walker's Gorbals teeth on edge.

'Now, you *have* declined to have a solicitor present, so—'

'There really is no point!' Wilding spoke testily now, in the voice of the outraged citizen. 'As I have said repeatedly, I was at *home*. And I do not drive a maroon Sierra or Mondeo. I drive a Rolls-Royce.'

Walker refused to react or show he was in any way impressed.

'When was the last time you visited your boathouse?'

Wilding shrugged.

'Not since I sold the boat . . . months ago, anyway.'

'Couldn't you be a little more precise?'

'Not without checking my desk diary.'

Walker leaned back and glanced at Barrow.

'Make a note to pick up the diary later, will you? So, Mr Wilding, can you confirm that there is only one set of keys? And that you have had these with you all the time?'

Wilding nodded. He was calm now, and measured in his responses.

'Yes, but there are a number of people, as I have already told you, that have borrowed those keys in the last few months: a locksmith, a painter and decorator and earlier in the year an entire rowing eight!'

'To your knowledge has anyone been there since last Tuesday?'

'Not unless they broke in, no. And since I have not had the chance to speak to my wife yet, I couldn't say for sure.'

He sighed and cast a glance at the door.

'Look, how much longer do you intend keeping me here?'

Walker smiled.

'As long as I need, Mr Wilding. Would you be prepared to take part in an identification parade?'

'A what?'

Had Wilding looked disconcerted? An identification parade of course was serious. It involved standing up in public and exposure to other people, witnesses, members of the public. The fractional moment of panic, if that was what Walker had seen, passed instantly. Wilding went on, quite placidly.

'Of course. No problem. If that's what you want.'

*

Coming off her shift, North arrived home by six twenty – a good result, given the traffic. She ran a bath and poured into it her favourite scented gel.

After the bath she dressed carefully. She wanted just the right balance – to look great but not as if she'd made a great effort. After she had applied some discreet make-up she looked in the mirror, moistening her lips. Not bad, she thought, for an ageing copper. She left the flat, climbed into her car, put on a Sheryl Crow CD and drove away.

Across the street a second car, a green Volvo, came to life. Its driver engaged first gear and began to slip the clutch, but then he changed his mind. He switched the engine off again and sank back against the driver's head-rest. He would wait, he thought, wait and see . . .

At three, Walker had tried to reach North at her office to say he'd probably be late home. He'd spoken to Hutchens but, increasingly sensitive to the police gossip machine, he hadn't left his name or a message. Three hours later, suspending the interrogation, he was back in the car park lighting a cigarette and trying to contact her number on his mobile. The battery was dead. He went up to the Incident Room, where Detective Constable Holgate came bustling over to him.

'The ID parade's been set up, Guv. Mrs Greenway's down at Brixton ID suite now. She's a little—'

'I know,' Walker cut her off. 'She's elderly, right?'

'Yes, but very sprightly. I don't think she gets out much. What about Wilding?'

'Very, very confident. You've got hold of his desk diary now, yes?'

Holgate nodded.

'I'll look at it later, but you might check through and find out what he was doing on the days Cassie Booth mentions seeing her "Uncle W".'

'Is Wilding admitting he knew her?'

'No, he's denying it – so far. But I've a sneaky feeling that that bastard and the seriously creepy "Uncle W" could be one and the same. In which case . . . Barrow!'

He summoned the Detective Sergeant from across the room with an imperious gesture. Barrow came hurrying across.

'Arrange to get Wilding over to Brixton ID suite now. The sooner we get the parade over the sooner we can all go home tonight – all except, with a bit of luck, Mr Karl bloody Wilding.'

When Barrow came back a few minutes later, having dispatched Wilding off to Brixton shepherded by a couple of the more experienced Detective Constables, he found Walker propped up against his desk idly flipping a coin and looking periodically at his watch.

'I'm bloody starving,' he said.

He reached behind for his phone and started dialling his home number. She should be there by now, surely.

'Want me to send out for something?' said Barrow.

The idea was appealing and Walker shook his head reluctantly.

'No, I'm expected home.'

Barrow's eyes twinkled.

'Little lady cooking up a storm for you, is she? Nice. They always start out that way, but of course give it few weeks and she'll—'

He ducked as Walker, listening to the phone, aimed a ball of paper at his head.

Eventually, after about twenty cycles of the ringing tone, Walker gave up and instead dialled Vice at Embankment. She wasn't there either.

Ross came over.

'Guv, we've contacted the locksmith and decorator who Wilding says had access to the boathouse. I'll interview them in the morning, OK?'

Walker grunted but the Detective Sergeant lingered.

'What do you think?' he asked.

'Very diligent, what more can I say?'

'No,' said Ross. 'I meant about Wilding.'

Walker screwed up his face and shook his head. He didn't know *what* he thought about Wilding, except that he was guilty of something. Precisely what remained to be established.

But Ross had what he reckoned would be music to the ears of the Detective Superintendent.

'*Crimewatch* are definitely interested. Their schedule's pretty full, but that video footage we got of Cassie's birthday party might tip the balance in our favour.'

Crimewatch. Many of the cases investigated by AMIP were ideal fodder for the famous TV programme, through which the police solicited help in tracking down criminals. Along with its imitators it consistently rated highly, with more than 10 million viewers, and the video reconstructions of the murders, rapes and robberies that were its weekly fare often prompted hundreds of calls. For the police it could be a mixed blessing: the switchboards were swamped in a mudslide of mistaken identities, prejudiced blindness and blatant malice, all of which had to be carefully sifted. Sometimes, a few grains of pure, golden evidence were produced. Sometimes, an entire crime was solved.

Jaundiced junior officers, whose job it was to pan through the sediment, sometimes wondered if the whole exercise wasn't about the senior officers having their fifteen minutes of fame. Walker on the other hand loved it.

Walker couldn't concentrate on this yet. He would not get away until they heard the result of the ID parade. And he knew he should contact Pat – but where was she?

And he wanted a cigarette.

CHAPTER 7

HAVING GUTTED so many genuine Victorian pubs in the nineteen-sixties and seventies, breweries had recently been stuffing their properties with fake Victoriana. The pub which Detective Inspector North entered was a prime example, full of unconvincing stained glass, false hand pumps, laminated non-tarnish brass fittings and several shelves of unreadable, job-lot books. The place was not crowded on this Monday evening. A few office workers sipped their lagers round the bar, a lone drinker idly fed the fruit machine, a soap opera played unregarded from an overhead TV.

North looked round for the man she had arranged to meet. Not seeing him, she headed for the ladies', where she checked herself in the mirror. Emerging a few minutes later, she saw him almost immediately, a tall, broad-shouldered figure carrying a pint of lager towards a secluded table.

'Hello, Jeff,' she said, trying not to sound nervous.

Detective Inspector Batchley of Oxshott police station jumped to his feet when he heard his name spoken.

'Hello, Pat.'

He seemed awkward at first, unsure how to greet her until settling for a hand on the shoulder and a light kiss on one cheek. Then he stood back and looked into her eyes. He'd always considered she had superb eyes.

'You look great,' he said.

There was another ungainly pause, until she snapped them both out of it.

'What are you having?'

With her drink bought, they talked about their respective careers, breaking the ice that had formed between them since their last date six months previously.

'So how is it down among the dirty macs?' said Batchley, after describing his move to Oxshott and some of the eccentricities of his colleagues there.

'It's different, all right,' she said, sipping her drink. 'A different feel, but I'm enjoying working in Vice and . . . and being right in town's very handy.'

It sounded a little lame. Handy for what? North felt she wasn't carrying this off terribly well. Batchley shook his head.

'To be honest, I can't wait to get back to the action.'

He picked up his glass and swigged, meeting her eyes again over his glass, which he put down deliberately. There was a moment's pregnant silence before he said, 'Haven't we skirted around this long enough, Pat? I know about you and Mike Walker and that you're . . . you know, living together.'

North frowned, then shook her head as if to clear it.

'I know who told you! Hutchens, right?'

'Don't blame him. There've been rumours. I just asked him if those rumours were true. You certainly kept it quiet. I thought . . . Well, I *thought* we had something going, the two of us.'

North's smile was a little forced. No one likes being in this position – made to feel you are in the wrong when you know you're not.

'Oh, come on, Jeff!'

She looked into her glass, refusing now to lock eyes with him.

'If you want to know the truth, it's still all a bit of a shock to me. But I just felt it was time I made a decision. I'd probably have dithered around for ever with . . . oh, I don't know.'

'You mean with people like me? Well, as we're being so truthful, I was cut up about the way you started avoiding me. Never returning my calls.'

'Jeff, I'm really sorry. I know I wasn't completely honest with you at the time. It was just that we didn't want anyone to know – not until we were more sure ourselves what we wanted to do.'

'And Walker's what you want, is he?'

North swirled the remaining drink in her glass.

'Right now, yes, he is.'

She drained the glass and at last looked at him again.

'Can we drop the subject now, please?'

It took a second or two for Batchley to react. Then he smiled and held out his hand to take her empty glass.

'Sure,' he said. 'Just wanted it all straightened out, that's all.'

North put her hand on his arm, pressing it to the table.

'I'm truly sorry if I misled you. You're a lovely guy.'

She leaned over and kissed him on the cheek. Batchley shut his eyes in mock-bashfulness and then, seizing both empty glasses, stood up to go to the bar.

'So's your friend Stephen Warrington,' he said as he left.

When Batchley was back with the drink she asked him about the Warrington case.

'Three schoolkids under twelve said he not only exposed himself but made lewd gestures . . .'

'In those words?' said North, incredulously.

'No, they probably said *dirty*, didn't they? Lewd was the teacher's word. She didn't actually catch him with it out, but heard the girls screaming, ran after him and caught him putting it away as he got into his car.'

North sighed, shaking her head sadly.

'He told me he was just taking a leak!'

'Well, he's not going to court, anyway. Charges have been dropped because the parents refuse to let the kids be subjected to any further "emotional trauma".'

He made the inverted commas gesture with his fingers – a habit which North had always found faintly annoying.

'Does he know yet?'

Batchley shrugged.

'Only knew myself this afternoon.'

'But Warrington did do it?'

'Course he did,' said Batchley. 'Want another? Or shall we get something to eat?'

North suddenly felt hollow with hunger. She stood up.

'Good idea – I'm starving!'

First she remembered to call Walker but his mobile was switched off.

*

'WHAT?'

At Southfields, Walker couldn't believe his ears. Barrow had hurried over with news from the ID suite in Brixton and was now being blasted with the full force of Walker's displeasure, both barrels.

'It's true, Guv,' he said, trying to convey his own innocence. What was that phrase? Don't shoot the messenger . . .

'OK – let me get this straight,' Walker said, pushing his face close to Barrow's. He spread out one hand and rapped the points out with the fingers of the other. 'Our eyewitness, the old lady, we schlep her all the way over to Brixton and feed her toasted cheese butties all afternoon and now she says she has – what is it? Tunnel *what*?'

'Vision,' supplied Barrow, haplessly.

'Tunnel vision. And what does that mean exactly?'

'Well, she sort of sees only, er . . .'

He raised his hands flat in front of his eyes, making a narrow gap through which he peeped.

'She only sees this much, like. No peripheral vision. Like looking down a narrow tunnel.'

'Just *how* bloody narrow?'

'Well, she's actually been clinically diagnosed as blind, Guv. We've had to send her home.'

Walker bared his teeth. Clinically blind! Christ, armed with this information a defence lawyer would think it was his birthday, Christmas and Cup Final day all rolled into one. There was no way they could hold on to Wilding now. He had to be released.

*

Looking up as he approached the main door of the apartment block, Walker saw that the flat was dimly lit. He checked his watch by the porch light: eleven forty-three. After the identity parade fiasco, he'd needed a pint and had been to the pub with Barrow. He'd still had nothing to eat.

Already in bed with a book, North looked at him a little guiltily as he put his head through the door. The only light came from her reading lamp.

'Hi,' he said. 'Where've you been? I'm starving. Any leftovers?'

'No. I ate out.'

'Oh?'

In the dark of the kitchen area he hung his raincoat behind the door and opened the fridge. The pale, harsh light showed how little it had to offer: cheese, bread. The makings of a sandwich at least.

'If I'd known you were going out for dinner, I'd have had something at the pub.'

North laid down her book.

'I didn't intend to. But I met Jeff Batchley for a drink and he suggested it. I called here and tried your mobile . . .'

'*Batchley?*'

Walker grabbed the cheese and slammed the fridge shut. Then he swept back into the bedroom, pulling off his tie.

'The rugby prop?'

She nodded.

'What did you see him for? He's a waste of space!'

North frowned,

'No, he's not! Anyway it was work-related. I needed some details of a case in Oxshott.'

Abruptly, Walker laughed as he dropped his tie on a chair and, still carrying the lump of cheese, made for the door again.

'Oxshott?' he said sarcastically. 'Is that still in the Met area? You want a cup of tea?'

From the moment he'd first met Jeff Batchley on the Morton inquiry, Walker had treated him like a rival. Not without reason, of course. But still, North resented his belittling of a man who she knew was a good officer and a decent man. By way of rebuke, she refused to respond to his offer of tea and turned towards the bedside light. She turned it off and rolled on to her side, ready for sleep. Seconds later there was a loud crash from the other side of the door followed by a volley of swearing. She reached out and switched the light back on.

'You OK, Mike?'

Walker was feeling for the obstruction which had tripped him in the dark – a wooden box such as might contain a dozen bottles of wine. Issuing a further expletive, he put on the light, retrieved the dropped cheese and filled the kettle. Soon he was sawing at the loaf of bread, a slice at least an inch thick.

'*Did* you want tea?' he inquired five minutes later, coming into the bedroom. North stirred and, opening her eyes blearily, she observed Walker placing a mug of tea on her bedside table, then sitting heavily on the edge of the bed. He immediately levered off his shoes, peeled away his socks and began unbuttoning his shirt. She struggled into a sitting position.

'Why do men *do* that?' she asked.

'What?'

She gestured across the room.

'Well, there's two chairs – but they never sit in one to take off their socks.'

Walker looked at her, puzzled.

'What you talking about?'

'Nothing. Just an annoying habit men have.'

Walker's hand snaked pre-emptively under the duvet and took a hold of her foot. She shrieked.

'Experienced many, have you?' he asked playfully.

North wriggled until he let go. As she reached for her tea, Walker dug out a slip of paper from his trouser pocket and perused it. It was a schedule of jobs which he thought he ought to take charge of. They had already agreed that a systematic division of labour in the household would ease the stresses of their new life together. So far, after much thought, Walker had written down: *papers, Saturday supermarket, off-licence, gas bills, TV licence, own washing, dishes, hoover lounge.* He thought it a responsible rota.

'Right, I've got my list,' he said. 'Now you have to make out yours.'

North groaned, blowing on the tea to cool it.

'Do I have to now? I've got a full day tomorrow, and—'

'And I don't? That is the whole point! If we don't start right now, we're going to get off on the wrong foot, Pat! I've got to get used to you not—'

'*Not* waiting on you hand and foot – like your wife obviously did?'

Walker's face darkened momentarily. Then, despite himself, he grinned.

'Whoops! That was a bull's-eye.'

With his palm he found the lump of her knee sticking

up under the duvet. Gently he stroked it in a circular motion.

'Sweetheart, we both have to work and therefore we both need to get our priorities straightened out. That means—'

'You don't expect me to shop, clean and cook?'

Walker nodded.

'Correct. We organize it.'

'OK, let's get started,' she said briskly. 'First, your socks and shoes will not walk into the wardrobe of their own accord. Ditto wet towels, shirts and . . .'

She sipped her tea and pulled a face.

'And I don't take sugar!'

Leaning back against the prop of one arm, Walker cocked his head to one side and smiled sweetly.

'I know. That's my tea. And I do.'

They looked at each other, right into each other's eyes, and in that moment it occurred to North that this look was a bridge between them – the most honest and confidential look they had ever exchanged. He said, almost in a whisper:

'Are we going to make this work, Pat?'

North swallowed hard but she knew when she spoke her voice would be husky.

'I hope so! We'll give it a good try, yes?'

She opened her arms to him.

'Come here.'

He slid forward, pillowing his head on her breast. He closed his eyes.

'What colour should we go for in here, then?' he murmured.

North stroked his hair and looked around, into the shadows of the bedroom.

'Maybe pale yellow?'

It was a question but Walker didn't answer. His eyes were still closed.

'I've been looking at some colour charts,' North went on. 'And wallpaper samples. What do you think of . . .'

She leaned across and picked up a Dulux colour strip.

'What do you think of "Lemon Buff" for in here?'

She waggled the card above his head then looked down at him. Walker was already asleep.

In his living-room, Stephen Warrington sat at the baby grand, his long fingers rippling across the keys. Although a latecomer to music, when he finally discovered his facility for the piano, he instinctively knew also that he had found the best diversion, the most complete absorption, the greatest drug and finest therapy he could hope for. As he played he closed his eyes, making the sonorous chords of the piano transcription of Beethoven's triumphant Fifth Symphony ring and chime like church bells. He forced all his churning thoughts and fears into those chords and runs. He left earth altogether. He floated, eyes shut, in a realm in which anger, persecution and desire were set free from earth and granted the grace to fly. He thought of a bird tumbling down the wind and was, for a time, released.

CHAPTER 8

TUESDAY, 13 APRIL

EXPLORINGLY, NORTH patted the bed to her left and found it empty. She slipped from beneath the duvet and stood up, yawning and stretching, then reached for her robe. It was just after seven. Listening, she could hear no noise in the flat. She called his name, but had no reply.

The bathroom was wet. A soggy towel had been left in the middle of the floor. Puddles lay under the basin and in front of the bath. The mirror was misted over and the toothpaste had not been recapped. Worst of all, Walker's shaving water, cold and scummy, still stood in the basin. Grimacing, she hauled up the sleeve of the robe and plunged her hand into the stagnant, grey soup. She groped for the plug chain, pulled and listened as the water gurgled its way into the drains. Carefully she wiped away the tidal ring of soap embellished with bits of his beard.

Walker's trail of havoc continued into the kitchen. The tea mugs from last night, and another from this morning, had not been washed. The worktop where he'd made his midnight sandwich was a litter of bread-crumbs, rinds of cheese, dropped pickle. Bread lay unwrapped, a milk carton gaped open, the hacked and gouged block of butter still had a table knife plunged into it, Excalibur-style.

'God!'

If this was his idea of the division of labour, he'd better think again. With a sigh, she collected the mugs and dumped them in the sink. Then she cleared the worktop, collecting up milk, butter and bread to put them in the fridge. But, as she moved to do so, she kicked against the box which Walker's foot had pushed under the table the previous night. With a puzzled frown, she bent to examine it.

Wrapped in the eternally reassuring aroma of fried bacon, Walker phoned Barrow from a café he had noticed close to Southfields police station.

'I'm in the greasy spoon around the corner,' he said. 'Join me. I want an overnight update, especially on the frogmen.'

While waiting for Barrow, he ordered a cup of coffee and the full fry-up. By the time the Detective Sergeant strolled in, Walker's knife and fork were poised for the assault.

'What's this?' asked Barrow, indicating the plate which overflowed with bacon, egg, sausage and two fried slices. 'Doesn't she do breakfast?'

Walker pointed his fork meaningfully.

'If I have to listen to your wisecracks every day, it's going to get right on my—'

'Just an enquiry,' Barrow broke in, innocently.

He drew out the chair opposite his boss and sat down.

'OK,' he said, suddenly businesslike. 'The bad news is *Crimewatch* have given us the thumbs-down.'

Walker grunted his disappointment, his mouth full.

'But there's this new show on ITV,' Barrow went on. 'It's pulling in big viewers.'

The Detective Superintendent swallowed his food.

'Oh yeah? OK, get me on *Who Wants to be a Millionaire?*. As long as you're not my phone-a-friend.'

Barrow smiled indulgently.

'No, I mean Angela Rippon's show – *Crime Night*. They'll show Cassie's birthday party video and do a reconstruction of the paper round. You know – with a look-alike.'

Walker nodded his approval.

'Angela Rippon? I always liked her.'

He began cramming another generous mouthful on to the prongs of his fork.

'Still nothing from the river search?'

Barrow shook his head.

'Not yet. Costs a bundle too. But you wanted them to go further down the river and the tide's fairly strong.'

Barrow's remark about the tariff on underwater searches, and its sapping effect on Walker's inquiry budget, was all too characteristic of the way policemen are forced to think now. When Walker first started catching murderers, money was the last thing a senior officer had to worry about. Today, there is a special accountancy of murder and no killer can be caught without the cost of every police action being counted and settled.

A mobile phone trilled.

'That yours?' asked Walker.

'No,' said Barrow. 'I've got Mozart on mine.'

Walker groped in a jacket pocket for his phone while the Detective Sergeant wandered over to the counter.

'Yeah?' said Walker when he had finally silenced the electronic bleat.

It was North.

'Mike, it's me. Good morning. You left quietly.'

'I didn't want to wake you.'

Walker heard her sip tea. He pictured her, in the white towelling gown, standing in the kitchen – *their* kitchen. His imagining delivered a rush of unexpected pleasure.

'Well,' she went on. 'The reason I'm ringing is, what's this wine doing here?'

'What wine?'

'In the kitchen. A case of wine. What's it doing here?'

Walker remembered.

'Oh, yeah. It was left outside the front door. I didn't know what it was. We've got crates and boxes all over the place. Is there a problem?'

He noticed her hesitation. There *was* a problem.

'No, no,' she said. 'Talk to you later. Oh, and have a good day.'

'OK – you too, sweetheart.'

As Walker disconnected, Barrow rejoined him with a coffee and a plate bearing two pieces of toasted Wonder-loaf, on which slabs of yellow butter were slowly liquefying.

'What do you think of this Wilding bloke?' he asked, drawing out the chair opposite and sitting down.

Walker mopped up the remains of his egg yolk with a square of fried bread. He chewed briefly, thinking, while Barrow helped himself to marmalade.

'I want to talk to his wife. And check his bank statements and credit-card bills for toy-shop purchases. See if he could be "Uncle W".'

'We've got to tread carefully, though,' warned Barrow. 'Wilding's got a lot of contacts in high places. And we've got nothing on him.'

Barrow was spreading his marmalade with loving attention but his meticulous care was unavailing. Quite abruptly, Walker drained his coffee and stood up.

'Not yet. Come on, let's go.'

Barrow looked at his uneaten toast. Walker intercepted his unspoken protest.

'Leave that, we've got work to do. You can eat later.'

Sipping from a glass of cold Chablis, Rebecca Wilding strode through the kitchen and into her elegant living-room, full of what Walker could tell must be valuable antiques. She was in her mid-forties and wore her carefully groomed dark brown hair in a chignon. In her ears were pearl studs and Barrow, who knew more about these things than Walker, was confident that inside the neck of her simple black dress would be an expensive designer label. The wine bottle, gleaming with condensation, was placed on the low table between them but she did not offer the two AMIP men a drink.

'We'd had rather a late night,' she was explaining in answer to Walker's enquiry about the morning her husband had gone to Paris. 'So we slept in until at least nine. We got up, had breakfast and my husband left for the airport about eleven.'

'So neither you nor your husband left the house before eleven?' Walker asked.

'No.'

'And you're sure your husband didn't nip out to get anything?'

Mrs Wilding looked up, irritated by the man's persistence.

'Not unless he went out in his pyjamas while I was in the shower.'

'And neither of you has recently owned or driven a maroon Mondeo car, or perhaps a Sierra?'

She tapped the table impatiently.

'No, never.'

With a sudden movement her hand darted out and seized the bottle of wine. She up-ended it into her glass, looking defiantly at Walker and Barrow.

'Will that be all, Detective Superintendent?'

She had had a slight problem hitting all the consonants in Walker's title. He thought, the woman's been through the whole bottle!

'Yes, Mrs Wilding, That'll be all – for now, anyway.'

'Good. Well, perhaps we can all get on with the day.'

A priority for Detective Inspector North's day had been to get rid of that accursed case of wine, which had boomeranged back to haunt her. It was obviously from Warrington and so now, for the second time, she presented herself at his door in the shape of the upright, uncorruptible officer of the law.

'I am sorry, Mr Warrington, but as I have already said, I really cannot accept any personal gifts of this nature.'

Standing at his front door and immaculately dressed in his accustomed clubman's style, Stephen Warrington received the news of this second rebuff with spread hands and (as it seemed to North) a carefully calculated smile.

'But this is ridiculous! All it is . . . I mean, all I wanted to do was thank you. What harm can there be in that?'

'I really do appreciate your generosity, but I absolutely must refuse.'

Warrington looked down, like a rueful naughty boy, at his scorned gift on the doorstep. North continued to press her complaint.

'And I would also like to know how you got hold of my home address.'

Warrington's smile returned, a little more strained this time.

'You happen to live so close by. I noticed you coming out as I drove past last night. Pure coincidence.'

'Well, I can't accept the wine – but thank you.'

North hadn't meant to say that. She shouldn't be thanking him – she should be showing how angry she was. She tried to glower at Warrington, who continued insouciantly.

'Well, in that case, you and Detective Superintendent Walker must join me and my wife for dinner one evening. And I *won't* take no for an answer.'

Good God, did he never give up? And how in bloody hell did he find out about her and Walker? Absolutely confounded, she opened her mouth to speak but no words came out. Warrington went on, smoothly.

'He's investigating the disappearance of Cassie Booth, isn't he? Have there been any developments?'

North turned on her heel. She must go – now. This was outrageous.

'I wouldn't know,' she said over her shoulder. 'Good afternoon, Mr Warrington.'

She dropped down the steps and began walking

smartly back towards her car. Warrington took a step out through the door, as if to pursue her.

'They dropped the charges, thanks to your intervention,' he called out.

She reached the car, sensing Warrington behind her.

'I had nothing to do with it, Mr Warrington. Believe me.'

He touched her on the arm, a sly rub up and down of his hand and a momentary squeeze.

'All the same, I appreciate it, Pat.'

North felt her gorge rising at his touch and the use of her first name. She yanked open the car door, slipped into the driver's seat and rammed home the ignition key. Then she drove away without another word. She was damned if she was going to speak to him ever again.

As she drove away, the curtain of an upstairs room moved aside. Susan Warrington, the muscles in her cheeks working, watched the Detective Inspector leave. She was glad to see the policewoman go but she felt no relief, just a growing sense of puzzlement and inexplicable, impending disaster.

'OK, what we got?' asked Walker of his team, assembled in the afternoon at the Southfields Incident Room. Gwen Holgate consulted a clipboard.

'Not a lot, Guv. We've eliminated the locksmith and the painter and we've checked out the rowing team. Nothing.'

Ross's phone rang and he went to answer it. Walker was fiddling with a fresh cigarette packet, trying to pick off the cellophane wrapping.

'I got nothing out of Rebecca Wilding except that

Wilding's a heavy sleeper and I expect she is, as well. Sank almost a whole bottle of wine while we were there and never offered us so much as a cup of tea.'

Gwen held up her pencil.

'Wilding's secretary sent a list of his appointments in France. They all checked out as legit. His first was just after he arrived – he booked into the Ritz.'

Ross was waving his telephone receiver.

'Angela Rippon on line two, Guv. She wants to rehearse your dance routine.'

Ross grinned around the room as Walker glowered at him.

'Just a joke!' said Ross. 'It's her researcher again.'

Walker strolled across to the phone, feeling oddly self-conscious. Meanwhile it was Barrow who picked up where Ross had left off. He spotted a red ring file on a nearby desk and he tucked it under his arm.

'Lights, camera and . . . *action!* . . . Detective Super-intendent Walker: this – is – your – *life*.'

Walker had the handset now. He flapped his free hand to quieten the buzz.

'Shut it!' he mouthed. 'Yes? Walker here.'

'Mr Walker – it's Lydia at *Crime Night* here. We're all ready to go tonight with the Cassie Booth story. Just making sure you can be here by eight o'clock, that's an hour before we go on air. Angela would like to go over the details with you first and then we'll have a complete run-through – OK?'

The television always seemed to be turned on in the Warrington house but, apart from news, Stephen Warrington rarely watched it. He lacked interest in sport, soaps and game shows, though he dutifully watched the classic serials with Susan when they came on. It was expected at work that he should have seen them. The others liked to talk about the 'brilliant' performances and 'astronomic' production values, basically to show how cultured they were. It could also be useful with clients. Instant classics were exactly what Warrington was trying to sell in wine – it was 'synergy', as they like to say in the business world.

Tonight, however, it was not Jane Austen but Angela Rippon who commanded his attention as he stood alone in his living-room, holding the video recorder's remote-control unit ready in his hand. He was dead set on watching the programme, a fierce determination which was to bring him into a rare struggle for power over the family set.

'. . . *The two men, both dressed in overalls and posing as Water Company officials, said that they had an appointment to install a new water meter,*' the presenter was saying. '*The two paintings stolen were large canvases with ornate gold frames . . .*'

Susan came in, trailed by her daughter Charlotte.

'Oh, Stephen darling, can we change the channel? There's a new series starting.'

'. . . *If anyone saw these two men leaving the gallery on that day, or have been offered these paintings, would they please contact the number on the screen . . .*'

'No,' said Warrington sharply. Susan did not like being studiously ignored. She tapped her husband on the sleeve.

'You don't want to watch this,' she said. 'There's this new thing about Nelson. Costume drama.'

'. . . *And now our main item this evening,*' Angela

Rippon was saying. *'The disappearance of teenager Cassie Booth . . .'*

Deliberately Warrington pressed 'Record' on the remote-control.

'We all like that historical type of thing, and Charlotte's doing him in history, aren't you, sweetheart?'

Trying to keep his attention directed at the screen, Warrington made a gesture of dismissal at Susan and his daughter.

'Then look at it on one of the other sets. We've got enough of them, for God's sake!'

'Well, why don't you, if this is so important? The girls want to see it. It's educational.'

'Why do you always have to make a scene?' Warrington spoke crossly, his voice rising in pitch and his fists closing. 'I want to watch this programme, in here. If the girls want to see something else, they can go somewhere else!'

'But it's three against one, Stephen!'

Suddenly Warrington lost control. He yelled, 'DON'T argue with ME! I want to watch THIS, all right? And you're making me miss it. Shut up, and get out. Go on.'

'For goodness' sake, Stephen. What on earth's the matter with you? You're being so childish. I've made some hot chocolate.'

'I don't want any. Just leave me alone. Now – you see? You're making me miss it.'

Susan clicked her tongue. She moved around and looked him full in the face.

'Are you taking your medication?'

'Yes, yes! Now leave me alone. Get OUT!'

As Susan ushered Charlotte out of the room, Walker was on screen, appealing for witnesses. By an act of will, Warrington calmed himself. He had been waiting, with a tingling sense of dread mixed with curiosity, to know the looks of the policeman who lived with Pat North. He tried to assess him. Small man, but tough-looking and quite intense. Quite formidable, Warrington judged, though a bit crude. He couldn't altogether see what an attractive woman like North saw in him.

'We received an anonymous call,' Walker was saying. *'It was to advise us that items of clothing worn by Cassie on the day she went missing were to be found in a boathouse in Putney. We urgently need to speak to whoever made that call.'*

As he watched, Warrington was moving his head rhythmically from side to side, in the action that can be seen among certain caged beasts at the zoo. He watched intently as the footage of the birthday party was shown, Cassie blowing out fifteen candles on her white-iced cake. A beautiful child was what she seemed to Warrington. Some people see the mid-teens as virtual adulthood, but Cassie still looked so young, thought Warrington. So young and so vulnerable.

Much later, he joined Susan in the bedroom. She was used to his meticulous nightly ritual – the folding of the discarded clothes, the double tooth-brushing, the opening of the window by exactly three inches. Sometimes Warrington's obsessions and rituals were endearing, but tonight they irritated her. Lying in bed as, now in his pyjamas, he carefully calibrated the setting of his trouser press, she snapped her novel shut, a signal that required him to placate her or not be spoken to.

'Susie,' he overtured hesitantly. 'I'm sorry . . . Sorry for getting all tetchy. You know the way I am when I get stressed. And I've had a lot on my mind recently.'

He slipped into bed beside her.

'I've made it up to the girls. Am I forgiven?'

Susan laid down her book and looked at him.

'I don't know why you're so uptight at the moment, if you really are taking your medication.'

Warrington reached for his wife, caressing her breast and stomach with his right hand, then leaning over to kiss her mouth.

'I love you. You know that, don't you? I adore you. I am so, so sorry. Let me make it up to you . . .'

Pat North was fast asleep under a small heap of fabric sample-books when Walker came banging into the bedroom. It was well after eleven.

'Pat! PAT! You asleep?'

He was eating a sandwich, out of which cheese crumbs were falling on to the carpet. North rolled over, felt the sample-books digging into her side and was awake.

'It went fantastic!' said Walker in reply to her unasked question. 'We got loads of calls. Including a woman who says she saw Cassie with a man in a maroon Sierra car on the morning she went missing . . .'

He took another crumb-cascading bite of the sandwich and began levering off his shoes. He was high on adrenalin, though TV hospitality must also have contributed to his euphoria.

'That's the good news . . . the *bad* news is that it was at a service station on the M1!'

'What time is it?' she asked thickly.

'Late. They gave me a tape of the show. If this woman's ID pans out, that's my number-one suspect off the hook. He was well on his way to France at the time.'

He began to undress untidily, throwing his shirt and socks to the floor with abandon before putting on his dressing-gown.

'Anyway, Gwen's going to check her out tomorrow. By the way, did you ever find out where that case of wine came from?'

'Oh, it's this real crank I've been dealing with,' said North, yawning. 'It's gone back to him.'

'Uh-huh? I'm going to watch the vid. You want a cup of tea?'

He hurried back out and North found him asleep only a few minutes later, slumped in front of the screen. It showed a group of fresh-faced teens singing 'Happy Birthday'. She picked up the remote-control and began to rewind the tape.

'Not fair, is it?' said Walker sleepily, his eyes half-open again. 'Sweet, innocent little thing and BANG! Some bastard takes it all away.'

He patted the upholstered arm-rest of his chair.

'Come here, you!'

She sat down on the arm-rest and he hooked his arm around her waist.

'I suppose it's too late for decorating decisions, now?' he whispered.

'Yes,' said North. 'But there's plenty of time. Cassie Booth has the right to all your attention right now. I do understand, you know . . .'

He smiled. He knew.

'I love you,' he said as she bent over to kiss him.

A matter of a few streets away, at 18 The Gables, Stephen Warrington was also in his dressing-gown, also watching a video recording of *Crime Night*, though he had made this himself. Upstairs his wife and daughters slept and he relished the chance of an uninterrupted viewing of this evening's programme. His thoughts were strikingly similar to Walker's. Cassie Booth was a young innocent. She was unformed and so fresh. She had not deserved this.

CHAPTER 9

S CRATCHWOOD IS the first of the service stations
strung along the M1 motorway, which thrusts
north from London towards Yorkshire and the
north-east. Around its plastic interiors the crowd milled,
devouring late breakfasts or looking for snacks to comfort them on their long journeys.

Holgate and Ross had been sent to meet Angela Bentall,
the *Crime Night* caller who swore she'd seen the missing
girl with a man in a Sierra. After spending an hour showing
pictures to anyone working in the area who might have
seen Cassie on that day – and drawing a complete blank
– they settled down to coffee and doughnuts in the café
while they looked out for their interviewee. She had quite
deliberately been asked to return to the scene of her
sighting at approximately the relevant time of day.

'Walker was funny on *Crime Night*,' Holgate was
saying as she stirred her drink. 'He looked so nervous to
start with, but he was loving it by the end. But let's face
it, he's no Clint Eastwood.'

Ross wasn't quite like Barrow. He didn't mind the
practice of gently taking the mickey out of a good senior
officer like Walker but he thought it should be definitely
discouraged in Detective Constables.

'Got results though. This eyewitness sounds the business.'

After sipping experimentally from his cup, Ross's face contorted in surprise. He peered quizzically into the warm drink.

'I don't know if this is tea or coffee.'

Holgate tapped his arm and jerked her thumb at the window. From the description of Mrs Bentall's car, and her own general appearance, she reckoned she'd spotted their witness cruising by in search of a parking space.

A few moments later, picking her way towards the building, they saw a dainty, middle-aged woman carefully dressed as if for a big occasion. Holgate waved as soon as she made her entrance in the café area.

'I'm Detective Constable Holgate,' she said, standing with Ross as Mrs Bentall approached. 'This is Detective Sergeant Ross.'

The witness produced a dimpled smile and nodded to both officers.

'Have a seat,' said Holgate. 'Can we get you a coffee?'

'No, thank you. Are you going to interview me here – not at the police station?'

Mrs Bentall was clearly disappointed at not getting a glimpse behind the scenes of a working police station and a murder inquiry.

'If you don't mind,' said Holgate. 'We just want to take a witness statement then we can go over to the petrol pumps and establish exactly where you thought you saw Cassie Booth.'

'OK. I'd actually not come in for petrol, just a sandwich from the shop. As I came out of the shop, I noticed a blonde girl in the back of a maroon Sierra car parked by the pumps.'

'Why are you so sure the girl was Cassie?'

'Well, she was wearing pink hair-slides and a red jacket, like the one they showed on *Crime Night*.'

Ross was scribbling hard in his notebook. Holgate continued with the questioning, as they had previously agreed she would.

'And where was the driver?'

'Putting petrol in the car.'

'Can you describe him?'

'Yes . . . he was white, tall, about five eleven, I'd say. Wearing a tweed jack— No, a raincoat. Dark haired.' She shrugged, shaking her head. 'But I wasn't paying any attention to him.'

'Did the girl try to get out of the car at all?'

Mrs Bentall's face showed she was trying to recall the scene.

'I can't really be sure. She did turn to look towards the shop. That's when I saw her face.'

After a few more minutes they repaired to the petrol station, where the witness was asked to park in the same place as she had on the day in question. But driving over, following Mrs Bentall's Mini, Holgate privately confided in Ross.

'There's something wrong.'

'What do you mean?' he said loudly. 'That was a great statement. Looked solid as a rock.'

'Well, we've not found anyone around here who thinks they saw her. And anyway it *isn't* solid at all. There's something wrong about it. I just can't put my finger on what it is. I need to look at the file of witness statements.'

Ross tipped his head.

'In the back.'

So, after they'd parked, it was Ross who went over to Mrs Bentall to confirm the details of her sighting, while Holgate thumbed through the bulky file of statements from Mrs Booth, Mrs Greenway and the others. When Ross returned she still had not found what she was looking for. The Detective Sergeant leaned in at the car window.

'Anything yet?'

'Not yet . . . Oh shit, I *think* I'm right.'

She scrabbled some more paper aside and settled on Mrs Booth's account of the last time she saw her daughter.

'Yeah – here it is. On the day she went missing, Cassie's hair was tied up with a silver scrunchie . . .'

'Scrunchie?' asked Ross. 'That's something you eat.'

Holgate cast her eyes up towards the sky.

'Takes a man! It's those elasticated rings of material, with a sort of ruffle, that are used for holding a pony-tail.'

'Oh yeah, those!' said Ross as if he knew what Holgate was talking about. In fact he hadn't a clue.

'Anyway, the point is,' she said, slapping the file smartly, 'there's no mention of pink hair-slides. But on the video of the birthday night that was shown on *Crime Night*, that's what she is clearly wearing! That bloody woman's lying.'

'Let's go!' said Ross, sharply.

With long, menacing strides he returned to where Mrs Bentall was waiting. He asked her to repeat her description of the girl.

'Blonde,' said the woman, nervous now, and with just the hint of a question mark in her voice. 'About fourteen, red jacket with, er, two pink slides in her hair. But I've said this. Told you this.'

'You are sure about the hair-slides, Mrs Bentall?' asked Holgate, rejoining them.

'Yes.'

'And you contacted us as a result of watching the *Crime Night* programme?'

'Yes.'

'You don't think you could have been mistaken, do you? Only no one else we've talked to here can recall seeing her at all.'

Mrs Bentall stuck out her chin obstinately.

'Well, I'm absolutely certain the girl I saw was Cassie Booth.'

'Not a figment of your imagination?'

Mrs Bentall looked puzzled.

'I'm sorry?'

Holgate began to explain as gently as she could that she didn't believe the statement that had been given.

'Mrs Bentall, Cassie Booth may be still alive and time could be running out for her. Now everyone wants their fifteen minutes of fame. But please, don't try to get famous by sending the police in the wrong direction and wasting valuable time and resources.'

She stared hard at Mrs Bentall, who said nothing. But her head was bowed.

'I think you've made this up,' stated Holgate firmly. 'You did not see Cassie Booth on that day, did you, Mrs Bentall? You have made this up, haven't you?'

Still the witness remained mute. Her only reaction was a slight, almost tremulous, shaking of the head. Now it was Ross's turn to play the nice guy.

'Perhaps,' he suggested tactfully, 'you saw someone who looked like her?'

Mrs Bentall had nothing to say to him either. He pressed on.

'Did you see a maroon Sierra as you have stated? Or is that made up also?'

The woman was visibly shaking now, as the motion of her head increased.

'You were very specific about those hair-slides because she was wearing them on the TV, right? But I have to tell you that on the day she was abducted Cassie was wearing her hair in a pony-tail. There were no slides.'

Mrs Bentall's head went down even further. And when she finally spoke it was with a catch in her voice.

'I'm sorry . . .'

'Sorry?' said Ross, as if seizing on the word. 'What exactly are you sorry about, madam?'

Mrs Bentall had started to cry. She looked back and forth between the officers, her face crumpled and defeated. She looked down again but continued to move her head from side to side, slowly and sadly.

'Because I don't really know why I did it . . . or what I'm doing here.'

She lifted her head and looked up. A jumbo jet roared overhead. She narrowed her eyes against the brightness of the sky.

'No,' she said, her voice still trembling, but with a new harshness to it. 'No, I didn't see Cassie Booth that day. I didn't see anyone like her. I wasn't even *here* on that day! Are you satisfied?'

She groped in her bag and found a Kleenex, sniffling into it.

Holgate said, 'It's not a question of being satisfied, Mrs Bentall. You have admitted making false statements to the police. That is an offence, I'm afraid.'

'I'm sorry. I just— Well, if you *knew* what my life's been like the last few months! I just thought— Oh, I don't know what I thought. I wasn't thinking.'

North's vow to have nothing further to do with Stephen Warrington was broken by mid-morning. She was working on a pile of witness statements from a porn-shop raid when the telephone on her desk shrilled. At first she didn't realize the voice was that of the smooth-talking *poseur* who had only yesterday invited her to dinner. This was a gabbling voice, a desperate voice.

'Hello, I want to speak to Inspector North . . . Hello, is that you, Pat? Pat? This is Stephen Warrington. It is imperative I see you.'

She closed her eyes. What had she done to deserve this?

'Mr Warrington,' she said, 'I'm very, *very* busy.'

From his gasping breath, she guessed he had been running – if not hyperventilating.

'It's happened again!' he wheezed. 'It's happened again! You have to see me. I don't know who else I can turn to. Please. Please agree to see me!'

'Mr Warrington, if this is about the house opposite—'

'No, no, it isn't. It's far more serious. I think I'm going to be arrested again.'

She was shaking her head now in disbelief. This man was a walking, talking disaster. So what had he been doing this time? Taking a pee in church?

'But the charges against you have been dropped . . . Haven't they? . . . Mr Warrington? . . . Hello?'

Warrington's breathing had hardly slowed. He

swallowed hard and when he spoke again his voice had risen close to the pitch of hysteria.

'I am going to be arrested, and I didn't do it. I didn't do *anything*!'

He was interrupted by a rapid series of bleeps. He was out of money for the pay-phone.

It sounded also as if Stephen Warrington was out of excuses, not to mention out of his mind.

She spent the next half-hour hiding in Records, to avoid the chance of Warrington getting through to her again. On her return, Jack Hutchens wandered in, eating from a packet of crisps.

'That Warrington bloke's been on the phone. Seems to have taken a shine to you, Pat.'

'I know. I spoke to him earlier. He was hysterical. I couldn't make out what he was saying – something about being arrested again. Then his money ran out. So please tell the switchboard that if he calls again, I don't want to talk to him.'

'I'll sort it.'

She nodded her thanks. He was dependable in that way, Hutchens.

'Maybe the parents of the kids he flashed at in Oxshott decided to press charges after all. Anyway, I'm not wasting any more time on him. We're due in court.'

Hutchens crumpled his crisp packet and dropped it in the bin. He moved quickly to the door.

'Want me to contact Batchley – about Warrington?'

She shook her head.

'No – forget it.'

As Hutchens ducked out through the door, Chief Superintendent Bradley appeared.

'Got a second, Pat?'

She cocked her wrist, checking the time.

'Sure.'

Bradley came in. He had the air of a man bringing unwelcome news.

'Uniform have just arrested your wine-merchant friend – Stephen Warrington?'

'What here? In town?'

'Yes. Exposed himself to a couple of schoolgirls in the park down by Embankment tube.'

North shook her head.

'I don't believe it!'

'You'd better. He's screaming blue murder and asking to speak to you!'

Suddenly weariness possessed her. Was she going to be haunted by this maniac for the rest of her career?

Walker was on the computer. Technologically, he had been a late developer, having only passed a Met computer course in the last year. Now he was trying to type a memorandum on progress with the Cassie Booth inquiry for the Assistant Commissioner, but suddenly the screen went blank.

'Shit – now what have I done?'

As Barrow came bustling up, Walker was furiously hammering at the 'Reset' key.

'There's something wrong with this keyboard. It's got different commands. I just hit "Save" and the whole screen went blank.'

Barrow dropped a slip of paper in front of Walker, the record from the switchboard of a call from a possible witness.

'Gwen just called in from the M1, Guv. The eye-witness at the service station turned out to be a hoaxer.'

Walker closed his eyes and slammed the desk with his fist.

'But there's something else,' the Detective Sergeant went on. 'We've got another woman who says her kid was approached by a man a couple of months ago, while doing Cassie Booth's paper round. She's coming in.'

Walker forgot his computer. He was interested again.

'Is she the same age as Cassie?'

'*He*. Twelve-year-old boy.'

Walker studied the slip of paper.

'Name of Mark Wilson. Mother accompanying him?'

'Yeah.'

Half an hour later, the two officers were in the so-called 'soft interview room', with its soft furnishings and the absence of any threatening recording equipment. Facing them were young Mark and his mother. He was a fresh-faced child with longish blond hair and a red baseball cap with bomber jacket to match. The mother held his hand protectively, taking it upon herself to tell them the boy's story.

'Apparently he did Cassie's paper round for a couple of days when she had flu, a couple of months back. Sneaked out of the house without telling me because he knew I wouldn't let him. Just wanted a little extra pocket money.'

She looked at her son with an intense smile. The boy blushed and looked steadfastly down at the floor. She went on.

'But when he saw *Crime Night*, he thought he'd better say something.'

Walker looked at Mark. The point was to get the boy's version of events, not the mother's.

'OK, Mark. You say this man got out of his car, approached you and frightened you – yes?'

'Yeah.'

The boy glanced up at Walker and then at the back of his hand. He scratched a red mark on the skin.

'Stop scratching!' exclaimed Mrs Wilson. 'He's got this nervous eczema rash, you see. It comes out all over his body. He's ever so nervous. Been off school because of it.'

Walker ignored her, keeping all his attention on the boy.

'Can you describe the man, Mark?'

Mark was rubbing the rash now with the palm of his other hand. He screwed his palm into it, as if to crush out the itch.

'Er, don't know. He was tall, white. Not fat . . . and he had dark hair.'

'And he was wearing a smart suit and glasses,' put in his mother.

Walker still paid her no heed.

'Can you describe the car?'

'It was a silver sports car. It was—'

'He'd driven past Mark,' Mrs Wilson broke in excitedly. 'Then he turned round. The man called out, then stopped the car and came towards him. That's right, isn't it, Mark? Tell him what the man said.'

The boy was scratching again.

'He said he had something for me,' he mumbled.

'But when Mark turned around to look at him, the bloke looked angry, didn't he?'

'Yeah. He just ran off.'

'I see,' said Walker. 'Any idea why he looked angry and ran off?'

Mark shook his head. Mrs Wilson opened her mouth to speak but Walker suddenly gave her a sharp look to shut her up. He turned back to Mark.

'Do you think it might have been because he was expecting to see someone else, maybe?'

'Don't know.'

'What were you wearing?'

Mark stopped scratching his hand long enough to gesture at his jacket.

'This.'

'And the hat?'

'Yeah.'

'Did anything happen on any other day you did the paper round for Cassie?'

'No.'

'Did Cassie ever say anything to you about this man?'

Mark shook his head.

'I don't know her.'

'How did you hear about the job, then?'

'From the paper shop. I was buying a comic and he asked me if I wanted to fill in.'

'Uh-huh. And you've never seen this man around the neighbourhood again?'

'No.'

When Walker then terminated proceedings, Mrs Wilson protested that it had been a bit of a short interview.

'Don't worry, Mrs Wilson, we haven't quite finished with young Mark yet. We want to try to get a picture of the man.'

Mark had an appointment to see the E-fit technician,

with whose help he would produce a computerized portrait of the man he had seen. Meanwhile, on the way back to the Incident Room, Walker was in an upbeat mood.

'God save us all from over-protective and interfering mothers!' he boomed when Barrow rejoined him. 'Well, the description fits Wilding.'

'Sort of,' said the Detective Sergeant cautiously.

'The boy could easily have been mistaken for Cassie, with that baseball cap on. Same height, blond hair and that red jacket's almost identical to the one she wore.'

Walker was thinking hard now, nodding his head as he agreed with his own conclusions.

'The guy said he had something to give Mark. But maybe if he thought it was Cassie, that's how he got Cassie into the car – enticed her in with a new beanbag toy to add to her collection.'

'Yeah,' said Barrow a shade more enthusiastically. 'I thought that too. But we're looking for a maroon car and little Scratchy said this bloke was driving a silver-coloured sports car.'

Walker punched Barrow lightly on the shoulder.

'Wilding's wife drives a silver Fiat coupé! Let's put surveillance on that bastard, eh?'

Entering the Incident Room, they both had a sense that the inquiry had, suddenly, acquired a new momentum.

CHAPTER 10

A SMART YOUNG officer, Detective Constable
Vivien Watkins, of Divisional CID, dropped into
North's office just as the Detective Inspector was
getting ready to leave for court. She was due to give
evidence in the Saunders case, an unsavoury business
involving a father and son from South London who had
disseminated hard porn over the Internet, as well as
selling it in the father's shop.

'Thought you'd like to hear the SP on this Warrington guy, Pat, since he keeps asking for you. We've got
him in the interview room.'

'The less I hear about him the better, Viv. He's a
bloody nightmare . . .'

But before she could push on to her appointment,
curiosity overcame her distaste.

'So?' she asked. 'What's happened?'

Watkins took a deep breath, enjoying the drama she
was about to relate.

'He'd exposed himself to these two young girls in the
little park down by Embankment tube station and then
legged it. There was a patrol car about a hundred yards
up the street. They saw Warrington running like hell

straight past them and round the corner to pick up his car. They gave chase but eventually lost him. Anyway, they managed to get his reg number, so we arrested him at home.'

'Are the girls OK?'

'Pretty shook up. One of them got especially traumatized because he tried to make her touch him. She almost got herself killed in front of a bus, running away.'

'You know he was arrested for the same thing in Oxshott?'

Watkins didn't.

'Really? Was he charged?'

'No. And for some reason he thinks I got him off. God, he freaks me out.'

'You know we found a bottle of lithium carbonate on him? Apparently its prescribed to treat a condition called cyclothymia.'

'What's that?'

'A form of manic-depressive illness. Means he's prone to violent mood swings: depression one minute, supreme confidence the next. When he was brought in he told the FME who did the medical on him that he'd recently stopped taking the drugs – which might explain his bizarre behaviour.'

North nodded. Bizarre was only the half of it.

'Anyway,' went on Watkins, 'he seems desperate to speak to you.'

But Detective Inspector North was determined not to let that happen. She picked up her briefcase.

'Look, I'm late for court. I really, *really* don't want to talk to him. Just say you couldn't get hold of me, will you?'

Watkins nodded as North made a hurried exit. She'd

known the Detective Inspector several months and she'd never seen her so agitated. This guy was getting to her, no question.

She made her way back to the interview room where Warrington was sitting with his head down, like a contemplative monk at prayer, observed by another plain-clothes officer acting as Watkins's back-up.

'So,' said Watkins briskly. 'What can you tell us about your actions in the Embankment park today?'

Warrington raised his head, defiantly. He was bristling with righteous indignation.

'I will say only that this is a gross and terrible misunderstanding.'

Stephen Warrington's meticulous received pronunciation was more obvious than ever now. He was confronting the police with beautifully modulated outrage.

'Mr Warrington,' warned Watkins. 'You were seen running from the park.'

'I had no idea anything untoward had occurred. I was running to get my car, as I didn't want to get a parking ticket. And until my solicitor arrives and until Detective Inspector North can speak with me, I absolutely decline to say any more.'

'I'm afraid I've been unable to contact Detective Inspector North. She's in court this afternoon.'

'Well, I refuse to say another word. I know my rights and I want my solicitor present.'

It was nine thirty when he finally reached home, his solicitor having organized his release while they sorted out identification by one of the girls in the park. Warrington found Susan in an agitated state. She'd been shopping in the West End when the police came for him. He ignored her, going straight through to the living-room and switching on the south-east news. Susan followed him through.

'What's been going on, Stephen? Where have you been? Mrs Morrissey across the road came flying out as soon as she saw me arrive back. Said the police had taken you away.'

'Well, I'm back now,' he said, without looking up from the screen. The newsreader was detailing a murder in Uxbridge. 'So you can tell that nosy bitch it was all a misunderstanding.'

'But why did the police come to the house?'

'I've *told* you – because they got me mixed up with someone else. It's preposterous. My solicitor said we could sue them.'

Susan Warrington stood uncertainly. Her husband's outbursts had led him into trouble before and she had a tried and trusted remedy.

'Do you want me to talk to Daddy?'

'NO!' snapped Warrington. 'I'll sort this out myself, and Pat North will help me. She works at the same police station.'

'What do you mean, "help"? You said it was just a mistake.'

'Yes. Yes, it was . . . is! Susan, if I had been involved in this thing in any way at all, do you think they would have released me?'

She felt utterly unenlightened, unable to see whether this latest emergency required action on her part.

'So they *were* mistaken?'

'Yes, yes! How many more times do I have to tell you?'

He pressed his palm to his forehead and massaged.

'I don't want to talk about this any more. I've got a terrible headache.'

She came across and knelt beside him, taking his hand tenderly.

'Would you like me to get you a Disprin?'

Still watching the screen, he nodded and, without another word, his wife rose and left the room. He heard her climb the stairs towards the bathroom, where the medicines were kept. Then he noticed that the story on the television had changed. There were frogmen, a riverside scene. He reached for the remote-control and upped the volume.

Police divers today continued to search the Thames near the boathouse where a blood-stained jacket belonging to missing teenager Cassie Booth was found a week ago . . .'

Warrington was shaking his head.

'No . . . no . . .' he whispered, and then he jumped to his feet and yelled.

'NO!'

Jack Hutchens, with Nurse Emily from 21 The Gables, had enjoyed a film and a curry and was turning in at her house when Warrington's car came surging out of his own gateway and, with screeching tyres, took off down the road behind them.

'Jesus! He's in a hurry,' said Emily. 'Did he see you? I'd hate him to get you into trouble.'

Hutchens shook his head, smiling grimly.

'No, he's in enough trouble of his own. The guy's a flasher.'

'No! You're kidding me,' said Emily, her mouth open wide. Then it split into a delighted grin. 'Oh, that's beautiful. Just let that pervert try anything against us now.'

Hutchens patted the air as if to dampen down her enthusiasm.

'Eh, don't broadcast that, or I *could* get into trouble.'

But she was still smiling as, nudging him, she broke into a salacious Mae West imitation.

'Ah well, honey, you gonna come in and lemme show yah mah tricks?'

Hutchens did not need a second invitation. He put the car in gear and drove smartly into the decayed driveway of her house.

Five minutes later Detective Inspector North was at home, thinking about how to cook the swordfish steaks she'd bought for herself and Walker. She was almost absent-mindedly snacking on a salad she'd found in the fridge while at the same time looking through wallpaper samples and colour charts. Then the door-bell rang. She checked her watch – ten to ten. Had he lost his key?

'Who is it?' she called.

Instead of an answer the bell rang again, longer and more insistently. She applied her eye to the peephole. It was Warrington! The bloody man wasn't under arrest, and he was still hounding her.

'Mr Warrington!' she called. 'I am not opening the door. Please go away.'

Warrington's voice was shaky, his face bathed in sweat.

'Please. I know I shouldn't have come here, but I have to talk to you.'

'I'm sorry, but I'm not letting you in. Please go away.'

'What'll you do? Call the police?'

Suddenly he sounded irate, aggressive, but the tone changed again almost immediately and there was the edge of a sob in his voice.

'You *are* the police and all I need is two minutes of your time, please. Please!'

'Mr Warrington you are on private property. I know what this is about, but I can't discuss your case. Please LEAVE.'

She heard him stumble away at last, muttering to himself in the curious sing-song way of men on the edge of tears.

At Southfields, Dawes, just beginning the night shift, had phoned Barrow's mobile at ten fifteen.

'Something's come up,' he said. 'Where are you?'

'Pub round the corner. What's up? Want me back in there?'

'Er, if you don't mind, just for a minute. Looks important but I'm not sure how important.'

Five minutes later Barrow bustled into the Incident Room.

'I was half-way through my second pint. So this had better be worth schlepping back in for,' he warned.

'It's a tip-off call again,' said Dawes, hesitantly. 'Another phone box, but this time in Barnes.'

'And? Come on, Dawes, spit it out.'

'A male caller said that, quote, "The cops are searching for Cassie Booth's body in the wrong place."'

'Uh-huh. Time of call?'

'Twenty-two-oh-two.'

'And this caller claimed to know where we should look?'

'Yes.'

'So where?'

'Didn't say. Just rang off.'

'And was it the same male caller who tipped us off about the boathouse?'

Dawes shook his head.

'Could be – I don't know. So what I want to know from you, Sarge, is how do we get the voice analysis done?'

Walker's arrival home, at about the time Dawes took his apparently momentous call, reactivated North's ambition to rival Delia Smith. Aproned and with cookbooks spread open, she was chopping onions when he wandered into the kitchen unscrewing a fresh bottle of Scotch.

'It should be shallots. But we've only got onions,' she was saying. He leaned across and looked at the swordfish marinading in a pudding-basin.

'Looks great,' he said. 'I'm starving.'

He collected a wine-glass from the cupboard and poured her a glass of white.

'You know, I think I may have something on this guy Wilding after all now,' he told her. 'A boy was approached by a man while doing Cassie's paper round for her.'

He poured himself a large whisky and put the bottle down on the table, which was already laid for two.

'The mother wouldn't let him do an ID parade, more's the pity. Over-protective type. But they've done an E-fit with him and it looks remarkably like Wilding.'

North smiled, only half-listening. She swept the onions into a pan and started to soften them in the hot oil. As Walker started to browse absent-mindedly through the wallpaper patterns the phone rang.

'I'll get it,' she said, but returned with the cordless phone a moment later. 'It's for you.'

Walker's face creased with irritation.

'Oh, for Christ's sake! I've only just got home!'

'It's not the office,' she told him. 'It's your wife.'

He took the phone and his whisky out to the stairs.

'Yes, Lynn.'

He listened.

'Uh-huh. Of course. We're still at sixes and sevens here, but when is it? *Tomorrow?* Jesus! . . . OK, OK, let me think. Tomorrow . . .'

He swigged from his glass.

'Well, it'll be a squeeze, but yeah, they can doss down in sleeping-bags . . . What? . . . Well, because we've only just moved in here and I've not got . . . Lynn, will you just calm down? I've said they can stay over but . . .'

North presented herself in front of him, wanting to go up the stairs. He reached up and caressed her bottom before letting her by.

'Yes, I can pick them up, or I'll arrange for them to be collected . . . Why? . . . Lynn, just listen to me. If I am free I will collect them. If I am not, I will make sure someone else is there and I'll call the school. What's the head teacher called again?'

Lynn's voice rose a few more levels. Walker let her talk for a while then broke in.

'Lynn, I'm under a lot of stress at the moment, so if I don't remember the woman's name, it doesn't mean I'm— What? Mrs Hawley! Fine, I'll call Mrs Hawley.'

North was on her way down now. She had done a quick change into her dressing-gown. She showed him her watch face and tapped it. Walker covered the mouthpiece.

'Lynn's mother's been on the waiting list for a hip replacement and they've had a last-minute cancellation for tomorrow. Lynn wants to take her to hospital – can the kids stay over tomorrow night?'

North shrugged as Walker said, into the phone, 'Just a second . . . just hold on, Lynn.'

'Sure,' said North. 'No problem.'

'Lynn?' he continued, raising the handset again. 'I'll pick up the kids and drop them back to you in the morning. OK? . . . Hello?'

But the line was dead.

'I can't talk to her,' he said, switching the phone off. 'It's impossible to have a sane conversation with the woman any more.'

'And *can* you collect them from school?'

'Yeah, yeah. I can nip out for half an hour. Pat – you don't mind, do you, the kids staying here?'

'It's your place as much as mine – and your kids'!'

Walker stood up. She was standing at the bottom of the stairs, he on the first step. It made them about the same height. He rubbed the side of her face with his hand and kissed her lightly on the mouth.

'Yeah, well, I know that. But I'm asking if *you* mind them staying over.'

She shook her head.

'No, I don't mind,' she lied. And she knew he could tell she was only placating him, because she did mind. She minded like hell, not just because of the kids – though God knew she had enough trouble relating to those unscrupulous little monsters – but because she knew that Lynn would not scruple to use those kids to get at her.

Oh well, it would probably always be like that. Might as well get used to it. She rapped Walker lightly on the head.

'Hey! Are we going to eat? I'm starving,' he said again.

CHAPTER 11

THURSDAY, 15 APRIL

THE POLICE divers had been out on the river since first light, to take advantage of an exceptionally low tide. Working from an inflatable boat, they had combed the south side of the river bed, going as far out as fifty yards offshore and working their way upstream until they were almost at Hammersmith Bridge. The tide had been ebbing when they began. Now, four hours later, it was about to turn – as was their luck.

They were motoring back to the jetty, setting off in a wide sweep which took them out of the strict search zone and closer to the northern shore, where a pleasure boat rode at anchor. One of the divers pointed.

'Hold it, guys. Can we get a bit closer? There's something attached to the anchor chain.'

The water around the boat was shallow and, as they drew nearer, passing between the boat and the shore, one of the frogmen dropped over the side into the oil-dark water. He was within his depth as he waded towards the chain. There, bobbing up and down, was what looked like a large sack. A considerable quantity of other rubbish had gathered around it, forming a mass of flotsam jammed between the hull and the anchor chain.

The diver grasped the sack but couldn't shift it. Its neck had been closed by thick twine and the long loose ends had wrapped themselves around the massive links of the chain. A second man went into the water and joined him. Using his knife, he hacked at the twine and gradually, pulling one way and another, the two men worried at the sack until it began to come loose. But the cutting of the string meant that the sack now fell partly open.

'Oh my God!'

The flesh revealed at the sack's opening was mottled white, black, brown and blue and its general appearance was bloated and sheeny. The divers made out the curve of a knee, and a foot still with the remains of toenail varnish, before one of them closed the sack again and pulled hard.

Slowly, as if trying despite their disgust to be respectful to the corpse, they towed it back towards the inflatable.

'Is it our girl?' asked Walker, hurrying into the mortuary where Barrow awaited him.

'Don't know yet. But she was a blonde, about the right age. She was wrapped in a heavy sack tied with rope. They found her quite a way down the river from the boathouse. If it wasn't for the low tide they might never have found her.'

Walker checked his watch. It was one thirty. In a couple of hours he was due to pick up the kids from school.

'Has Mrs Booth been contacted?'

'Yes. We warned her that the body was in a bit of a

bad way and she asked if her ex-husband could do the identification.'

'He's here?'

'On his way down from Manchester. Be here in a couple of hours.'

'*Two hours*? Shit! What am I going to bloody do? I've got to stay for the PM and the kids have got to be picked up from school. Can't be in two flaming places at once!'

Barrow looked at him curiously as Walker whipped out his mobile phone and keyed North's number. As he waited for the call to connect he winked.

'Just family life, post-divorce,' he told the Detective Sergeant. 'Something you in your innocence have yet to learn of.'

North was in court all morning, hearing the end of the Saunders case. Walker had left a message saying he'd call back and, by the time he did, she had returned to her office. At the time the phone bleeped, she was talking to Chief Superintendent Bradley.

'Saw Mike on *Crime Night*,' Bradley was saying. 'I wouldn't like to be in his shoes on that case – lot of pressure.'

'Hello,' said North, after lifting the phone. 'Detective Inspector North.'

Bradley moved off towards the door.

'I'll leave you to it,' he said, then turned back, struck by an afterthought.

'Oh, I heard you had a good result on the Saunders case.'

North said into the phone, 'Hold on a sec, Mike.'

She turned back to Bradley. It was a relief to talk about something that wasn't anything to do with Stephen Warrington.

'Yes, they got six years. When the kid heard his sentence, he screamed out he'd kill me, and old Judge Middleton gave him an extra six months. So he threatened to shoot the judge! The snazzy Raymond Luff who was defending Saunders, jumped to his full five feet two inches and said, "Your Honour, my client's in shock. 'E doesn't know what 'e's sayin'." '

Her rendition of Luff's cockney tones was flawless.

'Then Saunders pointed at him and shouted, "Oh, yes I do, you useless, two-faced pillock. I'll cut your froat an' all . . ." Middleton gave him another two months for threatening behaviour and suggested the accused be removed from court before he worked his way up to a life sentence. It was classic.'

Bradley laughed and waved, leaving the room. North, who could hear Walker's muffled voice calling her name impatiently, put the handset back to her ear.

'Sorry, Mike. Go on.'

'Listen, I need a favour. No way can I get off at four, we've got a big development. Can you collect the kids, Pat? I'm sorry to lay this on you, but I think we've found Cassie Booth's body.'

North rolled her eyes. She had a suspect to interview this afternoon. Hutchens, standing beside her now, had just dropped the guy's file in front of her.

'It's a bit short notice, Mike. I mean, it's impossible for me to—'

'Can't you work something, sweetheart? I'm really

stuck here, and you're a good twenty minutes nearer to the school.'

North sighed.

'OK. What's the address of the school?'

She jotted it down to Walker's dictation and said to Hutchens, 'How long do you think we'll be?'

Hutchens, hurrying out now, didn't know.

She said to Walker, 'OK, Mike, I'll sort something and get back to you.'

'Look, I really appreciate this, sweetheart, I can't tell you. You don't have to worry about their tea. I'm sure there's baked beans or eggs and bacon or something they'll like at home. The head teacher's name's Mrs Hawley, by the way, that's H-A-W-L-E-Y. Got that?'

'Yes, and I've really got to go now. I'll call you, don't worry.'

Briefly, with her elbow up on the desk, she dropped her head on to her hand. It was the last thing she needed right now. Then she pulled herself together, snatched up her bag and headed for interview room 4. When she was half-way to the stairs, Vivien Watkins intercepted her.

'Have you got a minute, Pat?'

'Is it important?'

'The thing is, it might not be as cut and dried as we thought, about the Warrington business.'

North sighed again. Was anything ever cut and dried about Warrington?

'Can we talk on the move, Viv? I've got an interview set up. What's the problem?'

'Well, I was hoping you'd agree to liaise with us on this. As I said, Warrington kept on asking for you. He

123

said he wouldn't discuss the incident unless you were there. At the moment he's released pending identification by one of the girls.'

Everything – her personal feelings, her experience as a copper, her visit from Warrington late the previous evening – was telling North not to get involved. The man's inexplicable obsession with her meant she might quickly become a part of the problem rather than an assist to the solution. And she could easily be accused of muscling in.

'Come on, Viv. You know how paranoid everyone gets. If I start nosing around someone else's case—'

'Pat, this isn't coming from me. I wouldn't dare interfere. Don Shaw's heading the inquiry. He wants a word about this previous incident Warrington was picked up for.'

They were in the lobby now. North said, 'I'll get back to him, but not right now.'

She noticed that Watkins was holding her car keys. Watkins wasn't married. A thought hit her.

'You off home, Viv?' she said.

Watkins nodded.

'You couldn't do me a *major* favour, could you?'

She explained about Walker's kids in their school out in Essex, how they had to be picked up about four and brought back into town when both she and Walker had unbreakable commitments.

'You couldn't get out there, could you? Bring them back for me? Be there in twenty minutes if you know the back doubles.'

It was Watkins's turn to sigh reluctantly, but she had nothing particular doing after her shift and said she could make the pick-up. Gratefully North gave her the details and, as they parted, reassured her.

'And don't worry, Viv, I'll talk to Don Shaw about Warrington, maximum cooperation – OK?'

Quid pro quo.

As Watkins pushed through the main doors of the station, North pulled out her mobile to call Walker and tell him the good news – she'd sorted out his problem with the children.

Dawes had been having an interesting day, tailing Wilding. Two things struck him straight away: the man was seriusly wealthy but his businesses seemed to happily run themselves. Wilding had little or no serious work to do. One of his factories was somewhere off the Great West Road – computer printed circuits, chips, disk drives – and this was where he had his main office. But he had spent no more than an hour at work on this Thursday morning.

A little before lunchtime he'd left and Dawes trailed him to a Waterstone's. Moving rapidly through the ground-floor sales area, Wilding disappeared into the basement and it took Dawes, not over-familiar with the layout of large bookshops, a while to locate his man. He was leafing through a sporting book, in a section adjacent to the children's literature. Dawes thought this highly significant. At one point, keeping a careful distance, he was certain Wilding was winding himself up to speak to a child of about eleven. But the mother came up and took her away before anything happened.

Wilding had left the shop and walked rapidly, decreasing his pace only when he came abreast of a park.

Eventually he had slowed to a stroll as he found himself opposite the mesh fence of a children's playground. Yes, thought Dawes. The guy's a nonce for sure – just look at him looking. The Detective Constable, loitering some distance away, noticed Wilding had something of shiny metal in his hands. What was it – some toy or gizmo to attract a child's attention? No, it was just car keys. A few moments later, he had stopped beside a silver Fiat two-seater, bleeped it open and climbed in.

Dawes would have liked to have something more definite to report to Walker. But this was a start: there were indications they were on the right path, for this wasn't exactly the behaviour of a normally adjusted, happily married company director.

The buzz around the Southfields Incident Room, where Walker was due to hold a briefing, was about the imminent identification of the body discovered between Putney and Hammersmith Bridge. It was a difficult moment in many ways. On occasions like these, the officers of AMIP are torn between, on one side, a natural desire for a missing person to be found alive and, on the other, the near-certainty that the finding of a body would lead them half-way, if not all the way, to a killer.

While they waited for Walker to get off the phone, Holgate buttonholed Ross.

'Have we got the body ID'd yet?'

'No. Barrow called in from the mortuary. Cassie's father's just arrived. They're treating it as a special PM and hoping to jump the queue.'

'All right, listen up everyone!'

Walker was back. He was patting his pockets which, as all who knew him could tell, was a sure sign that the Detective Superintendent needed a smoke.

'Now, the body was wrapped in a canvas sack, secured by strong plastic ropes or thick twine.'

He had his packet of Marlboro out now, and was ripping the filter tip off a cigarette.

'We don't yet know how long she has been in the water, *or* if she was sexually assaulted. It's always a tough one when the body's been in the water. From what I saw, it was very bloated.'

He tipped the truncated Marlboro into his mouth and lit it fast, using a butane lighter. He inhaled deeply while the officers in the room exchanged glances.

'Other developments. We had this phone tip-off last night which all of you know about. Detective Sergeant Ross! Any luck with the voice recognition on this second tip-off, compared with the one which led to us finding the clothes?'

Walker was pacing around, as he always did on these occasions, leaving not one available carpet tile untrodden. In this office, with its tough clean-air policy, his sinful smoke could be smelt by all.

'No, Guv,' said Ross, concealing a smile. He knew what was coming. 'Same problem as we had with the first. His voice was too quiet and muffled to get a definite pattern.'

With a piercing, electronic shriek the smoke alarms sounded. Walker looked around, bewildered.

'What the *fuck*?'

Suddenly every officer who smoked was waving an

unlit cigarette in the air. It took Walker a couple of beats to see the relevance and then he relaxed and laughed.

'I forgot!' he shouted above the din. 'Why didn't you dirty bastards remind me?'

Defiantly he took another drag before stubbing the cigarette out on his shoe.

The journey from Grays in Essex to central London was fun. The Walker children had been with strange police officers before but Vivien Watkins turned out to be especially good company, telling stories about investigations she'd been on, and about the bizarre things that sometimes happened to police officers. At Embankment station they had to hang around a few minutes, after which (they were told) they'd be introduced to Detective Inspector Pat North, who would take them home to their father.

'I know who she is,' whispered Amy to her brother as they waited. 'She's that cow.'

'What cow?'

'The one who took him away from Mummy, of course. They're *living together*.'

'Oh, that cow,' said Richard, nodding knowingly. He was in his school uniform but wore a blue bug-eyed fleecy hat with ears and long floppy antennae.

Eventually North emerged from her office and took the children out to the car. Watkins, who had surprised herself by how much she'd enjoyed the chore, came out to see them off.

'Put your seat belts on, kiddoes, else you might get arrested!'

'Bye-bye, Auntie Vivien,' said Amy with ingratiating politeness.

'You're a big hit, Viv,' said North. 'And I really appreciate this. Thanks.'

'No problem at all,' said Watkins. 'Just remember – you owe me one!'

The smoke alarms seemed to go on squealing interminably and forced a halt to the briefing. Walker left the office ten minutes later, and it was a blessed relief. He went as far as the off-licence, where he bought a half-bottle of Glenfiddich and, on his way back, lingered in the car park where he could smoke and think in peace. It was here, perched on a brick dividing wall, that Ross found him a few minutes later.

'Been looking all over for you.'

Walker showed him his lighted cigarette.

'Just having a crafty one, unlike the last! Unbelievable, isn't it? The most stressed job on the planet and they don't even allow—'

Ross, a non-smoker, was unimpressed.

'Yes, well, the smoke alarms have finally stopped.'

'Anything come in from the surveillance on Wilding?'

Ross's head indicated a negative.

'Nothing concrete, not yet. But Dawes says he's been sniffing around the children's section of a bookshop – reckons he could be sussing out his next victim.'

He indicated the half-bottle of whisky which stood on the wall next to Walker.

'What – having a quiet snifter as well as the fag?'

Walker smiled conspiratorially.

'No, got the big boys coming in to check the policy

129

file. We only just found a body, but as always they want a result by yesterday.'

He tapped the top of the bottle.

'But a few sips of this quality malt, and they'll be eating out of my hand. At least we've got something more to go on now – the body.'

'So you think it's her?'

'Yes, course I do. Who else could it be?'

Walker's question was rhetorical but, as it turned out, an answer to it would soon be required. By four o'clock, Barrow was at the mortuary to meet up with Cassie's father, Daniel Booth, who had arrived to carry out the identification. Clutching, for some reason, a photograph album, this nervous, haggard middle-aged man himself had the pallor of a dead man.

The mortuary attendant, moving silently on rubber shoes, speaking only in murmurs and whispers, conducted them down the stairs to a small chapel-like room. In the centre was a raised platform, on which lay a sheeted shape. Unlike the other parts of this starkly clinical building, the room was carpeted, with warm air being pushed out through mumbling vents in the skirting.

Booth refused Barrow's offered help with the thick book, laying it reverently on the floor. Then he stood, as if at attention, beside the shape on the platform. The attendant gently ghosted back the covering sheet.

Booth looked for a long time. The attendant in turn looked at him, and then glanced at Barrow. Booth's expression was difficult to read at first. He had seemed puzzled, but this soon gave way to emotion. He stared for perhaps fifteen, twenty seconds, very slowly shaking his head, his shoulders seeming to heave and slightly tremble. When he turned around to address Barrow, his eyes were filled with tears.

'This is not my daughter,' he said, in a thin, almost inaudible voice.

Barrow felt the man must be in some kind of denial. He kept the thought to himself, watching as Booth crossed to the album of photographs and bent to pick it up. There was a low table beside the wall and he placed it there and, utterly absorbed in what he was doing, began to turn the pages. Barrow didn't like to interrupt him and just waited. After a few moments, Booth seemed to come to himself. He dabbed his eyes with his sleeve, sniffed deeply and beckoned to Barrow. He showed the Detective Sergeant one of the pages, a single enlargement of Cassie as she had been perhaps a year earlier on a beach. Her smile was toothy, her hair flew in the breeze, and she looked happy.

'This is her, this is Cassie,' said Daniel Booth quietly, the tears now streaming down his face. 'Not that poor girl there.'

Barrow looked closely at the photograph and back at the body on the platform. Immediately he could see it. Booth was not simply refusing the fact of his daughter's death, he was telling the simple truth. The girl they'd fished out of the Thames looked superficially similar, but really she wasn't Cassie Booth. She was someone else entirely.

He sighed. They were almost back to square one.

CHAPTER 12

RICHARD AND Amy said nothing at all in North's car as she drove them back to Barnes. She tried to jolly them along by pointing out sights along the way – Big Ben, Lambeth Palace, the MI6 building – but their stony silence was unyielding. North decided she had no gift for dealing with children: the childish behaviour of certain junior male officers in the canteen was a doddle compared to real kids. So it was with a sense of relief, coupled with renewed anxiety about feeding, that she showed Walker's progeny into the flat.

'Just let me see what's for your tea . . . Take your coats off and put them . . .' She looked around at the ambient chaos. 'Just dump them anywhere.'

It took her thirty seconds to check the kitchen. There were no cans of baked beans or spaghetti, no eggs and bacon. Apart from a carton of Moroccan pea soup and a jar of rough country pâté, it was a situation Mother Hubbard might have identified with. North made an executive decision not even to ask if they would try the soup or the pâté.

'Right,' she said, bustling back. 'Your dad didn't shop, so we'll go out and eat. What's it to be? Hamburgers? Pizza? Fish and chips?'

They turned their white faces to her, big eyes unblinking, but did not respond. What was this – some kind of social ostracism? Or just a game? Deciding to face them out, North planted her hands on her hips. Whatever they were playing at, it could not go on.

'OK,' she said. 'I've had the silent treatment in the car and at the police station. But I won't have it in my own home. What's this all about?'

Finally it was Amy who spoke up for them both.

'Mummy said not to speak to you. She said Daddy's supposed to look after us.'

North looked from the girl to the boy and back again. She sighed and shook her head slowly. How to put this?

'Yes, well, your daddy's not like most kids' dads. His work's special and much more important because . . . Well, because he doesn't just look after you, he looks after all the kids that get lost, or hurt . . .'

They continued to stare while she fumbled for an explanation.

'OK, I'll call him!'

As she went to the phone she muttered, 'Are you sure you two didn't star in *The Omen*?'

There was, however, no prospect of speaking with Detective Superintendent Walker at the moment, as he was closeted in his office with the Top Brass.

'What's going on?' asked Holgate, bringing in coffees for herself and Ross.

'Guv's got the big boys in – Area Commander Crime and Area Commander Operations.'

'Sounds heavy. Does he know yet that the body isn't Cassie Booth?'

'He does. Anyway, apparently he says he'll have them eating out of his hand – that's vintage malt he's got in there.'

But the only person in Walker's office drinking the twelve-year-old malt was Walker, watched with unspoken disapproval by the two Commanders. They insisted on drinking fruit juice for which, with a sinking heart, Walker sent Ross down to the canteen.

His spirits revived as the spirit he was drinking began to have its effect. Walker now became animated, not to say pugnacious, in response to the suggestion that he could do with some extra help in the area of new investigation techniques. Walker was not impressed by trendy theories taking the place of practical evidence-gathering. And he told the senior officers that the lack of progress in the Cassie Booth case was more apparent than real.

'We did a copybook house-to-house exercise, incredibly thorough. We did a successful TV appeal—'

'How successful?' broke in the Area Commander Crime, draining his orange juice. 'You mean *you* enjoyed yourself!'

Possibly it was an attempt at humour but more likely this was a criticism disguised as humour. Walker felt himself bristling.

'Over three hundred bloody calls, sir. All right, I admit none of them has led us to the body, but we've already had one about the blood-stained clothes. That means there's somebody out there trying to communicate with us, tell us about what happened to Cassie. He's done it once, he'll do it again. In fact we think he *has* done it again – a phone call from a guy who suggested we were looking for Cassie in the wrong place.'

But the Commanders didn't want to talk about the details of the case.

'Mike,' said the ACC, 'our main concern here is the overall operational situation. For instance, how's the budget?'

The fact that Walker had anticipated this question did not much help him. He was known in the Met for his maverick approach to budgeting but, however hard he tried, he could never put up a convincing impersonation of a bookkeeper. This had always in the past been compensated for by good end results, but how long would his luck hold?

Slowly he unfolded the single sheet of A4 paper on which he had scribbled some (pathetically few, it seemed to him now) calculations. The Area Commander Operations, who had hitherto remained ominously quiet while downing half a pint of juice, listened with a long face to Walker's account of his expenditure.

'Anyway, the point is,' said Walker in conclusion, 'this inquiry has been carried out with no stone unturned.'

'And, with the greatest respect,' said the ACO, 'our concern is that you may be letting yourself get a mite too close to the detail on this case. Don't be afraid of bringing in specialists. There are so many new, efficient ways of identifying which stones should be turned first, psychological profiling being a case in point. Academic studies have shown you can save a lot of time and money. For instance, a profiler might have told you whether this very costly river search was really necessary.'

Walker gulped at his drink and took up a defensive stance, pointing his finger in the air.

'Look, sir, in my judgement a thorough search of the river was absolutely vital. Don't forget we found blood-stained clothes in a boathouse, right? And the search team was fantastic, recovered all sorts of stuff you wouldn't believe – there was a whole car down there which turned out to have been stolen in Glasgow seven years ago.'

'It sounds like an expensive way of clearing up a missing vehicle, Mike,' said the ACO with a bloodless smile. 'And, by the way, have you got any more of this juice?'

'What? Oh, yeah, I'll send someone down.'

He opened his door and beckoned Ross while he continued to talk to the Commanders.

'I *was* aware of the cost. But what was I supposed to do? We got a result, didn't we? Only it wasn't the one we wanted.'

He strode over to his coat, hanging on a peg outside his office, and checked the pocket for cigarettes. He found none. He spoke over his shoulder, more loudly than he meant.

'I just don't feel that at this stage the investigation requires the assistance of someone from the outside.'

Ross came over.

'Yes, Guv?'

'Get some more orange or apple juice from the canteen, would you? And have you got any fags?'

'Sorry, Guv.'

'Get along, then!'

He returned to his office and closed the door.

'You want psychological profiling? I'll give you my psychological profile of this guy. This is a killer who *wants* publicity because, one, it has to be him who tipped us off about the body in the boathouse and, two, when the press and TV put it out that we're searching a wide stretch of the river he tips us off again. Says we're looking in the wrong place!'

The Area Commander Crime tapped his lip.

'Could be, Mike. Could very well be. But we've got specialists coming out of the National Crime Faculty who've trained in this psychological stuff. There have been some remarkable successes, as you know. So I've attached an officer to your team who will be joining you today. He's just been to the NCF and he's a very good Detective Sergeant. He'll be invaluable. Oh, and have you seen the new *Murder Investigation Manual*?'

He picked a fat ring file from his briefcase and handed it to Walker.

'It's been issued as a kind of Highway Code for AMIP teams – you know, what to do, what not to do. Make sure you read it, OK?'

Murder Manual? Did these men think he didn't know his job? Walker took a last, large gulp of his whisky. It was good stuff but, from his face, you'd think he was swallowing paint-stripper.

A small and dapper officer wandered into the Incident Room, looking about him. He was nearly cannoned into by Ross, carrying a tray with bottles of fruit juice.

'Hey!' said the newcomer. 'Hitting the juice, are we?'

Ross turned and immediately recognized Detective Sergeant Dave Satchell, who had been with AMIP nearly as long as Walker, but had been away for months on some kind of attachment.

'Hi!' said Ross, holding the tray in one hand and shaking with the other. 'What you doing here?'

'I've just come off a profiling course at Bramshill – a blinder. Brilliant it was!'

'Well, you don't have any fags, do you? Guv wants a fix.'

Satchell pulled out an unopened packet from his coat and tossed it over.

'Give him these. I've not started again, but I like to test my will-power.'

'Well, this place'll do that. A murder inquiry without a body!'

Satchell waved his hand in the air.

'Leave it to me. I'll find one,' he said with a touch of smugness.

It was too late for the fruit juice because now the meeting in Walker's office was breaking up. The Area Commanders filed out of the room, nodding cursorily to members of the team standing by like curious spectators. In their wake came Walker, treading with a tell-tale slowness, carrying the empty bottle of Scotch between thumb and forefinger. His face lit up when he saw Satchell.

'Hi, Satch. What you doing here?'

'Didn't you get the memo?' said Satchell. He nodded at the malt-whisky bottle. 'And I hope you've got another one of those, mate.'

Walker dropped the empty bottle into a bin and it clanged loudly. He looked at it, saying in a melancholy voice:

'They are bringing in some pen-pusher. A wonder man, who can apparently solve any crime via his crystal balls.'

'That's me!' said Satchell with a delighted grin, as Ross handed him a bottle of vodka produced from a desk drawer. 'National Crime Faculty trained. I've just done the course.'

'Oh yeah, yeah,' said Walker tiredly. He assumed Satchell was joking, of course. Satchell was a regular police officer, a great guy with whom Walker had worked many times. Not some smart-arse from the Crime Faculty who reckons he's a shrink first and a copper second.

Walker wandered back to his office. He caught sight of the *Murder Manual* lying on his desk. He snatched it up and re-emerged, waving the offensive file.

'This here is the Met's latest detection strategy, boys. A *Manual*, no less, a fucking *Murder Manual*!'

He lifted his arms in mock-dismay.

'Oh my God!' he said, 'a murder victim. Now hang on, let me check . . .'

He turned pages feverishly.

'C . . . C for Crime Scene. "Do not touch the body . . ."'

He threw the book down again.

'It's a bloody insult!'

He picked up his coat to put it on. The others watched with mounting amusement mixed with a slight unease. Inebriated, Walker became unpredictable and inarticulate.

'So, I am in def'cit, a very *large* def'cit but what the hell . . .'

He was trying to find the armhole of the coat but couldn't. He gave up.

'I am, I think, about to be shafted. They skirted round it, but I know this prick they've foisted on me from the Crime Unit'll take over and – Christ! – it'll be Oxshott next for me, alongside Batchley . . .'

Satchell was cruising around looking for something to drink from when he passed the photograph of Cassie Booth.

'This is the missing girl, right?'

'Correct,' said Walker, who was now over by the water dispenser, helping himself from the plastic-beaker dispenser. 'Didn't you see me starring on *Crime Night*? And we've got a body now, but not the right body.'

'What, you got *two* bodies?' said Satchell, surprised. 'You think we've got a serial killer?'

'No, she turned out to be that missing Soho hooker. Central Area are dealing with it.'

'What if they're connected, though?' put in Ross. 'She was found close to the boathouse.'

'Read my lips, Ross,' said Walker. 'They're not connected.'

Walker brought back two beakers. He seized the vodka from Satchell, unscrewed the cap, poured a large slug and handed it to Satchell. Then he poured a second.

'Guv,' said Ross, in concern. 'It's vodka. You've been on the malt.'

Walker glared at Ross and handed him the second beaker.

'I know that, big man. I was pouring one for you. I might be pissed, but a malt man would never touch a Russian woofter's tipple.'

He snorted.

'And those two pricks'll get the running shits from all that orange juice they seem to prefer.'

Instead of putting on his coat he balled it up and jammed it under his arm.

'G'night. See you in the morning.'

Unsteadily he wandered out.

Ross and Satchell stood together in the now almost empty Incident Room. Neither could think of a suitable remark to cover Walker's retreat. Instead Ross handed Satchell the policy file. The Detective Sergeant opened it, flipping through its relatively light contents.

'This all you've got after . . . how many weeks?'

'Ten days.'

Ross pointed to a mound of files stacked on a table near Walker's office door.

'They're the house-to-house. We've had hundreds of statements. This . . .'

He tapped the file he had just handed Satchell.

'. . . is an update.'

Suddenly Ross yawned and looked at his watch.

'Keeping you up, am I?' said Satchell.

Ross smiled.

'I don't need sleep – I'm an athlete.'

Satchell gestured towards the door.

'Walker's not. He was well away. Oh shit, he's not driving, is he?'

'No. He'll get a lift in a squad car.'

Ross proffered the vodka bottle.

'Just relax. Enjoy another slug of the Russian poofter's tipple.'

Satchell poured and shook his head, still thinking of Walker.

'He thought I was joking. I really have done the course – ask me anything.'

He tapped his head.

'It's all up here. I'm a highly trained, perfectly tuned criminal profiler.'

But Ross's mocking look said, 'Pull the other one.'

The children had decided on pizzas and, at about the time Walker's meeting with the Area Commanders was beginning, North drove them to Putney High Street where they found a chain restaurant with seats near the window.

'OK,' said North, scanning the menu. 'I'm going to have the Deep Pan Hawaii with extra peppers, mushrooms and extra cheese.'

She was letting rip on her diet, as she was well aware, but what the hell. She deserved it. Anyway, she felt incredibly hungry and in need of reserves of stamina if she was going to get through the evening.

The waitress looked at eight-year-old Richard, who simply said, 'I want number four.'

His two-years-older sister shook her head pityingly.

'Four? He can't even read. So he doesn't know what number four is.'

North made a calming gesture with her hand.

'Just hold back the abuse, Amy. Richard has picked . . .'

She consulted the card.

'Oh my goodness, spicy salami with extra cheese! It's the best!'

'He hates salami,' said Amy, flatly. 'He never eats it. I told you he can't read – he's dyslexic.'

She turned to her brother, taking charge.

'You do want some chips, Richard, don't you? And

how about pizza just with mushrooms and cheese? And I'll have a pepperoni thin crust with a side salad, OK?'

She sat back, satisfied that she had bested North again.

'Any milkshakes, Cokes?' asked the waitress. 'We have great raspberry and a terrific iced chocolate shake.'

Richard chimed in, 'Oh yes! I'll have that.'

North looked towards Amy. She resembled Walker physically, or at least you could see she was his daughter. She had also clearly inherited his intelligence, but none of his character came through from her – neither his bluster nor that underlying vulnerability. Amy's personality seemed to derive almost exclusively from her mother.

'What would you like to drink, Amy?'

Before the little girl could answer, they were interrupted. A tall, thin man in a dirty jacket and crumpled shirt – he looked like a dosser – approached the table. He was pulling faces to amuse the children, popping his eyes and puffing out his cheeks. It took North two or three seconds to recognize Stephen Warrington.

'Hi!' he said breezily enough, in spite of his dishevelled appearance. 'I was walking past and looked in and saw you, Pat. And these two amazing people – are you kids from the Land of Oz? Can I sit with you, yes?'

Amy and Richard looked delighted as Warrington slid into the one vacant place and picked up a menu. They watched fascinated to see what he would do next.

'I'm going to have a huge chilli pizza, so hot it makes your tongue throb.'

He stuck out his tongue and rolled his eyes. The children giggled.

'Mr Warrington,' said North, finding the power of speech at last. 'Please leave the table. I would like you to leave us alone.'

He ignored her, leaning across instead to Amy.

'What does your daddy do?'

'He's a police officer,' she said proudly. 'He's a detective – Michael Walker. And my mummy's called Lynn.'

'*Really*? Is that so?'

Warrington produced a coin from his pocket and started rolling it across his knuckles. He apparently made it disappear before producing it again from behind Richard's ear. North signalled towards the waitress and immediately Warrington was alert to the danger.

'Please,' he said, 'don't let me spoil your evening, Pat. I just want someone to talk to.'

He slid off the seat and began to move around to North's side of the table. She tracked his progress but said nothing.

'I needed to speak to you,' murmured Warrington. 'I really did. It was an awful situation, all a mistake. It'll be cleared up. I was just, well . . . I was scared.'

North was looking away from him but he still edged nearer.

'No one likes the police at their home,' he went on. 'Luckily my girls weren't there, didn't witness it. It was just terrible – been a bad sort of week all round, really . . .'

The waitress appeared with three pizzas and placed them in front of North and the children. Although still unsure what to make of the strange intruder, and fascinated by the way he was making North crosser and crosser, the children's appetite took over. They settled down to voracious eating.

'Those stupid girls in the park . . . they're lying. I was not even close to them.'

He was right behind North now, murmuring his justifications in her ear. She shuddered, forcing herself to turn and face him.

'Then why did you run away from the police, and then drive off, knowing they wanted to speak to you?'

'I ran towards my car. If they say I ran away from them, they've got it wrong. They frightened the life out of me, suddenly putting on their sirens so close behind. I thought it was some sort of emergency and they wanted me out of the way, so I drove faster.'

North shut her eyes. Her appetite had gone. But, although overwhelmed by the desire for him to go away, she forced herself to be calm.

'Please leave us to our meal now, Mr Warrington.'

Deliberately she turned her attention to the children, offering to cut up Richard's pizza and get Amy a drink. What did she want?

'Orange juice,' said Amy imperiously.

'Please!' offered North.

Warrington took up the theme, calling to the waitress.

'Orange juice! Orange juice for the beautiful young lady, the princess!'

He turned back to Walker's daughter.

'You look like a princess, has anyone ever said that to you before?'

At this North felt even queasier than before. But Amy glowed.

'Yes, Daddy. My daddy calls me Princess.'

Warrington glanced down at North with a warm, embracing smile. What *did* he think he was doing?

'My oldest daughter is called Charlotte,' he said to the children. 'And my youngest is Lucy. My two princesses. I adore them.'

He turned to North again, his eyes soulful and moist.

'Pat, please answer me. You don't really believe that I did anything that would in any way frighten a little girl, do you?'

'No,' said North, herself forcing a thin smile. She would say anything now to get rid of him. 'I'm sure you didn't. Goodnight, Mr Warrington.'

But it wasn't time for him to leave them yet. He leaned forward, over her shoulder, close to her ear.

'I get very anxious, Pat. I have to take medication, just to calm down. Things worry me, spiral out of control. On the TV I saw that they were trawling the river for Cassie Booth. I bet her body *won't* be bloated. I bet it'll be crawling with maggots!'

North's head jerked upwards in disgust. But before she could properly piece together the import of what Warrington had just said, he was patting Amy's curly red hair as she ate. Warrington was leaving, but he had one final question for North.

'Are you sure,' he asked, 'that you're looking in the right place for that girl?'

He moved quickly, almost loping, towards the exit and pushed out into the street. As he passed the window beside which they were sitting he paused, put his hand on the glass and favoured them with a farewell smile.

It was almost ten by the time Walker got back to the flat. Richard was in a sleeping-bag on the floor, Amy on the sofa. He got down laboriously on his hands

146

and knees and kissed his gently breathing son. Amy stirred.

'Daddy?'

He spotted Richard's blue felt insect hat and pulled it on, vaguely thinking it would amuse Amy. Then he shuffled towards his daughter.

'I'm sorry. Sorry I couldn't get away. You won't tell your mum, now, will you?'

He fussed around her, drawing up a blanket which covered her sleeping-bag, rearranging the pillow under her head.

'I know I haven't been around as much as I should have. I know that . . .'

He sighed and looked into his daughter's face. She stared back at him, half smiling at the blue hat that looked so bizarre on her father's head.

'But I always used to kiss you good-night, whatever time I got in, never missed.'

He felt a surge of emotion – alcohol-enhanced, to be sure, but real enough for all that.

'Sometimes, when I come home now, I miss that . . . Miss it a lot.'

His voice was almost breaking.

'I love you both, so much,' he whispered. 'I'm your daddy – don't you ever forget that.'

Amy reached up and clasped her hands around her father's neck.

'Good night, Daddy.'

She kissed him then pulled back, wrinkling her nose.

'Yeuch. You've been on the Scotch!'

Walker smiled indulgently, gazing at his tangle-haired daughter with love and pride.

'Sleep tight, Princess. Night, night.'

He gave a final adjustment to her bedding, stood up, still wearing the silly hat, and crept none too quietly out of the room. As soon as he'd gone, Richard turned over.

He whispered loudly, 'I pretended to be asleep. Will it work, Amy?'

'Oh yes, keep it up, and just before we get picked up by Mum, give him a hug and ask for the . . . what is it you want?'

'A Multi-Warrior with five different weapons, batteries not included. But it's twenty-five quid!'

'Trust me, it's your turn. I got the new Barbie wardrobe and Honolulu beach holiday wear. And when it's my turn next I'll get her pony.'

'Night-night, Amy,' said Richard softly. He turned over and went satisfied to sleep, picturing the Multi-Warrior in his hands, flashing and roaring.

'Night-night, Richard,' said Amy.

'They adore you,' said Walker to North, without the slightest shred of evidence.

She was still in the bathroom as he heaved himself into bed and pulled the duvet up to his ears.

'You are a wonder woman. What would I have done without you?'

North came through in her nightdress, wiping at her make-up. There was a glass of whisky on her bedside table. She said nothing, but was thinking of Cassie Booth.

'Ah! I dreamed of this all evening,' he went on. 'I am knackered. Totally wiped out. Oh, Pat, I've had such a day, and one I never want to repeat. For a few minutes I thought we'd got another serial-killing nutter. The body we found was another girl. About the same age as Cassie but a prostitute, missing for three weeks.'

North turned off the main light, leaving only her bedside lamp. She got into bed and sipped her drink. Still she kept her counsel.

'Then I had a little visit from a couple of Area Commanders. Apparently I'm too "hands on", so they said. I should take a step back.'

He rolled over and found her hand, squeezing it under the duvet.

'God, there's hardly any real detectives left in the Met. New management are only interested in nodding dogs who don't get their hands dirty. Makes me sick.'

He yawned cavernously. She looked at him. His eyes were closed.

'Pat, I really appreciate it. Thanks for taking care of my kids.'

North took another sip of whisky.

'Mike, it would be freaky, I know, and maybe too coincidental, and I could be wrong. But you know you often go on about intuition, that gut feeling about something . . .'

She laid the glass down beside her and huddled down into the bed.

'So, Mike, I don't want to worry you, but there's this guy I've been dealing with – Stephen Warrington. He's the one who left me that wine, remember? Well, I *think* he might know something about your case . . . Mike? Are you listening?'

She looked at him again. His jaw had gone slack, his breathing was noisy and metronomic. Soon he would be lightly snoring.

With a sigh she switched off the light.

Chapter 13

THIS TIME it was North who left the flat first, Walker who lay on in bed groaning and virtually unable to communicate until he'd drunk the cup of coffee that she had left helpfully beside his bed as she left for work. She did not mention Stephen Warrington to him – she had wanted to last night but she now felt the need for something more substantial by way of evidence than the three bare words 'crawling with maggots', however fiercely whispered. Neither that nor Warrington's generally odd behaviour constituted a crime. What she wanted now was to know more about him and why, out of nowhere, he had brought up the subject of Cassie Booth.

She called Hutchens into her office. He'd been on the night shift, but now she asked him to spend the morning quietly investigating Warrington.

'It's just background, Jack. His business, his movements in the past fortnight, three weeks, the cars he drives or has access to. And especially any Ford Mondeos.'

She didn't tell him specifically why she wanted this. She didn't want to invite ridicule. Unless and until something solid came up to connect Warrington with the Cassie Booth case, she preferred to keep her suspicions dark. The tension she felt about everything connected with Warrington surprised and slightly frightened her.

Towards mid-morning, Hutchens was back in her office.

'Got anything, Jack?' she asked.

Her voice had an intense quality Hutchens hadn't heard before. He grinned good-naturedly. He'd got some answers for Detective Inspector North, but he'd be wanting some himself, too, before he left the office.

'You *do* know I've been off duty for one hour and fifteen minutes . . .'

'Come in, Jack. What you got for me?'

He sat down.

'OK – you after cut-price wine? Well, he's your man. And Warrington's bargain-basement wine company isn't owned by him at all. In fact he's really a sales rep, but a glorified one, their numero uno in fact.'

'Did you speak to anyone about vehicles?'

She sounded incredibly wound up about this. She had a pencil gripped so hard in her hand he thought she would break it. Of course, Hutchens knew that Warrington had been hounding her a little bit. So what was this all about?

'Yes, I did. Their salesmen use a rental company. Warrington himself leases a green Volvo estate.'

He could see the news had deflated her. He went on.

'I don't know what you're after, but . . . well, a few weeks back, Warrington was having trouble with the car's air-conditioning. Does this still interest you, by the way?'

'Yes, yes. Go on.'

'Well, they rented him a 1996 maroon car, a—'

'Mondeo, yes? I'm right, aren't I? It *was* a Mondeo!'

Hutchens was nodding and smiling and North felt a sudden surge of confidence. This was even better than she had hoped.

Stephen Warrington was in front of the mirror, preparing for his ID parade at Brixton identification suite. This was in connection with the supposed flashing incident at Embankment. He had dressed, as requested, in the same clothes he had worn in the Embankment park, but he now combed his hair differently. How old was this kid? Six, seven? She'd never remember him!

Susan came in.

'What time did you get in last night?'

'I told you. I had dinner with Adrian Riply. Business.'

'I was going to call the police.'

He swung away from the mirror and looked at Susan, appalled.

'Police? What on earth for?'

'Peggy's still missing. I called the RSPCA again, but they've had no Jack Russells brought in.'

Warrington strolled to the chair on which his jacket hung. He put the jacket on.

'I never liked her anyway. She was always ferreting into everything.'

She came up to him and straightened his collar, brushing off some fluff from the lapel.

'Stephen, really! The girls are awfully cut up. Where are you going?'

'None of your business!'

She looked at him sharply.

'Well, OK,' he conceded. 'I wasn't going to tell you, but they're making me do an ID parade.'

Susan Warrington took a step back from her husband, biting her lip.

'What?'

'It's appalling the way they're harassing me. Just terrible.'

'I'll come with you.'

'No, no. You've no need to.'

'I want to!'

'But she'll never be able to identify me, Susan – not a chance in hell.'

Laura Davies was in fact seven. When the man in the park had taken his willy out in front of her, she'd screamed and he'd run away. Now a kind lady was explaining that they had quite a few men here, but they weren't sure if any of them was the man who showed Laura his willy.

'So you've got to help us, all right? Try to identify him,' said the Child Protection Officer to Laura. 'Let's do a practice. We asked you to bring your favourite dolly – Tippy, yes?'

Laura nodded.

'Well, I'm going to show you some dollies lined up in a row. Each of them has a number in front. If you see Tippy, tell me her number.'

They did it several times. Sometimes Tippy was in the line-up of dolls and sometimes she wasn't. When she was, she always had a different number. Laura did well. She identified Tippy easily on each occasion that her doll was in the line-up and spoke up clearly when she wasn't.

'So you know what to do now, don't you, Laura? If you see the same man, the man from the park, just tell me what number he's sitting in front of. Are you ready?'

Laura nodded her head.

By coincidence, North's unit had an ID parade an hour after Warrington's. She decided to show up early, to learn the upshot of his parade, and bumped into Vivien Holgate in the car park outside.

'Hello, Viv. Have they done Warrington yet?'

Holgate nodded.

'She didn't pick him out.'

'What? I don't believe it!'

North was astounded but Holgate just shrugged.

'She's seven. *I* wouldn't have been certain. I mean, come on . . . At the time the poor kid was terrified.'

'Well, I suppose so . . .'

'Anyway, I've got to go, see you later.'

On her way out of the building, North suddenly caught sight of Warrington himself exchanging a few parting words with his solicitor. Before she could get out of the way, he'd seen her too and was heading over.

'Hi, Pat!'

He was greeting her like an old friend. He spread his arms wide.

'No case! Innocent!'

His voice was full of geniality, until it suddenly turned nasty.

'She couldn't pick me out, the silly little bitch. They should never have wasted their time.'

It was hard to believe this was the suave wine buff she'd met at his home – let alone the snivelling near-down-and-out who'd interrupted last night's pizzas. Today, he was swaggering and loud.

He leaned towards her, winking.

'I fooled them all again, didn't I? I could get away with murder!'

As North flinched away from him, Warrington glanced across her shoulder. His wife was standing close by, beside her Volvo just a couple of parked cars away. Without another word to North, he almost ran to her.

'Darling – I told you this was all a big misunderstanding.'

He moved to embrace her, his arms wide, but Susan Warrington became suddenly rigid and took a step back.

'Stay away from me, Stephen. Don't touch me!'

North watched him step towards his wife again but she raised her hands to ward him off, flushed and furious.

'DON'T TOUCH ME!' she shouted. 'Stay away from me. You disgust me!'

She wrenched open her car door, stepped in and drove away, leaving him with his arms still wide in the middle of the car park's tarmac. North, now in the driving seat of her own car, started the engine. It had been a scene to savour, but what did it mean?

At Southfields, with the inquiry not making too much headway as it entered its second week, Walker was having a meeting with his new criminal profiler, his old mate Dave Satchell. They'd been discussing Dawes's surveillance reports on Wilding.

'He looks like a classic paedophile,' said Satchell. 'In my opinion, Wilding's in what's known as precursory mode, which means—'

Walker grimaced at the artificial jargon. Satchell was not to be easily put off.

'Which *means* he is hanging around places where there are children, observing them and building up a fantasy which will eventually become so vivid that he does something.'

'Maybe,' said Walker sceptically. 'Maybe not. Cassie Booth was fifteen – hardly a child.'

'Yeah, but she was very small for her age.'

'OK, so what do you suggest we do?'

'At this point you should keep an open mind, yeah? We don't want *you* getting tunnel vision, like Mrs Greenway. Wilding's not a registered offender, so there's not much we can do except continue to stick to him like glue and try to work out what he's going to do next.'

So why, thought Walker, was someone tipping them off? It didn't make sense to him. But before he could raise this with Satchell, he saw North walk into the Incident Room. What the hell was she doing here? He jumped up and, telling Satchell to get on with his analysis, intercepted her.

'What's happened?' he said.

'Nothing serious. But I need a quick word.'

She had a typewritten report in her hands, which she handed firmly to Walker like someone serving a writ.

'First, read this.'

He glanced at the title: *Stephen Warrington*. He looked around. Various faces were turned towards them. One or two of his colleagues were offering their opinions to each other behind their hands.

'Come on,' he said brusquely. 'In my office!'

Five minutes later Walker had read the report and was frowning deeply. If the evidence was beginning to point to Warrington, who was Walker to argue? At least it had been gathered by normal, old-fashioned methods of detection. And yet he was annoyed: she should have told him this before. *And* the memo seemed to let Wilding off the hook. Walker had invested so much of his suspicion on Wilding that he positively *wanted* the man to be guilty.

'Warrington's made a lot of extreme statements,' North was saying, 'to me in particular. But I put a lot of what he says down to his illness. He's cyclothymic.'

Walker hissed through his teeth. More jargon, he supposed.

'It's a form of manic depression and means he has violent mood swings if he doesn't take the proper medication. Anyway, he's developed into a right pest. First I get sent down to appease him as a persistent complainer. Next thing I know he's found out where we live, and sent over that case of wine. Then he gets arrested twice within a few days on indecent exposure charges and demands to speak to me at the station. He obviously sees me as an ally because, although I refused to speak to him, he must have followed us to the restaurant where I took Richard and Amy last night. Scared the daylights out of me. He kept ranting on about his flashing offences and that he was innocent. But what's so weird is that he keeps going on about the Cassie Booth case.'

'And according to this,' said Walker, tapping North's memo, 'he drove a maroon Mondeo until, when? Last week, yes?'

'Correct. It's back with the rental company now, being used by a Tony Levine.'

She pointed to the bottom of the second page.

'That's his address, there.'

Walker still felt angry. He flipped back to the memo's front page and scanned it again. He simply said, 'I'll see you later.'

'Look, if you're pissed off that I came here, I'm sorry. I thought it might be important.'

'It is important. But it's hard to deal with feeling two foot high – as well as the fact that you've kept this to yourself.'

He waved her out.

'I'll get over it, thanks.'

It was not the reception she had banked on. Confused, frustrated and by now just as angry as Walker, North left the building.

He sat at his desk, thinking hard. He lit a cigarette. Then he noticed that some of the detectives were beginning to pack up for the day, calling out their good-nights or discussing plans for the evening. He tore a piece of paper from his desk pad and scribbled some words copied from North's memo. Then he strode out of his office, slamming the door behind him.

'Ladies and gentlemen,' he called out harshly. 'Listen up. We have another suspect.'

The hubbub immediately gave way to a profound, an almost shocked silence. Everyone was looking at Walker.

'His name is Stephen Warrington. He leased a maroon Mondeo during the time Cassie Booth was abducted. It's presently being driven by a Mr Tony Levine. Ross, Gwen, get over to his place – here's the address – and get forensics to check over that car. Go!'

SATURDAY, 17 APRIL

Levine had been an unassuming, middle-management, family man. He had been a little aggrieved, to be sure, that the police were taking such an interest in the car, but he realized there was nothing he could do about it and the car was swiftly removed to the forensics garage. The examination of the Mondeo was at first hampered by sackloads of cans, toys, sweet-wrappers and discarded clothing left by the little Levines, whose mother had been using the Mondeo as a runabout. But with that lot finally removed, they had the car stripped back to the condition it was in when Levine took it over from Warrington. After that, it didn't take much for Walker's next step to be clear to him.

One of the examiners found a small dark spot on the carpet taken from the boot of the car. Spectroscopic examination proved encouraging.

'I think it's dried blood,' he told Walker on the phone.

'Can you prove it?'

'Yes, but it'll take some more tests. At the moment, I'm merely confident.'

'Confident enough for me to bring someone in for questioning, though?'

'That would be for you to decide, Mr Walker. I'll just stick to being confident.'

Walker didn't want further tests done until Monday. At the weekend they would be cripplingly expensive as well as wasting time. Instead he got on the phone to the Incident Room.

'Tell uniform to go to 18 The Gables, SW13. They're to bring in Stephen Warrington. I'll be waiting at the nick to talk to him. Hurry!'

CHAPTER 14

WARRINGTON'S EXTREME behaviour had helped turn his second arrest into a major theatrical production. The handcuffs, the impressive uniformed presence and the several marked cars combined to terrify him, and his hysterical shouts and screams made this an event the street would talk about for months and years to come.

Alan Napier, Warrington's solicitor, was quickly on the scene at Southfields police station, to be present when his client was questioned by Walker under the eye of the video camera and with Detective Sergeant Satchell in attendance. He fully understood what this matter was about. Cassie Booth, a fifteen-year-old girl, was missing and (by some) presumed dead. The police were suggesting, on the basis of a possible spot of blood found in the boot of a car previously used by his client, that Warrington was involved in the abduction of the girl. As Napier saw it, this was a lousy prosecution case and unless it strengthened considerably, so he told his client, the matter would probably never get to court, let alone achieve a conviction. Warrington was buoyed up by the news and he presented a shining, confident face to his interrogators.

Warrington had given the police what he claimed to

be a full disclosure of his activities on the morning of Cassie Booth's disappearance. There had then been a short adjournment after which Walker had returned to ask Warrington to go over his story again. Napier knew exactly why the Detective Superintendent had done this: lies were not fixed as firmly as truth in the memory. A second telling of an elaborate lie did not always tally with the first.

Warrington sighed, dramatically, when asked to retrace the ground.

'I drove my daughters to the local swimming-pool on Barnes Lane,' said Warrington, with mock-weariness. 'That was sevenish. I remained there for about an hour. I spoke at length to their swimming instructor, Don Clark, I think his name is, then I returned home at about eight o'clock and had coffee with my wife, as my first business appointment wasn't until about eleven . . . Ah, yes! This is something new and very interesting.'

He had put his finger indicatively in the air.

'And I suppose it's the reason for you asking me to repeat myself. Now I remember something else that might be helpful.'

He glanced sideways at Napier, as if appealing for corroboration. But Napier's help had so far been confined to urging his client to answer direct questions directly.

'Good,' said Walker in encouragement. 'And what might that be?'

'I tried to fix the espresso coffee-maker. I fancied a strong coffee and it's not been working for a while. So I took it apart. In fact, it made me a few minutes late for my meeting with Adrian Riply of Riply Wine Merchants, established 1896, in Oxshott.'

He flicked another look at his solicitor.

'Who can verify these times?' Walker wanted to know.

'My wife, obviously. And, look, I do apologize again for not advising you about the car. Obviously, I now realize how important it must be to eliminate it from your inquiry. That said, I think your abusive behaviour and unreasonable display of force at my home was totally unnecessary.'

Walker took a deep breath.

'Mr Warrington, there has been extensive media coverage of this case. You can hardly have been unaware of the importance we have placed on tracing the car.'

'My poor wife was beside herself,' continued Warrington, as if Walker had not spoken. 'Not to mention the gossip I shall be forced to endure from my neighbours.'

'Well now, if you were that concerned about your image in the community, would it not have been more sensible to have contacted us immediately with regard to the car?'

'Gossip is gossip, Mr Walker, and innuendo is innuendo. I wished to avoid any involvement in something I knew I had nothing to do with.'

He was beginning to get more agitated now, touching his hair and waving his hands about.

'I can really see no reason why I'm being held here unless you are intent on persecuting me because you are privy to facts relating to my private life – facts that I can only assume Pat North has relayed to you. Well, for your information, no charges were brought against me and neither of the two cases will ever go to trial.'

At this point, Napier tapped his client on the arm and asked Walker for a moment's intermission.

'Stephen,' he murmured, 'I wouldn't mention those charges—'

'Are you deaf?' demanded Warrington brashly. 'I just *said* – there were no charges.' He pointed his finger across the table. 'And you, Mr Walker, have no right to insinuate that I was in any way guilty of deviant behaviour.'

Walker raised his eyebrows and caught Satchell's eye: this was getting better and better. Napier didn't think so, though. Again he plucked at his client's sleeve.

'Stephen, please!'

'Shut up! Can't you see what this man is doing? If you are trying to upset me, Detective Superintendent, then you have succeeded. I was completely exonerated in both cases.'

Walker thought, The man's completely hyper, a class-A loony.

'Mr Warrington—'

'No, I have given you exact details of my movements on the morning Cassie Booth went missing. And as for you, Alan, considering how much I'm paying you, you should get me out of here – with a full apology.'

Napier's eyebrows jerked upwards and he shook his head. He said, 'Detective Superintendent, may I speak with my client alone?'

'Why, for God's sake?' burst out Warrington. 'I haven't done anything wrong!'

'Just calm down, Stephen,' said Napier.

But Warrington was unstoppable.

'DON'T tell me what to do!' he snarled.

Tactfully, Walker and Satchell removed themselves and stood in the corridor. From there one half of the 'private' consultation could be clearly heard –

Warrington's tirade against the police for negligence in not closing down the brothel he'd reported in his street, and then their coming down in force to his place, hell-bent on making a violent arrest.

'All for a simple inquiry into whether or not I'd leased a maroon Ford Mondeo,' he boomed. 'It's bordering on the ridiculous, Alan.'

Barrow swung into the corridor and joined Walker and Satchell.

'Got anything?' he asked.

Walker snorted.

'Loves the sound of his own voice. And he's got smooth-as-silk Napier in with him. I need you to check out his alibi.'

'Got a good one, has he?' asked Barrow, sceptically.

'Says he was taking his daughters to their swimming lesson, then coffee with his wife, then meeting with Riply Wine Merchants in Oxshott. Satch has the details.'

'I'll get on to it,' said Barrow.

'Any news on the blood from the Mondeo?'

'Still to be tested. Results in a couple of days.'

Walker sighed. Why was it always 'a couple of days'?

'All right – you get on to the swimming-pool and the wine people and we'll have a chat with the wife. OK?'

Satchell had gone upstairs to phone the Warrington household, checking that Susan Warrington would be at home. Walker returned to the interview room to explain why he wanted to keep Warrington as his guest for the time being. This caused an explosive scene.

'I said we'd like to keep him with us,' Walker told the Detective Sergeant as they drove out of the Southfields car park on their way to Barnes. 'At least until we'd checked out his alibi. At which point he threatened to sack Napier!'

'I know he comes over as a major fruit and nut case, Guv, but believe me, he's enjoying the attention. Apparently it's typical of a cyclothymic. Look at his mood swings. One second depressive, the next manic, over-confident and acting like he could conquer the world.'

'So what do you think?' asked Walker, then held up his hand. 'And *cut* all the psychobabble. Is he our man?'

Satchell shook his head slowly.

'I'm not convinced.'

'Yes, I'm right,' said Susan Warrington, leafing through a spiral-bound diary. 'Stephen took the girls to their swimming lesson.'

Walker and Satchell were seated on the sofa, side by side, while Mrs Warrington paced nervously between the fireplace and the baby grand, with its thick plantation of family photographs.

'What time would that be?'

'About six thirty. Lesson starts at seven, and if he doesn't have an early appointment he usually comes back for coffee.'

She put a hand to her mouth.

'Although, now I come to think of it, that was the morning he decided to try and fix the espresso machine, for some strange reason.'

She passed the diary to Walker who glanced at the relevant days. He pursed his lips. So far Warrington's alibi was looking good.

Mrs Warrington was still talking about the coffee-machine.

'Stephen never does anything around the house, but he suddenly got really het up because he couldn't have a cup of real coffee.'

'So what time exactly did he get back from the swimming-pool?'

'Oh, about eight o' clock, I think.'

'And did he have any more appointments that day?'

'Yes, he went off to work about ten, came home about teatime.'

'And what car was he driving?'

'Well, it would have been the hire car. The Mondeo. He only got the Volvo last week.'

Walker, still listening, had spotted something that interested him on the bookshelves next to the fireplace.

'And what colour was the Mondeo?' he asked as he got up to take a closer look.

'Dark red.'

Walker picked up his find from the shelf, a small beanbag toy.

'Whose is this, Mrs Warrington?'

She looked startled at the sudden change of subject.

'That? Oh, Lucy's. Our Jack Russell, Peggy, went missing recently, so Stephen bought her that to cheer her up.'

'How long ago was that?'

'That Peggy went missing? About a month.'

'No, no. I mean, when did he buy the toy?'

She shrugged.

'Oh, a couple of days later.'

'Do you know where he got it?'

Yes, I think it was a place on Putney High Street. It's

called something like Playbox or Toybox. Why? What's the significance of it?'

'It might be significant. I can't say more at this time, I'm afraid.'

To Walker the woman looked suddenly terribly puzzled, alone and frightened. She was surrounded by questions she didn't understand and answers whose significance she couldn't guess. He knew it was an inadequate emotion, but he pitied her. She didn't know if she was helping her husband or condemning him. Nor, he thought, did she know which of these she would rather do.

Don Clark, in a crisp, clean tracksuit and with a whistle and a stopwatch around his neck, looked a fit and well-organized individual. Barrow told him he wanted details of the Warrington girls' lessons, and especially the one eleven days ago. Clark retrieved a file from his small cupboard of an office and turned the pages.

'OK,' he said, 'Tuesday the sixth. Yes, Lucy and Charlotte Warrington were here for the first class – registered in.'

He screwed up his face, remembering.

'Yes, I spoke to their father that morning. He was very upset his younger daughter Lucy hadn't been picked for the inter-school swimming challenge. In fact, he was quite abusive.'

Barrow smiled slightly, as if he could well imagine the reaction, but did not comment.

'And what time was that – when you spoke with him?'

'Well, it was before the lesson started, so I guess around five to seven.'

'Did he stay and watch the girls swim?'

Again Clark tried to remember that one morning among so many.

'I can't be sure about it,' he said finally. 'But I don't think I saw him once the lesson had started.'

'And one more thing, Mr Clark. Did you by any chance happen to see what car he was driving?'

Clark was sure about this. He shook his head.

'No, sorry.'

Barrow snapped shut his notebook.

'Thanks, Mr Clark. I think that just about does it.'

Riply's Wine Merchants was a hundred-year-old firm and thought of itself as occupying the quality end of the market. This was no low-cost warehouse outlet, always with a range of cheap reds and whites available for tasting by the public. Riply's customers were a conservative bunch, on the whole, who relied on the owner's taste and experience. Adrian Riply himself, a substantially paunched man in his thirties who wore a blazer, rugby tie and grey trousers, liked to congratulate himself that they were rarely disappointed.

'Stephen Warrington?' said Riply in answer to Barrow's question. 'Yes, I met him that day.'

'You see him regularly, Mr Riply?'

'Fairly. We've always got on. And I must say, he's a brilliant salesman. Managed to sell me six dozen cases of exactly the same Bordeaux wine, same bottling and from a château with a particularly nothing reputation, that I rejected from another source a year ago. *And* he got a higher price. I don't think I'm an easy touch, particularly. I'd be out of business if I was. But to this day, I don't know how Stephen did it. Nor how we sold it on, come to that. But now he's surpassed himself: he's talked me into an enormous Georgian wine promotion. I ask you! No one, in the UK takes wines from Georgia seriously.'

He shrugged.

'On the other hand, they once said that about Bulgaria, Romania . . .'

Barrow, with little time for wine trade reminiscences, chipped in.

'Can you confirm the times during which he was here on the sixth of April?'

'Yes, I think so.'

He turned the pages of his desk diary.

'Here's my diary entry – Stephen was here at eleven. We had about half an hour's talk about the Georgia thing, did a bit of tasting. I suppose he left about twelve.'

'I think that's all I need, Mr Riply. Thanks for your time.'

Riply walked him to his car. He was frowning thoughtfully.

'What's this all about then? Stephen in some kind of trouble?'

Barrow climbed into the car.

'Just inquiries, Mr Riply. Thanks for your help.'

Walker had been unable to locate his wallet.

'I was so bloody hungover this morning I'd have forgotten to bail my granny, never mind look for my wallet,' he told Satchell as they left Warrington's house. 'I expect it's in my other jacket. We'll pop in and pick it up – it's just a couple of streets away.'

Satchell didn't mind. He was curious to see the place where the two lovebirds had made their nest.

'Very nice,' he was saying as they went through the living-room and into the kitchen. 'So you bought it or what?'

'Renting. Couldn't find anything for sale that we liked, not in our price range. OK, bedroom there, nice bathroom and big kitchen, lounge. Right, I'll just grab my wallet. You want a quick coffee while we're here?'

Satchell nodded, just as his mobile phone started bleeping. It was Barrow, with a verbal report. Walker bustled around looking for the coffee and filling the kettle, and meanwhile listened to Satchell's end of the conversation.

'Right, got that . . . he's sure about the day? . . . Yeah, well, we all know about Mr Warrington's temper! . . . Any luck with the car? . . . OK, too much to expect, really. Any security cameras?'

When the call ended there were two steaming cups of instant coffee on the kitchen counter and Walker was hunting for his missing wallet.

'The wine buyer at Oxshott has confirmed that Warrington kept the eleven o'clock appointment,' said Satchell. 'And the swimming coach verified he was at the pool but couldn't say how long he stayed there.'

'Security cameras?'

'They have a roaming CCTV camera overlooking the car park but they don't keep tapes more than a week.'

Walker, who was tucking the retrieved wallet into his backside pocket, clicked his tongue.

'Well, it looks like we're going to have to let him go.'

Satchell sipped his coffee and flicked through a thick volume of wallpaper samples.

'I said he was a time-waster, didn't I? It's Wilding. Wilding's your man. Uncle W? Uncle Wilding!'

'Mmm. Or Uncle Warrington . . .'

Still perusing the wallpaper pattern-book, Satchell had stopped at a blue striped design.

'This is very nice. I like stripes.'

'Must be because you're a sergeant.'

'No, one wall plain, one striped, same colour as the carpet. I can just see it . . .'

Walker drained his coffee. Wallpaper was the last thing on his mind.

'Can you check out that toy shop Susan Warrington mentioned, see if her fruitcake husband bought any more beanie animals there?'

'Sure, OK,' said Satchell absently. His mind was still on interior decoration. He took the pattern-book into the living-room, cocked his head to one side, looked down at the book and again at the walls and said, 'Yeah, stripes'd look good here.'

'They'd look good on your arse, son. Come on, we've got work to do.'

CHAPTER 15

'STEPHEN!'

The front door of 18 The Gables had slammed. Susan Warrington was in the living-room, but she heard him moving in the hall. Then there was no sound for several moments. What was he doing? Listening?

'Stephen! Come in here. I want to talk to you.'

'What?'

His voice sounded testy but she persisted.

'Come in here and shut the door.'

Warrington appeared in the doorway. He mooched into the room, not looking at his wife. He seemed to notice something in the garden and went to the window. Crossing back to the open door, she slammed it and leaned against it, as if to bar his escape. Her face was set.

'I have just had two police officers here, asking me questions.'

Momentarily, she shut her eyes and shook her head.

'I can't take much more of this.'

Warrington turned around, suddenly animated.

'*You* can't? What about me? They are persecuting me – and do you know why?'

He swung his arm, pointing expansively out of the window.

'It's because I complained about that brothel—'

'Stephen! Why did they want to know where you were on the morning that poor girl went missing?'

'Her name is Cassie Booth. It's all connected to that bloody company car I hired. What did you tell them?'

'Why did they want to know about the car?'

Warrington breathed in deeply, calming himself.

'They want to question everyone in the area who drives a maroon Mondeo. Now please. I've already had one interrogation today. I don't need another.'

'They *interrogated* you?'

To Susan the word was alarming.

'Questioned! They questioned me! And then, as you can see, they released me. May I go now? Is that all right?'

He moved towards the door and grasped the handle. She gave way, moving aside. As he was going out she said, 'Oh,' remembering. 'You had a call from Adrian Riply.'

'What?'

Riply? Warrington stopped in mid-stride. Of course! The police would have been to see him, would have told him God knows what! He turned back to Susan.

'What did he say? What did he *say*?'

Karl Wilding had felt irritable all day. Rebecca had gone off to the supermarket in the morning and had not returned, so there was no sign of any lunch. In the end he made do with biscuits and cheese. Then when he tried to nap he found he couldn't drop off. He tried to soothe himself with a session on the Internet when, through the window, he saw her car, its headlights unnecessarily switched on, sweeping through the gate, clipping the hedge and narrowly missing his Rolls.

He went to the door. His wife struggled out of the silver Fiat with bags of supermarket shopping. Leaving the car door wide open, she climbed the steps unsteadily towards the front door, where by now he was waiting for her.

'I'll make lunch,' she said.

'Lunch?'

He looked at his watch meaningfully.

'Lunch? It's half-past five!'

She stopped half-way up the steps, frowning. She shook her head.

'Oh sorry, dear. I got held up.'

He ran down the steps and leaned into her car to switch off the lights and remove the ignition key. Then he slammed the door and pressed the security lock.

'The only thing holding you up,' he said, 'is the booze. Get inside, go on, you stupid bitch. Go and sleep it off.'

Later that night, Wilding was again sitting at the PC when Rebecca reappeared with a glass of whisky in her hand. He was looking at a screen folder of files and systematically, one by one, he was selecting and deleting them.

He nodded at the whisky.

'I would have thought you'd had enough at lunchtime.'

She approached and put the glass on the desk next to his keyboard.

'It's for you.'

'I'm sure it is – but I take it with soda.'

'Oh, I'm sorry. I forgot.'

Wilding rose brusquely and crossed to the sideboard where on a tray of drinks he found a soda syphon.

'I'm surprised you even recall your own name.'

She was looking at his computer screen, where a dialogue box showed, saying: 'Are you sure you want to delete Babes in the Wood?'

'Lucky for you I don't remember everything.'

He turned, with the syphon in his hand.

'What's that supposed to mean?'

Rebecca put a hand on the mouse and placed the pointer on 'OK'. She clicked and the box, and file, disappeared.

'You know full well.'

She picked her words cautiously, swaying a little on her feet.

'And Karl, don't give me the "protecting my image" spiel. That morning, when that girl went missing, I—'

'Hey!' snapped Wilding. 'Don't go down that road again. You may not give a damn about your reputation, but I do. You need treatment.'

A sneer crept across Rebecca Wilding's face.

'And you don't? If the police were to find that filth on your computer, it wouldn't be my reputation anyone would care about. But I suppose that's why you're deleting those files.'

She swayed towards the door, adding, with a touch of alcoholic grandiloquence, 'Unfortunately for you, you can't delete *my* memory.'

He sat down again when she had gone. He selected a file on the screen as he muttered, 'Stupid drunken bitch.'

Using the mouse, he dragged the file to his virtual wastebin. The computer asked him: 'Are you sure you want to delete Lisa Lollipop?'

Deliberately he clicked on 'OK'.

It was Saturday night and Walker and North had thought they would go out, to the cinema and then for a curry. They showered and he made tea while she dried her hair.

'What happened with Warrington in the end?' she asked when he came back with two mugs of tea.

'His alibi seemed to pan out. So we had to let him go.'

She stopped the drier to listen.

'He's certainly a head case—'

'Say *that* again!'

'But I'm not convinced he's capable of murder.'

'Well, if not Warrington, who?'

'I still think Wilding's our man. The surveillance team seem to think he's behaving pretty strangely. And – you know what? I don't think Cassie Booth was snatched at all. I think she got in the car of her own accord.'

'How on earth would you know? Wasn't the bike found knocked sideways and the papers everywhere?'

'Good girl! So it was. But you see, if she propped up the bike and then hung the newspapers bag on the handlebars – thinking she was just leaving them temporarily, right? – the weight of the bag might easily have toppled the bike over. I tried it with her bike and papers in the property room. It works.'

'But that would suggest it was someone she knew, if she got in the car herself.'

Walker snapped his fingers.

'Right again! You're on form tonight. Did I tell you we had this boy come in who did Cassie's paper round a couple of times, as a stand-in? He described Wilding as well as the silver Fiat coupé that Mrs Wilding drives.'

North was brushing her hair now.

'OK, but what about the Mondeo? Are forensics still testing it?'

'They're testing a patch of blood but the results aren't back yet. It's pathetic. I feel I'm going round in circles, with no body and no murder site. She could still be alive, for all we know.'

'So, if he didn't do it, why do you think Stephen Warrington's so obsessed with the Cassie Booth case?'

The mention of Warrington made Walker snort with contempt.

'Obsessed with you, more like. If he comes near this place or my kids again I'll get an injunction slapped on the maniac. That's a promise.'

His phone was bleeping and he snatched it up.

'Hello? Oh, hello, Princess. How are you?'

North could hear Amy asking him something.

'What?' he said. 'Did Mummy ask you to dial for her? Well, put her on, then . . . Yes, Lynn? About tomorrow? Well, I'll pick them up in the morning, take them swimming maybe, bit of lunch . . .'

At this point North left the room.

CHAPTER 16

B Y NINE THIRTY, Walker had left the flat to enjoy quality time with his children, leaving North the best part of the day to herself. She decided on a morning workout.

As she was getting into the car to go to the gym an attractive blonde woman of about forty approached.

'Excuse me,' she said, diffidently. 'Are you Pat North?'

'Yes,' said North, startled.

She recognized the woman straight away from the Brixton car park: smartly dressed and with an accent that had been undoubtedly honed at a costly private school. But today, instead of anger and outrage, she seemed weighed down by anxiety.

'We haven't actually met,' she said. 'But I'm Susan Warrington – Stephen's wife.'

North's eyes narrowed warily. What was this about? She'd been plagued to distraction by the husband; was she now to be pursued by the wife? Nevertheless, there was something so vulnerable about the woman that North couldn't snub her.

'Hi,' she said, extending her hand.

'Hello.'

They shook hands briefly. Then North said, 'Are you OK?'

Susan Warrington certainly didn't look it, but she said, trying to sound cheerful, 'Yes, fine! But I just wondered if I could have a word.'

'Well, I was just on my way out, actually.'

Susan Warrington's face twisted and her eyes moistened.

'I'm so sorry to bother you, but . . . Well, I couldn't think of anyone else . . . anyone else I could speak to.'

North put her hand on Mrs Warrington's.

'Look, why don't you come up to the flat? It's just here.'

She refused tea and coffee, agreeing only to a glass of tap water.

'This is so kind. Thank you. It's just that I don't think I can take any more. This has been so awful.'

Seated at the kitchen table, she sipped her water. North stood by the sink and said nothing, leaving the woman time to unburden herself in her own way.

'I really need to know . . . Was there any truth in the accusations against him? I can understand there being a mistake once, but twice? And this Cassie Booth inquiry. He said he was being questioned just because he drove a maroon Mondeo.'

North nodded.

'I think they were eliminating all drivers of that make and colour of car.'

She sat down opposite her visitor, wondering about the professionalism of this. She knew too much about this case already, but it was nothing to do with her – she just happened to live with the Senior Investigating Officer. Yet she continued, 'Susan, if you know anything, you should speak to a member of the investigating team. Not to me. It's nothing to do with me.'

Mrs Warrington shook her head sorrowfully.

'I don't . . . know anything, I don't really. That's the whole trouble. I . . . Well; he did go on and on about it that morning she went missing.'

'About Cassie Booth?' asked North, suddenly interested. 'How do you mean – on and on about it?'

Mrs Warrington blew her nose into a Kleenex.

'Oh, just how terrible it all was. He's very protective of the girls. I was determined to have it all out with him today, but I don't know where he is and . . . I've tried so hard to make it work for the girls' sake, but . . . Well, I want a divorce, you see. Do you think that's what I should do?'

North took a deep breath. Shit! What was she doing with this woman in her house?

'I really couldn't advise you.'

'But if you were in my position, what would you do? I mean, *you* know what he's like!'

North shook her head.

'I'm sorry, Mrs Warrington, I'm a police officer not a counsellor. There must be someone – a doctor, vicar or priest?'

Mrs Warrington shook her sleek, fair head.

'No, really, there's nobody. Stephen's so . . . peculiar. He was always unpredictable – I used to say "dashing", because that's exactly how I saw him when I first fell in love with him. But he's become so much worse. His sleeping. I mean, sometimes he can't be woken up after nine, ten hours. Other nights he can barely manage three before he's up and pacing about bemoaning his

180

lot. He takes wild, reckless risks. I've been told it's all part of his illness. Once he did a tightrope walk along the pitch of our roof to rescue a baby sparrow. Another time he invested a huge amount of our own money in a single first-growth claret. It paid off, thank God, but the wine might have been unsaleable. On his day he's brilliant, persuasive and, well, *beautiful*. It's the only word I can give you. He plays the piano exquisitely. He can recite thousands of lines of Shakespeare, he sings terrible comic songs, he's a killing mimic. The girls adore him – well, they do on his good days. But I'm beginning to find the rages insupportable. I mean, last night's tirade against the wine trade because one lousy deal didn't go through. It's so wearing, so unnecessary. I'm struggling to cope, to be honest.'

She stayed quiet for a moment, staring vacantly at the tabletop. Then she roused herself.

'But what's all this to you? I've taken up enough of your time and you've been very kind. It was silly of me to suppose you could help – I can see you're a kind person but of course you have a job to do.'

She smiled shyly, sniffed, dropped her sodden Kleenex into her bag and stood up. Showing her to the door, North, despite herself, couldn't help saying something.

'Susan, nothing is ever as miserable as it can seem. I can't tell you anything about the case, because I hardly know anything, and what I do know is confidential. Perhaps you could talk, in confidence, to your husband's solicitor about these arrests.'

'I don't know . . . I've never met the man. It's all so difficult.'

North swung open the door.

'Goodbye,' she said. 'And I'm sure it'll all work out.'

Vengeance: that's what was on Stephen Warrington's mind when he woke up after a bare two and a half hours' sleep. He leapt from bed, leaving Susan snoring. She'd knocked herself out with sleeping-pills so it was no good looking to her for help. This was something he'd have to do alone. Bloody Riply. How dare he change his mind about the Georgian wines promotion? It was all agreed, tied up. But Riply said he had reason to believe that Warrington was having trouble with the police and it was of such a nature that Riply's Wines could not associate themselves with him. Bloody brass neck! Someone had been talking and it was slander, a black calumny. And it was the police who'd done it. It was that bloody North woman. *She* was at the bottom of all his troubles. *She* was the one who'd got to pay.

In his pyjamas, he emerged into the garden, stalking barefoot towards the grubby, unkempt end where the compost was. On his way he collected a spade from the shed. An owl hooted and, from somewhere, an urban fox answered with a single bark. When he found his chosen spot he started digging. He enjoyed the clean sound of the blade slicing into the soil, and the thought of what he was about to unearth. It would be covered in creepy-crawlies by now. Maggots, worms. Exactly what he needed.

Susan was not rational, that was clear. Talking wildly about divorce, taking the girls away from his influence, letting him have 'a bit of money if he agreed to have treatment' – the bloody cheek! The truth was they were all trying to get him. Calumny. He'd not let them get away with it.

The spade hit a piece of sacking. He probed to one side, and then the other, until he found the edge, driving the spade in hard to get leverage, but it wouldn't come loose. With an impatient curse, he threw the tool aside and knelt in the turned earth, scrabbling with his fingers to get the thing up. In a few minutes he'd have done it. Then vengeance would be his!

CHAPTER 17

'YOU'RE NOT going to believe this,' said Hutchens to North, entering her office early the next morning. 'He's back – bloody Warrington! He's refused to leave the reception area until he's seen you.'

North reacted savagely. She had decisively had enough; this time Warrington was going to get a piece of her mind.

'Right! Get him in here, Jack. And don't you leave me for a second. I want a witness.'

A couple of minutes later Hutchens was back.

'Mr Warrington to see you, ma'am.'

Warrington was such an extraordinary sight that it was as if he had mutated into another person. Unshaven, his skin greasy and his hair wildly awry, he was staring at her with a fixed, ferociously predatory look. Under a raincoat, he was still wearing his pyjamas. North could see that they were caked with dried mud from knee to ankle. On his feet, a pair of bedroom slippers were almost entirely dyed mud-brown. In his hand swung a plastic supermarket bag.

He started in on her right away.

'You have a lot to answer for, Detective Inspector North. I have lost the Riply account because of you.

And, if that wasn't bad enough, you have encouraged my wife to start divorce proceedings.'

'Mr Warrington—'

North had vowed to come in hard herself, but Warrington's anger was a wave of tidal magnitude, sweeping aside her puny forces.

'Don't MISTER Warrington me, you two-faced bitch!'

Suddenly he spat in her direction. She raised her hand as if to ward him off.

'Now look here—'

'I went out of my WAY to show how grateful I was for your help with the Oxshott business.'

'I had nothing whatsoever to do with that,' she said, desperately. She looked at Hutchens, who seemed as much at a loss as herself.

'DON'T lie. I asked for your help and they withdrew the charges. That is why I have trusted you. But now, to . . . to encourage my wife to divorce me!'

North tried again at calming measures.

'Sit down, Mr Warrington.'

'No,' said Warrington, red in the face, the cords on his neck standing out. 'I will not. But I have a present for you. I told you Cassie Booth would be eaten up by maggots by now, didn't I? I *told* you, didn't I? Didn't I?'

He was swinging the plastic bag now, with a ghastly smile on his face. Hutchens edged closer, hoping to get a hold on Warrington, though he was not exactly Schwarzenegger and was a good deal shorter than the visitor.

'Put the bag down, Stephen,' ordered North. She had tried reasoning with him and knew she should now try to assert herself. This was the nearest thing she could muster to a parade-ground voice. It had no noticeable effect.

'I've got Cassie Booth's head in here,' he said. 'If you'd been nicer to me, I would have shown you where the rest of her is buried . . .'

'Give me the bag, Stephen,' said Hutchens.

'RIGHT!' screamed Warrington. 'DON'T EVER SAY YOU DIDN'T ASK FOR IT.'

With an overarm swing of his right arm he hurled the bag down on to the desk. It split wide open and a disgusting mass of decayed flesh fell out, with earth and hair and, above all, worms, grubs and maggots. Black, white and pink, these were flung out in a gleaming, writhing cascade of subterranean life, covering the desk and the floor around North's feet. And on her feet, too. She sharply stepped back and tried to stamp them off. A moment later she realized, with an inner scream of horror and fear, that they were also in her hair and on her face. They were crawling all over her.

She turned, her features frozen, to Hutchens and then back to Warrington. Her mouth fell reflexively open and something alive tickled her lip and tongue. In a spasm of revulsion she spat it out. And then she was shuddering, helplessly, as she bent over and tried to sweep the disgusting things from her head, her shoulders, her skirt.

At Southfields, Walker's phone had been chirruping but he ignored it and went down to the car park for a smoke. He suspected it was one or other of the Area Commanders – the last human beings he wanted to commune with today. The call was diverted to Ross, who took the semi-coherent message from Detective Inspector North of the Vice Squad.

'When you see him, can you get the Guv to call Pat North?' he asked Satchell, whose desk was nearest to Walker's office.

Satchell had spent the weekend reading the policy file. Now, eager to prove his profiling skills, he was sitting at his computer, typing out his psychological report of the Cassie Booth abductor – or killer. He grunted to let Ross know he'd heard the request but was not to be further disturbed.

Then Barrow burst in, with a face flushed with the excitement of unexpected and dramatic news. He was holding a video cassette.

'Where's Walker?' he asked Satchell.

Satchell still did not look up from his keyboard.

'What am I, his secretary?'

But there was something in Barrow's voice that compelled his attention. He looked and saw the video.

'Got your own copy of the new *Star Wars*, have you?'

Something in Barrow snapped. It was bad enough Satchell arriving back full of his prowess as a profiler, as if he'd just earned a doctorate in astrophysics. What was worse was the way he'd so easily slotted back into his old partnership with Walker. In short, Barrow's nose was out of joint. He jabbed an irritated finger at Satchell.

'Listen, smart alec. It's the security video from the swimming-pool, on the day she disappeared!'

That certainly got the attention of everyone in the room. Responding, Barrow swung round, addressing the whole team.

'Can somebody let the Guv know it's here, please!'

He felt great inside. This would show full-of-himself Satchell who was Walker's most effective aide.

In the end Barrow, unable to sustain the suspense, went to get Walker himself. On the way back upstairs, he explained how he'd got the tape.

'There was a ruckus that morning in the car park, apparently. CPS needed the video as evidence against a couple of vandals. The solicitor had it. Turned out they were ten and eleven years old. Broke into a car and were collared by the leisure centre staff.'

'Your Don Shaw didn't mention any ruckus that day, did he?'

'Probably never even knew about it. He was inside, by the pool area.'

In the Incident Room everyone on the inquiry was gathered round the television screen which had been hooked up to the video replayer. It was like Royal Wedding day all over again.

'It's poor quality,' said Barrow, thoroughly enjoying his moment of pre-eminence. 'But Technical Support say they can clean it up. You ready?'

He pressed the 'Play' button and an image of sorts emerged. As the viewing eye got used to it, discounting the snow and fuzziness imparted to the black-and-white picture by an overused videotape, they could see that they were in a car park. The camera slowly panned through its fixed arc of movement, catching in its view a light-coloured two-seater car, two people-carriers and a four-by-four. Then there was a BMW with a pair of

188

small skateboarders in attendance, pressing their noses to the glass. Seconds later, in movements almost too quick to register, one of them had smashed the glass with his skateboard and picked out a purse from the front dash. The security tape was without sound, but everyone watching could imagine the car alarm wailing. Then, just as suddenly as the crime itself, came retribution. The leisure centre manager hurtled into view in hot pursuit of the culprits.

But, with total aloofness towards this criminal incident, the camera showed no inclination to follow the chase. Instead it continued implacably with its panning shot of the car park. And now, as another parked vehicle appeared, everyone in the room craned forward.

'My God!' shouted Walker. 'It's the bloody Mondeo.'

He was kneeling in front of the screen now, as if wishing he could climb into the shot itself. This was indeed recognizably the rear end of a Mondeo exactly like the one they had been interested in – and in fact, as Barrow would later verify, it bore the same number plate.

'And Warrington!' said Walker again, jabbing with his finger the screen figure of a tall, thin man near the back of the car, occasionally passing in front of it. 'That's Warrington, isn't it?'

'But wait,' said Barrow. 'There's more.'

As the pan continued to slide by millimetres rightwards, he moved closer to the screen.

'Look who's to the right of the car – see him? It's very blurred. See him?'

Walker did see. The man on the right was talking to

Warrington, and Warrington, pacing about and gesticulating in an agitated way, was talking back. But who was he talking back to?

'Fuck me!' said Walker, suddenly seeing. 'It's Wilding. Wilding! They bloody know each other!'

The silent drama continued to unfold. The men were clearly having a furious row.

'That could be the keys to the Mondeo or the boathouse he just handed to Warrington,' whispered Ross.

The boot of the car was thrown open and the men were examining its contents. Suddenly they moved slightly apart and the inside of the boot was revealed to the watching camera. The AMIP team collectively gasped. Was that a knee, a white arm, a shape curled around foetus-like to fit the space? Was that the body of Cassie Booth?

Wilding now moved away and out of shot.

Barrow said, 'I assume Wilding's heading back to his wife's car – the Fiat.'

The camera could neither confirm nor deny this, for it did not see Wilding again. It had almost moved past the Mondeo, with that possibly incriminating cargo, with as much indifference as it had earlier lost interest in the pursuit of the vandals. But first, the camera caught Warrington looking down for a single still moment at the body before pulling a rug over it, looking over towards Wilding and slamming the boot shut.

'Can they get us a clearer picture of the boot?' asked Walker. 'I mean, can you see anything? I can't. Can you freeze that frame?'

Ross rewound the tape until he found the moment

when the open boot was revealed. He pointed to the interior.

'Technical Support can enlarge that section. It looks like that's a leg . . . and maybe a hand resting against it. And *that* could be a fraction of her head showing.'

It was only after they had rerun the tape many times, freeze-frame by freeze-frame, and had discussed every aspect of the little scene played out between Wilding and Warrington, that Walker authorized the tape to go over to Technical Support. He also told Barrow to find a lip-reader, in case anything of Warrington's and Wilding's conversation could be recovered.

Only then did someone remember to mention he should phone North at Embankment. Half an hour later he was in her office, holding her in his arms despite the public embarrassment factor. For this comfort, she thought, she would be eternally grateful.

'Pat, I'm so sorry. I only just got the message.'

'There was no need for you to come over. I'm fine.'

But she pressed him so tight to her that it told another story.

'Well,' he whispered, 'I was worried.'

They stood silently for a few moments, then he said, 'Where's Warrington?'

'I arrested him for assault. He's down in the cells.'

Walker stood back now, holding her at arm's length. At last he could tell her of his breakthrough.

'I need you to drop the assault charge and have him transferred back to Southfields. Him and Wilding – they were in it together.'

She was stunned.

'You mean . . .?'

He nodded.

'They were caught on security camera in the swimming-pool car park, with what looks like Cassie's body in the boot of the Mondeo. I want to arrest them both on suspicion of murder.'

'Well, the sooner you get him out of here the better.'

He touched her cheek with the palm of his hand.

'Can I get you anything? Aspirin?'

She almost laughed. Walker could be so loving and tender one minute and so inept the next.

'I'm fine. Thanks for your concern but it's not a headache.'

'Did she tell you what happened?' asked Hutchens as he and Walker, led by the Custody Sergeant, were on their way down to the cells to see Warrington.

'No, I didn't ask her for a blow by blow. She looks bloody shocked.'

'Well, I was there. Saw it all. He came in and asked for her. Refused to leave. She said she'd see him in her office and he came up with this Tesco bag. He got so worked up and angry with her, then flung the bag down on the desk. It split open and she was covered in maggots. It was a rotting dog – Jack Russell, I think.'

'Crazy bastard.'

'You can say that again. The FME's been in to check him. He was freaking out but he seems to have calmed down now.'

They peered through the peephole. Warrington was sitting with a grey blanket over his shoulders, head bowed. His hair was sweat-soaked and hung in rats' tails, his face was drawn and strained after his exertions, flinging himself around the cell, beating the walls with his fists and hurling curses at the head of Detective Inspector North for what he thought of as her betrayal. They went in to talk to him.

'Thank God you're here,' Warrington said, breathing deeply and still sweating. He swallowed hard. 'I want someone to tell my wife that . . . that I will admit I killed her. I mean, I will admit to murdering Cassie Booth *if* she stops the divorce proceedings. Are you listening to me?'

He had seen Walker and Hutchens exchange glances. He stared hard at Walker. He was the man Warrington could do business with. Hutchens was just a flunkey.

'But *only* if Susan agrees. Then I shall give a statement admitting I killed Cassie Booth.'

The policemen were staring incredulously. A man would admit to murder to avoid getting divorced? This had to be a first.

'What are you staring at me for?' shouted Warrington, beginning to work himself up into a lather again. 'Are you deaf, stupid or what? I know where the body is, for God's sake. I KNOW WHERE IT IS!'

Walker took a pace forward and eyeballed Warrington.

'Stephen Warrington, I am arresting you on suspicion of the murder of Cassie Booth . . .'

He informed the prisoner of his rights and, as he did so, he noticed Warrington's face beginning to acquire a scheming look. When Walker had finished, he said, 'But, Detective Superintendent Walker, just one thing . . . I will *only* show you where the body is *if* Pat is with me – no one else, just Pat North.'

Walker turned half round and looked again at Hutchens.

'That's out of the question. You assaulted her and—'

'Assaulted? That wasn't assault! It was a warning. It was an object lesson in loyalty. Look what happened to the dog that was unfaithful, yes? OK, Walker, I seem to have your attention now so I'll tell you my proposal and you can take it or leave it because I won't vary it. You put me in a car with Pat and I'll take her to the place. No one else in attendance, mind. Afterwards, she can bring me back in and, subject to my earlier conditions, I'll make whatever statement you require about the murder. Is it a deal?'

It should, of course, have been out of the question but they couldn't budge Warrington and Walker was desperate to find Cassie's body. He offered himself, or any other male officer in his team, but the suspect was adamant. It had to be North or nobody. So Walker decided to put it to her in her office, in all reason, as a realistic proposition.

'You can do it. You're tougher than you think. And the Booth family need the body of their daughter back. You can give it to them.'

'No, I'm sorry, I don't want to put myself through another second with that man. There has to be another way. Get him to take *you* to the body.'

'I've tried that. But he won't go unless you're there. Pat, listen, I'd be right behind you. And we'd get you wired up.'

'What about his solicitor?'

'He doesn't want him around.'

She turned away from him.

'Pat, we've got the video, we've got the pair of them, but I need that body.'

North heaved a sigh from her shoulders down and turned to face him again.

'All right,' she said, 'if it really is the only way.'

'That's my girl! Thanks, love.' He kissed her on the mouth. 'And you'll be fine. I can persuade him that you must have a driver, so you'll have Myles with you in the car. It'll be a doddle.'

North looked at him. She didn't believe him. She was dreading having to deal with Stephen Warrington again because she knew just how bizarre he could be. But she knew too that somebody had to do this, and that this person could only, it seemed, be her.

Warrington played a game of consummate brinkmanship. Right up to the moment when they were all standing beside the patrol car at Embankment police station, he refused to concede the driver. But in the end, standing there with his blanket cast like a cloak over his shoulders, he said, 'OK, just Pat and the driver. That's the deal. Take it or leave it.'

'Fine,' said Walker stiffly. He glanced sideways at North, who stood beside him with the hidden transmitter strapped to her waist. She did not even attempt to smile.

'You'll be on your own,' Walker went on to Warrington, 'until you show Pat the body. Then she will radio for back-up.'

Warrington wagged a finger.

'Just make sure no one follows. If I catch so much as

a glimpse of you then the deal's off. You need me, Detective Superintendent, but I'm damned if I need you. I've nothing to lose either way. I could so easily be useless, if I chose.'

North stepped forward. She must try to assert her control. It would be the only way to get through this. His ranting made her sick; his incessant demands were revolting to her.

'Get into the car, Stephen,' she said.

Myles opened the rear door for Warrington and put his hand on his shoulder to guide him in.

She looked at Walker.

'I'm ready,' she whispered.

'Be right behind you,' he assured her.

She got in beside Warrington and told Myles to drive according to Warrington's directions. The car took off and Walker nodded to another member of the pursuit posse, a motorbike constable dressed in the dirty leathers and plastic overjacket of a motorcycle courier. He put out his cigarette, adjusted his goggles, fired up his bike and pushed off in the wake of Myles's car.

Walker said to Satchell, 'She's wired up to me and we've got a biker tailing her as well.'

They headed towards Walker's unmarked car, planning to keep in touch but out of sight the whole time.

'This is like the ultimate endgame for him,' Satchell was saying.

Walker grimaced. It was Bramshill-speak again.

'Thing is, he really believes he's in control,' Satchell went on. 'What'll be really interesting is to see which one of the suspects breaks first. They'll both incriminate each other. But we're giving Wilding a long time to elaborate on his side of the story.'

'Just get in the bloody car, Satch. We need that little girl's body.'

The tyres of the car spat gravel under Satchell's driving, as he set off in pursuit. Walker said, 'You know, we had the results on the blood. It wasn't Cassie's, but some animal.'

Satchell nodded his head, as if this confirmed his own thinking.

'I don't think Warrington's a killer,' he said.

'No? Well the rotting Jack Russell was his work, and it had had its neck broken.'

For the first few minutes Walker, with a receiving unit on his knee and an earphone in place, listened to the feed of Warrington giving his directions. It quickly became apparent that the suspect wasn't for the moment taking them anywhere in particular. He was directing Myles in a completely random way, with the result that they crossed the Thames three times by the same bridge. All the time he was trying to get North to open up about how she would persuade Susan Warrington to drop the divorce. North doggedly refused to commit herself.

'*We'll have to see, Stephen. When we have Cassie's body, we'll see what we'll say to Susan.*'

'Come on!' growled Walker, as he listened edgily to her stonewalling. 'Just bloody say you'll do it – anything. You don't have to actually *do* it, just satisfy *him*.'

She would only say they would have to see – if and when they had found Cassie – but Warrington persisted in directing Myles back and forth across the bridge. Finally they heard North's exasperation.

'*Stephen, the joke's really wearing thin now. This is the third time we've been across this bridge.*'

'*I know,*' said Warrington. '*But if you won't agree to talk to Susan, then why should I cooperate? She can't be allowed to divorce me.*'

'*But if you admit to this murder only because you want Susan to drop the divorce proceedings, then it's . . . well, it's ridiculous!*'

At this, Warrington seemed to laugh, with all the indulgence of a superior being.

'*Oh, Pat. You see, my mind works in a different way to yours. I swear before God that I did not kill Cassie Booth. But I will say that I did, to prove to Susan that I am prepared to be punished for the most heinous of crimes, just to keep our marriage intact.*'

'*But that's madness, Stephen. You'd lose her anyway, because you'd be put away for life.*'

'*Well, I know that, but it would prove that I love her. I love her, I love her, I – here, driver, turn round, here!*'

The car did a squealing U-turn, catching Satchell on the hop. By the time they were back on track, they found themselves southbound across Putney Bridge yet again. Walker was not impressed.

'Any more of this and I'm going to pull the son-of-a-bitch over. He's playing bloody games with us.'

'What did I tell you?' asked Satchell, with simple smugness.

This time the squad car kept on going south as North continued through gritted teeth to try to humour Warrington. But this apparent progress was illusory.

'*Driver, turn right at the next traffic lights and when you come to a traffic island, turn right and right again.*'

They were heading back to Putney again.

'*OK, I'm not playing your sick little game any more, Stephen. We need to find Cassie Booth. Think of your daughters, Stephen. Think what it must be like for any parent whose child is missing. Have you any idea of the pain you're causing? If you know where she is, then take me there. And if you don't then stop pissing about and tell me, now!*

Under this assault, Warrington had audibly wilted. All the strut and noise had gone out of him. He said something in a whisper which Walker did not catch.

'*All right, Warren,*' he heard North say loudly enough for Myles to hear. '*Please take us straight to Southfields police station, will you?*

Walker frowned. Warrington said something else he couldn't catch – something about his house and a migraine. He heard a rattle as Warrington agitated his handcuffs.

'*I don't want Susan or my daughters to see me in these. Can you take them off?*

'*Why should I do that, Stephen?*

'You shouldn't, Pat, you shouldn't!' Walker was warning. He said to Satchell, 'They might be going to his house, Satch. Pat's just asked him if the body's there. I think he said it is, but he's talking low. I can't hear him properly. Oh God! She's agreed to take the cuffs off him. Bad move, Pat.'

He heard her say, '*I'm only doing this because I trust you, Stephen. We trust each other, don't we?*

And to this Warrington said, '*Of course. Of course we do.*

They came to a level crossing in Barnes. The warning lights were already flashing but Myles's car sailed through just before the barrier came down. The pursuers were not so lucky. They could only watch helplessly as

199

Myles sped away into the distance. Then they had nothing to look at but the slowly moving train.

'Come on, come on!' shouted Walker in frustration, banging the dashboard with the flat of his hand.

But there was nothing he could do. This was a goods train, trundling endlessly past with its mixed rolling stock of hopper cars, tankers and flatbeds. Walker took the magnetic police car light out of the glove compartment, lowered his window and stuck it on the roof. Meanwhile he was listening to the transmission from Myles's vehicle, for clues as to its whereabouts.

The end of the train passed them at last, the barriers juddered and slowly lifted.

'Quick,' said Walker to Satchell, setting the light flashing. 'Warrington's house. You know where it is. They're there already. I can hear Pat talking to Myles outside the car. Warrington must be inside still.'

Satchell plunged down the accelerator, flinging the car this way and that to force a path through the traffic. For much of the journey he was hair-raisingly close to the right-hand pavement. Once he clashed wing-mirrors with an oncoming car. But ten minutes later they were flying along the leafy enclave of respectability that was The Gables.

Close to the Warrington house, Satchell slowed to a crawl. They could see Myles's car, with himself and North standing beside it looking up the road, obviously waiting for them. Suddenly they both saw the rear door of the squad car burst open, as Stephen Warrington hurled himself out. He cannoned into North and sent her staggering backwards. Then he took off through the gateway of his house. North and Myles looked at each other. It was every police officer's nightmare: their prisoner was on the loose, uncuffed and completely unpredictable.

CHAPTER 18

MONDAY, 19 APRIL, EVENING

JUST BEFORE Myles's car had left Embankment – biker, Walker and Satchell in pursuit – Walker had phoned Barrow to tell him to re-interview both Rebecca Wilding and Susan Warrington. He wanted to find out what they knew of the relationship between their husbands. Barrow sent Holgate and Ross to the Warrington house first.

The sound of piano practice could be heard coming through the living-room window as they mounted the steps and stood waiting for Ross's ring to be answered. Susan Warrington came to the door looking tired, but nicely turned out. She was of the school that did not, if possible, let major family disaster upset minor routines and appearances.

'Oh, it's you,' she said, glancing at Ross's warrant card. 'I don't suppose it's good news you bring, by any chance?'

'It's just a few more questions, I'm afraid, Mrs Warrington.'

She hesitated, about to make a remark, then thought better of it. Instead she said, 'Wait here one moment, would you?'

She carefully shut the door. A few seconds later the

hesitant arpeggios from the living-room stopped and there was a loud, resonant report as somebody dropped the keyboard lid. Then there were voices in the hall, which tailed away. Moments later Susan Warrington was back at the door.

'Please come in. I sent my daughter upstairs. She can finish her practice later.'

They filed into the living-room and the two officers sat on the sofa, while Susan Warrington moved nervously around, unable to compose herself.

'So, how can I help you this time?' she asked, lighting a cigarette.

'Well, a name has come up in connection with our inquiries,' began Ross.

'Inquiries?'

'The disappearance of a young girl – Cassie Booth.'

Susan smiled and nodded to show she was calm and in control.

'Yes. And you needed to eliminate men driving red Mondeos, as was my husband. Is it something else to do with the car, then?'

'In a way, Mrs Warrington. The name that cropped up is Karl Wilding. We wondered if it meant anything to you.'

She had taken just a couple of puffs of her cigarette before stubbing it out. Now she was at the mantelpiece, moving a piece of pottery a quarter of an inch to the right. She turned around.

'Wilding? No, we don't know anyone of that name.'

'What about his wife?' asked Holgate. 'Rebecca. Perhaps you've met her. They live quite close.'

Susan thought for a moment, then shook her head.

'No, I don't think so.'

'So you don't recognize the name Karl Wilding at all?'

'No.'

'Your husband never mentioned him? As an old friend, perhaps?'

She shook her head decisively.

'No, it doesn't ring any bells at all.'

'And if I may just show you a photograph, do you recognize this man?'

Ross produced a photograph of Wilding which Susan studied briefly. Then she shook her head again.

'No.'

Ross was getting nowhere and had no more questions to ask. He pushed himself up from the comfortable seat.

'OK, that's all. Thanks for your time, Mrs Warrington.'

He and Holgate ambled towards the living-room door but Susan Warrington had not finished with them. She said, her voice trembling and pitched low, 'By the way, I haven't told the girls yet, but you should probably know . . . I intend to divorce Stephen. I want nothing whatsoever to do with him any more. I don't even know where he is. I'm scared. He's very . . . unstable, you know?'

'There's no need to be scared,' said Ross. He flicked a glance at Holgate and continued. 'You do know your husband has been arrested?'

She put her hands to her face.

'Oh, my God. It's for Cassie Booth, isn't it?'

'Well, at this stage I can't reveal the details. But suffice to say, Mr Warrington is in safe custody at this moment in time.'

She showed them to the front door and they walked

down the steps and crunched across the gravel to the car. But before they could get in, to their complete astonishment, Stephen Warrington came running in at the gate, with a blanket around his shoulders and his eyes staring. He was even more disconcerted than they were. Seeing the two police officers, he veered off, plunging down the narrow alleyway at the side of the house which led into the garden. Ross looked at Holgate.

'That was Warrington! What—?'

'Go after him! I'll get on the radio,' she said.

'He's heading round to the back. Gwen, stay with Mrs Warrington!'

Ross took off down the side of the house and, before Holgate could reach her radio, the rest of the hue and cry came tearing in at the gate: first North and Myles on foot, then the car of Satchell and Walker and finally the 'dispatch rider'. Susan Warrington had opened the front door and was standing on the step.

'What's happened? What's happened?' she shouted, close to hysteria.

Holgate vaulted up the steps and took her inside.

'We'll stay in the house,' she said calmly. 'Your husband has escaped from custody and he has come back here. He's just run into the garden.'

'Oh my God, what's he going to do?'

Susan hurried through to the kitchen and locked the back door.

'I don't want him in here, at any cost.'

'Is there any other way into the house?' asked Holgate.

'No, that's it.'

Then she remembered her daughters and ran up the

stairs to check they were all right. Holgate crossed to the kitchen window and looked out. It was a substantial garden. She could see Walker and Satchell dodging in and out of some flowering currant bushes on the left, while Ross checked the garden shed. The motorbike officer was striding down towards the end of the garden on the right. Detective Inspector North was already at the garden's end.

North and Ross conferred briefly.

'The worst thing would be if he got hold of any of his family,' she was saying. 'I'm going to check there's no way he could have got into the house. Can you check out next door's garden?'

'Right!' said Ross, moving at speed to the lattice fence and jumping up on the spot to get a look over. He then raced along the fence to find a place to get through. Meanwhile, North started back to the house, past a clump of rhododendron next to the shed. Seconds later, she was on the ground, her legs crumpling under the weight of a man who had pounced on her from under the bushes. The smell of damp earth and dead leaves was in her mouth and nose as she was dragged by a pair of determined hands into the cover of the bushes. Stephen Warrington.

First he knelt on North's chest to knock the breath out of her. Then he stuffed the grey police blanket into her mouth to keep her quiet and tossed the rest of the blanket over her head. He was shaking with anger.

'You bitch! They were waiting for me. What have they been telling my wife? What have they told Susan?'

His knee was pressing on something small and solid under North's shirt. He put his hand in and felt the microphone. He grasped it and yanked until it came away. He flung it angrily aside.

'Nobody's going to hear you now, Pat! You *lied*, bitch.'

Walker, ranging around the garden, could see everyone except North. He doubled round to the front and pressed the door-bell. Holgate opened the door.

'Is Pat with you?' gasped Walker.

'No, Guv. She was outside.'

What had happened to her? And where was Warrington? Walker had assumed he would be legging it like hell, but he might have chosen another course. It was this second option that worried Walker.

'Where's Pat?' he asked Ross, who was emerging from the alley alongside the house, having failed to see Warrington in the next-door garden.

'She was headed for the house.'

'No,' repeated Holgate, shaking her head. 'It's been locked. Nobody's come in.'

Satchell appeared from the road, shaking his head. Walker beckoned him to follow and ran down beside the house back into the rear garden.

'Where the hell is she?' he said, crashing through the rhododendrons. Satchell followed more slowly, looking at the ground.

'Here, look at this!' he said.

He was holding up a wire and a small microphone.

'She must have come this way,' said Walker.

Behind the bushes was the garden wall, partly broken down and easy to scramble over. They did so, Walker almost immediately finding a woman's shoe.

'It's hers,' he said. 'Come on.'

This was a more orderly garden than Warrington's, with no possible long-term hiding places. The two AMIP men soon found themselves emerging at the front of number twenty, where Myles came up, holding a pair to the shoe Walker had found.

'I found this in the middle of the road, Guv.'

The microphone, the shoes. North would not have discarded them without a reason. To Walker it was clear the transmitter must have been taken from her by Warrington. The shoes she probably took off herself, to leave them clues.

'I think he's got her hostage, and they came this way,' said Walker, forcing himself to think his way out of incipient panic. 'They didn't run down the street because they'd have been seen – right?'

Myles nodded.

'If they'd gone any way down the street. There's a squad car at each end. They must have entered one of the other gardens. But which one?'

'The shoe was in the middle of the road, right? They must have crossed over without anyone spotting them. So now, we're searching on the other side, the odd-number houses, starting with nineteen and twenty-one. Look for anything she might have thrown down for our guidance.'

Five minutes later, Ross found North's transmitter unit, lying in the overgrown driveway of number twenty-one, the house which Warrington had called a brothel.

'Don't make a sound or I'll hit you with this spade.'

North was under the blanket still, but she felt the

hard steel of the spade prodding into her as she crouched in a mass of rotting leaves and sticks.

'Why are you doing this, Stephen? It'll only make things worse for you. I don't believe you killed Cassie and, if you let me go, we can sort this out together.'

It sounded pretty unconvincing to her ears, but it was worth a try. Anything was. Warrington was utterly irrational, so judgements about what would or wouldn't work with him were bound to be difficult. She crouched down, listening for his movements, too terrified herself to move. She tried to anticipate his intentions but her head was spinning too fast to allow her to think.

'You want Cassie's body?' she heard him say close to her ear. His voice was no longer snivelling but purposeful, as if issuing a challenge. 'Well, start digging, Pat! Right here in front of you.'

He pulled the blanket partly to one side and peered at her. She looked, as she felt, afraid. He smiled in satisfaction.

'Don't make me do this, Stephen.'

'Shut up and dig!' said Warrington, placing his foot on her back and pushing her down to the ground. 'With your hands. You won't have to go very deep. It's a shallow grave.'

She started to sweep aside the wet leaves and then to sink her hands into the soft wet soil, scooping it away to one side. At first it was easy enough, as Warrington had said it would be, but soon she began to encounter stones and broken bricks which broke her nails, and she feared somewhere below the surface broken glass waiting to slice into her fingers. But then she started to think about what she was digging for and she remembered the incident with the maggots in her office. The gorge rose in her throat and she started sweating.

'Dig faster, damn you,' hissed Warrington, who now sank to his knees next to her and started to scrabble at the ground with his own hands. Suddenly North froze. She had touched a piece of cotton material. She scooped round it and below it, trying not to move in towards the buried object which her hands sensed in the earth. But then, without warning, she came upon the unmistakable, cold texture of human flesh beneath her fingers. She recoiled with a horrified whimper and snatched back her mud-dyed hands. The white, limp shape of a small, decomposing hand protruded from the ground.

'I said I'd show you the body, didn't I, Pat?' crowed Warrington. 'Can you feel her? Yes, there she is, there! That's her hand.'

He put his hand on her back, forcing her down towards the buried corpse. She screamed once and then repeatedly, shuddering uncontrollably, moving her head from side to side. She stopped only when she heard Walker's voice calling from somewhere in this wilderness of a garden.

'Pat! You there? It's OK. Hold on, it's me. Just hold on.'

CHAPTER 19

WALKER WOKE up profoundly depressed and out of sorts. He had done his best to comfort North the evening before, holding her and giving her soup and sweet tea and holding her again, himself drinking whisky while she remained silent, thoughtful and withdrawn, except when she was weeping quietly. He knew they had all been cleverly manipulated by Warrington from the very first. None of them had even begun to take his measure, which had been their failure of judgement. But Walker had never known an operational cock-up – that was the only word he could use to describe what had happened yesterday – to hit him so hard where it mattered. The woman he loved was suffering because of it and no words of his seemed to make any difference.

After an emotionally exhausting (and supperless) evening, he'd lain awake in bed beside her. She had at last dozed off but the usual torturing, insomniac questions came to him from the darkness. How much of the cock-up was his fault? Should he ever have asked her to go with Warrington in the first place? Should he have warned – no, *ordered* – her never to remove the handcuffs?

These questions were no more comfortable or easily answered in the hungover morning light. Chief Superintendent Bradley had given North the day off, and detailed Vivien Watkins from Divisional CID to go over during the morning and, if necessary, keep quiet company with the traumatized Detective Inspector. Walker, on the other hand, knew his day ahead would be full of tension and upheaval.

But his first duty was to visit Cassie's mother and tell her the news. It was a duty he had performed he couldn't remember how many times. But he could never get used to it. Having Gwen Holgate with him helped, but only a little.

The Booth home was done out as a shrine to Cassie. There were prayers, poems, messages of sympathy, photographs, ribbons, soft toys and flowers everywhere. Mrs Booth, pale and drawn but extraordinarily calm, showed them in and Walker, refusing tea, told her in his usual stilted, awkward way that they had found a body which they were sure was her daughter Cassie. She had probably died on the same day on which she went missing. He couldn't give her any further information in advance of a post-mortem, except that two men were helping the police but no one had yet been charged.

'I expect to do that today, though. Mrs Booth, there's no easy way to tell someone all this. I'm sorry I've been so blunt. But you have my heartfelt condolences.'

'Thank you,' said Cassie's mother. 'I guess I've known for a while that I wouldn't be seeing her again.'

She sniffed and tears welled in her eyes.

'It'll be worse for Daniel, her father. He was very

211

shaken after he had to see that other girl. It gave him hope, you see, because it wasn't Cassie.'

Holgate stepped forward and put a hand on the woman's arm.

'Do you have anyone here with you, Mrs Booth?'

'No, I wanted to be on my own.'

She stood, shaking her head very slowly.

'You've been very kind. Everyone has. I wondered . . . I know you've been very busy, but . . .'

She turned and opened a drawer in a small cabinet-desk behind her, bringing out an envelope. It contained a pack of cardboard invitation cards held together with a rubber band. She handed one to Walker and on it he read Cassie's name, a date a few days hence and the address of her comprehensive.

'They're holding a service at the school,' said Mrs Booth. 'I suppose now it'll be a memorial. I'll understand if you can't.'

'I'll be there,' said Walker, gently touching her hand.

Wilding had been picked up from his home at nine in the morning and brought to Southfields. He had stormed at the police, denouncing them for what he called their strong-arm tactics and calling for his lawyer. Finally Derek Waugh of Clarence Clough, solicitors, showed up in the interview room, frowning with concern. He and his wife were bridge and golfing acquaintances of the Wildings,

'Derek!' roared Wilding, leaping to his feet. 'About bloody time.'

Waugh asked the officers in attendance for a private interview.

'Karl, I am very worried,' he said when they were alone. 'I have been told there is a very incriminating video recording.'

Wilding's jaw went slack.

'Video?' he asked. 'What are you talking about?'

'Security-camera footage from the car park at Barnes Lane swimming-pool, Karl. Taken on the morning Cassie Booth disappeared. Apparently you are on it.'

Wilding sat down, nonplussed.

Waugh said, 'I think this would be a good opportunity for you to speak to me openly and truthfully, Karl.'

Wilding closed his eyes and sat, leaning forward, as if he felt a heavy weight on his shoulders.

'Oh God! You have to believe me, Derek. I swear to you, I am totally and utterly innocent.'

Waugh adjusted his glasses and, with a deep sigh, sat down opposite his client and unscrewed his fountain-pen.

When Walker arrived in the Incident Room, he learned of everyone's concern about Pat North. Barrow especially found that his earlier, jocular approach to Walker's private life left a bad taste after what had happened yesterday.

'How's Pat, Guv?' he asked as soon as he saw Walker.

'She's OK. She's at home. Got a friend staying with her until I get back.'

He went to his desk and threw himself into his chair.

'OK. Mrs Warrington – what you got for me?'

'Susan Warrington was adamant she had never heard of Karl Wilding. Rebecca Wilding, whom we also spoke to when Wilding was out yesterday, was too blotto to be certain of anything.'

'Is Wilding here yet?'

'Yes. His solicitor's with him. Derek Waugh.'

'Oh, it's Waugh, is it? Excellent.'

Walker knew Waugh and didn't rate him too highly.

'Warrington's brief's here as well. Shall I go for him?'

Walker shook his head.

'No. He's mine.'

'Well, shall I take Wilding?'

But Barrow was disappointed.

'No,' said Walker. 'You're with me.'

At this point, Satchell breezed in and Walker's face brightened visibly.

'Satch! We all set?'

'Ready when you are.'

Here we go, thought Barrow. It was to be the Old Firm in action again.

'Right,' said Walker. 'You go for Wilding. Take Dawes in with you, as he did the surveillance. I'm saving Warrington for myself.'

Barrow was secretly disgusted. Satchell had just walked in on the case. It was he, Barrow, who'd been here since the start and he felt it entitled him to take the leading part in interviewing at least one of the suspects. He thought Walker's decision almost amounted to nepotism. Everybody knew that Walker and Satchell had worked together for years. But Barrow was a career policeman, a professional, and he knew that he was lucky to have been coopted on to the investigation in the first place. So he kept his thoughts to himself.

Satchell bustled out to find Dawes and have a last flip

through Wilding's case file. Walker tapped Barrow on the shoulder.

'Before we get to it, send someone back to Mrs Wilding. At this hour her head might be clearer.'

'I wouldn't count on it.'

'Worth a try, though. Having her husband arrested might have sobered her up, you never know.'

Warrington sat beside Napier in the interview room, looking subdued after his exertions of the previous evening. Walker and Barrow had introduced themselves to the video-recording equipment and Walker commenced the interrogation with a broad, open-ended question.

'Tell me what you did, please, on the morning of the sixth of April.'

Warrington nodded. He spoke quickly but, at this stage, in a quiet voice.

'I went to Barnes Lane swimming-pool on the sixth of April. Karl wanted to borrow my car. I said yes. He said it would be just for a short time and he couldn't use his own car for some reason.'

'So you did what?'

'I waited at the swimming-pool until he called me on my mobile to say my car was back.'

'You do mean the Mondeo?'

'Yes, the Mondeo, of course.'

'Whereabouts did you wait?'

'Round the corner from the lifts. I tried to read a paper but couldn't concentrate.'

'How long were you waiting?'

'It seemed like for ever but I guess about forty minutes.'

'You talk to anyone in that time?'

'Not that I remember. There's hardly anyone around at that time of the morning.'

'So what happened when you got the call from Wilding?'

Warrington was sitting slumped forward, his elbows on his knees, not looking at Walker but at the floor.

'I went out and met him in the car park. He said I had to help him.'

Warrington's voice was quavering now.

'He said I had to . . . Oh God! The body was in the boot of the car.'

'What did you do next?'

'I drove down to the river. I was going to throw her into the water but the tide was too far out, so I had to put her back in the car. That was when I purposely decided to leave her jacket and shoes in Karl's boat-house. So you'd be forced to question him.'

'How did you get into the locked boathouse?'

'I still had a key, from when I use to work for him.'

Walker looked across at Barrow, surprised. Wilding and Warrington had worked together, but neither of the wives knew about the relationship. That made it a strange sort of friendship – and perhaps a conspiratorial one.

Warrington looked up now, his head suddenly twisting sideways in the tic-like action that often seized him at moments of strain.

'I did not kill Cassie Booth, Detective Superintendent. I didn't!'

*

Meanwhile, Wilding was unfolding to Satchell and Dawes his own version of the events on that morning.

'I had a call from Stephen at about seven thirty.'

'Where were you when this call came through?'

Wilding waved his hand apologetically.

'I'm sorry, at home, with my wife. Stephen sounded slightly hysterical and said he needed to see me urgently. So I met him at the swimming-pool at Barnes Lane. He said he'd done something terrible and then he opened the boot of his car.'

He shaded his eyes from their view for a moment.

'Oh, dear God! The girl wasn't moving and, ah . . . I'm sorry . . . well, I asked if she was dead and . . . then I said I wouldn't have anything to do with it. I was in a state of total shock.'

Satchell nodded.

'Understandably. So why didn't you tell us this when we spoke to you earlier? Or even before that, when the case was so widely publicized you can hardly have failed to hear about it.'

'Well, it was unforgivable and I am deeply ashamed. But I admit, I am a weak man, very weak. I had helped Stephen a long time ago, you see. Fifteen years ago. Perhaps – and the more I think about it, it is still unacceptable, but maybe understandable – because back then I looked on him as a son.'

He produced a handkerchief and wiped his eyes.

'I did nothing, Detective Sergeant, because I was afraid. You see, I had once lied under oath to protect him.'

Walker asked Warrington how he had got to know Karl Wilding.

'I started working at Wilding's factory in nineteen eighty-four. Wilding made me head sales manager and gave me my own car. He'd buy me nice suits and silk shirts. He became, well, the father I had never had. He encouraged me to . . .'

There was a pause which Walker allowed to endure for five, ten seconds.

'Encouraged you to do what, Stephen?'

Warrington swallowed. His voice was husky now and the vowels were gradually flattening.

'Use my charm on the young girls. Persuade them to meet up with Wilding. He always employed a lot of young girls – as a matter of fact a lot of them were under age – at the factory.'

'Why was that?'

'Well, it's obvious isn't it? But I never touched them.'

'You didn't like these girls?'

Warrington's answer was given from a mouth distorted in disgust.

'No. They all reminded me of my mother. They smelt of body odour, cheap perfume and fag ash.'

'What did Karl Wilding do with these girls?'

Warrington snorted bitterly.

'Karl could do what he wanted. Have sex with them, then pay them off. But Heather Richards was different. She wanted more money.'

Barrow and Napier simultaneously noted down the name: *Heather Richards*.

'Go on,' said Walker. 'What happened with Heather Richards?'

'He sent me to warn her off. But she got dead nasty and that was why I . . . beat her up, see? It went to court but I was found not guilty of assault. She . . . she killed herself when she heard the verdict. I left the company, Wilding and the whole sordid business behind me.'

'So then fifteen years later you have a completely new life. Why did you allow Wilding back into it?'

Warrington looked up at Walker now. There were traces of the East End in his voice now. The well-spoken carapace of his respectability had begun to crack and the old Stephen Warrington was showing through.

'Because I was afraid if I didn't he would destroy it, right? I bumped into him again at some function my father-in-law was hosting.'

'When was that?'

'A couple of months ago. He said he wanted to borrow a car – my car, the Mondeo.'

'How many times did he borrow it?'

'Oh, four or five. He said he couldn't use his, as he had frightened some boy that he mistook for Cassie Booth. He was scared his wife would find out he was having an affair.'

Walker raised his eyebrows.

'An affair? Cassie Booth was only just fifteen, and very naïve. Are you saying she *agreed* to meetings with Wilding?'

'I didn't know her name then. I didn't know who he was seeing and, to be honest, I was too scared to ask.'

'Why was that?'

'I knew she'd be under age.'

'And that bothered you?'

'Of course! I have two young daughters. Can you imagine what Susan would have thought – or her father – if they knew I'd been mixed up with someone like this?'

*

219

'How did you get to the swimming-pool?' asked Satchell.

Wilding had blown his nose and composed himself but he was still emotional, his voice trembling a little. He was speaking very slowly and hesitantly.

'I took my wife's car. I suspected something . . . had an intuitive feeling that something was wrong . . .'

'*Wrong?*' exclaimed Satchell. 'Being shown a lifeless body in the boot of a car!'

'But Stephen said it was accidental. She'd suffocated when he'd tried to stop her screaming.'

A visible tremor ran through his body. He took off his glasses.

'I never touched her. I swear before God, I'm innocent.' He had raised his voice to make this declaration. He was sweating. 'Stephen Warrington is insane, you can see that. He's also a dangerous liar. He's very dangerous. I'm deeply sorry for not reporting this, deeply sorry. May God forgive me for being so weak, but I was just afraid of getting involved.'

Chapter 20

WALKER WAS surprised to find how eager Warrington was to talk about Heather Richards. During a short break he had asked for confirmation of the details from the police computer and they checked out. Under Warrington's real name, McClaren, he had been tried for assault. Wilding's evidence at the time had been decisive in exonerating him.

Napier was concerned about the amount of information his client was volunteering.

'Stephen, please wait for specific questions to be put to you before you make any admissions—'

Warrington suddenly stood up and turned sharply to his brief.

'Keep out of this, Napier.'

He turned back to Walker, but he was speaking also for the record, like a man back in the dock.

'I *do* admit it: I did it. I know it was a terrible thing but, right now, in front of you, Detective Superintendent Walker, I admit I assaulted Heather Richards and I should have been punished.'

'Please sit down,' said Walker wearily. 'I appreciate your honesty, Stephen, but what you did all those years ago is not directly connected with the murder of Cassie Booth.'

'Of course it is!'

Warrington did not sit down. He leaned forward towards Walker, growing red in the face and raising his voice.

'It proves without doubt that Karl Wilding is a liar. He knew I'd attacked Heather Richards. I should have been punished. But he lied under oath to get me off! Are you STUPID? Haven't you pieced it together yet? He knew I'd done it because he bloody WATCHED!'

It was Holgate who had gone over to interview Mrs Wilding. Around mid-morning she phoned in her preliminary report, which Walker received in the corridor outside the interview room with intense gratification.

'Good, good, good!' he told her.

Satchell interrupted him, after suspending his own interview with Wilding. He was looking pained.

'I had Wilding crying all over the place,' Satchell told him, shaking his head.

'I could weep! Holgate's just called in,' Walker said, waggling his mobile phone. 'She's been interviewing Wilding's wife, who now admits she had a blackout on the morning Cassie Booth was abducted.'

'She was pissed as a newt when we saw her.'

Walker punched Satchell lightly on the shoulder.

'It means, you thick prat, that Wilding no longer has an alibi.'

'What?'

Walker nodded, brimming with satisfaction.

'That's not all. Warrington used to work for Wilding!'

'You're kidding.'

'But under a different name – Stephen McClaren.'

'Why did he change it then?'

'Some incident at work. But anyway, I'm certain they're in it together. And I'm getting that bastard Wilding in a line-up.'

'Oh? But isn't our eyewitness blind?'

'Tunnel vision, Satch, tunnel vision, which isn't exactly *blind* blind. It just means she has no peripheral vision. According to Gwen, she can see as clear as day in a small corridor directly ahead.'

Walker held his mobile to his eye as if it were a small telescope.

'Let's hope she can ID Karl Wilding in that little corridor. Well, I'm going for a fag. When I come back I want every one of those inept amateurs in the Incident Room.'

Satchell raised an ironical salute and clicked his heels.

'Aye, aye, Captain.'

Walker returned to the Incident Room and swallowed an aspirin with his coffee. The thought of Wilding in a line-up had done much to chase away his headache but this should deal with the residue.

Barrow was holding forth.

'I'm telling you guys, Warrington didn't do it. He's telling the truth. If you dig under what he's just spieled, he's actually admitting to quite a lot—'

'Yeah,' said Walker gruffly. 'Burying that little girl's body! Driving around all day with her in the boot of his flaming car. So don't give me all this bullshit about Warrington not being guilty.'

He shook a second aspirin into the palm of his hand and bumped it into his mouth.

'Those two bastards are in this together. I'm convinced of it. And they're both lying through their teeth, each trying to hang the blame solely on the other.'

He looked up as Holgate swept in with a clipboard.

'Hello, Gwen. What you got?'

'OK, I spoke to Mrs Greenway,' she said. 'And she's willing to come back in.'

'Good. Wilding's agreed to take part, so let's set it up.'

Ross said, 'I'll get on to Brixton ID suite, see if we can get a priority slot this afternoon.'

Barrow cleared his throat.

'Guv, you sure you want to risk her not picking him out?'

Walker turned on him bitingly.

'Got any better ideas, Barrow? Because with what we've got at the moment we sure as hell can't charge Wilding with murder.'

As a matter of fact, Barrow could think of several things they could do, such as a new house-to-house with Wilding's picture and another trawl of shops selling beanie toys. Anything putting Wilding in the driving seat of the Mondeo would be useful too. But with Walker in this mood, he thought it best to keep his counsel.

'We now know Warrington changed his name,' Walker was saying to the team, still with an edge of anger in his voice. 'No thanks to any of you. It would have been good if one, just *one* of you had dug around and found that out. But now that we've got the information, let's look for anything on Stephen McClaren as a possible sex offender – or any other kind of offender.'

Walker dragged himself home by eight thirty, exhausted but knowing he would have to face North and try to help her. Nor would he find sleep easy.

The ID parade with Mrs Greenway had gone remarkably well. She had picked Wilding out without much hesitation.

'Number five,' she had said, 'that's the man I saw driving past my gate. I'm sure of it.'

When Walker came in, he found Vivien Watkins watching television.

'She's in bed, asleep. Doctor's been, gave her some sort of tranquillizer. OK if I get off now?'

'Yes, you've been a great, great help, I can't tell you.'

'Don't mention it. I'm glad to be of use.'

North was in bed, curled asleep and breathing deeply. Walker simply sat in the chair smoking and watching her. He stayed that way for an hour, thinking of his own mistakes and how they had hurt her so badly. Suddenly she woke and saw him sitting in the lamplight.

'Oh, hi!'

She sat up in bed and rubbed her face.

'Whatever they gave me knocked me for six.'

She looked again and saw that his eyes were damp and red.

'Mike? You OK?'

Walker shook his head sorrowfully.

'Sweetheart, I'm sorry I put you through that. If I'd

had any idea . . . I've never felt so inadequate, so . . . scared. I mean, if anything had happened to you—'

'It didn't, I'm fine!'

She patted the bed.

'Come here. Tell me how it's going.'

Walker stubbed out his cigarette, stood up and loosened his tie. At this moment the phone rang.

'I'll get it,' she said.

She reached for the bedside phone.

'Yeah?'

She listened for a moment and replaced the receiver.

'That was your wife. I mean, I presume it was. She hung up. That's what she does. If I answer, she hangs up.'

Walker sighed.

'How long has this been going on?'

'Since we moved in. It's all right. It doesn't bother me.'

Walker reached in his pocket for the mobile.

'Well, it bothers me. I'll give that stupid cow a piece of my mind, so help me.'

'Just forget it, Mike. At least for tonight.'

Walker made for the bathroom.

'I'll call her anyway. It might be the kids.'

He ran the basin taps so North would not have to hear his conversation. Getting on to Lynn, he learned she had a plumbing crisis, a burst pipe. She wanted Walker to go over and sort it out. He refused point blank.

'Just turn the water off at the mains – you know where that is? – and then get a plumber in . . . OK then. Oh and Lynn, if you can't be adult enough to talk to Pat when she picks up the phone, use my mobile number, please!'

He disconnected, turned off the taps and now could hear a sobbing sound from the bedroom. She was clearly *not* fine, or even OK. He went back to her and tried to hold her but she fought him off, deeply shocked and disturbed.

'I keep feeling them crawling all over my face, in my hair, on my neck and then . . . I can feel the body and . . . I can't stop, I can't stop thinking about it . . . and that smell, that God-awful smell!'

'I know, I know . . .'

He reached for her more gently now and she yielded herself into his arms. He rocked her until gradually her racking sobs subsided.

'Shush now. Shush,' he said. 'Hey, if it makes you feel any better, I've charged Stephen Warrington *and* Karl Wilding. Not for abduction or making false statements or anything trivial. I've got them both for the murder of Cassie Booth. What do you think of that?'

She sniffed and smiled wanly.

'I think it's great, Mike. Put them away for me, will you? Promise me?'

He nodded his head.

'I promise, sweetheart.'

CHAPTER 21

SIX MONTHS later, after a summer of legal meetings, evidence gathering, disclosures to the other side and plenty of other paperwork, the trial of Karl Wilding and Stephen Warrington, jointly accused of killing Cassie Booth, opened at the Crown Court. It had been a long wait, not least for the defendants, but this period is about par for the preparations ahead of a murder trial. Walker, despite his monumental capacity for impatience, had had to learn to live with that over the years.

The secure van carrying the accused men was like a mobile battery farm. The prisoners were locked like chickens in narrow cages which lined both sides of the van. These compartments were dimly lit by small windows, their glass darkened and toughened to bullet-proof standard. Throughout the journey Warrington called out for attention but Wilding sat silent, his jaw set and his gaze fixed.

They brought Wilding out first, spiriting him quickly into the courthouse. Then it was Warrington's turn to be unlocked and ushered out.

'Come on, sunshine,' said a broad security guard, whose form filled the narrow aisle between the cages.

'Didn't anyone hear me?' asked Warrington plaintively. 'There's something I wanted to ask.'

They brought him handcuffed down the van steps. He stopped at the bottom and asked the burly guard, 'Would it be possible to find out if my wife's in court? Only I've asked her not to be, and—'

The guard pushed Warrington hard from behind to keep him moving, all the time looking around for trouble. Warrington had no choice but to trip along in front of him.

'There's no need to get rough,' he snapped. 'I'm simply asking you a question. Don't push me!'

The guard made no reply as he prodded the prisoner through the doors and into the court building.

Susan Warrington, severely chic in a grey suit and dark glasses, was in court along with George Ashby, her father. They met Pat North passing through the public entrance and she introduced Ashby, tall, white-haired and giving every appearance of considerable prosperity and respectability. North could at least understand why Warrington had felt the need to conceal his past. Later, Walker and Satchell watched Rebecca Wilding debouch from a chauffeur-driven Rolls and head up the courthouse steps. She, too, was carefully and expensively dressed. What was more, she was walking steadily up the steps.

'She's sober, by the look of her,' said Walker. 'You notice the chauffeur? I doubt if Wilding'll be using the Rolls again, not for a long time.'

'Don't count your chickens, Mike. Is Pat here?'

'Yes – that's her car over there.'

Because North had been led to the body by one of the accused she was a vital witness. Not, it must be said, a very willing one. The thought of reliving her ordeals, first with the dead dog and then the shallow grave, was not a comfortable one and Satchell knew it.

'How is she?' asked Satchell.

'Says she's fine – why do you ask?'

Satchell had seen North perform at meetings with the Crown Prosecution Service. And he had his own views.

' "Fine" – you know what that word means, or can mean? Fucked up, insecure, neurotic and emotional.'

'No!' snapped Walker. 'She's just infuriated by the way she's been compromised by difficult circumstances. That's *all* she's pissed off about, OK?'

'OK, if you say so! You think she'll be called today?'

'I doubt it – this should be a long trial.'

'Well, look over there,' said Satchell, nodding in the direction of a black taxi slowly disgorging Mrs Greenway and a woman friend. When the old lady had climbed out she unfolded a white cane and went tapping off with her friend towards the court.

'I hope to God they don't call her,' Satchell continued.

'Christ Almighty! Satch, see if you can get someone to coax that white stick out of her hand – without her toppling over as she climbs into the witness-box, of course!'

The court was crowded. Many of the participants had been here countless times before but for others, such as the Booths up in the public gallery, this darkly panelled cockpit of justice presented an impressive scene. The judge, in his full-bottomed eighteenth-century wig, sat under a large heraldic shield, to emphasize that within this room he was monarch of all he surveyed. The barristers and clerks, also in their wigs and robes, carried with them the aura of important figures, completely at ease in their own element, yet utterly focused on the proceedings at hand. Speaking for the Crown was Willis Fletcher QC, a large florid man in his forties who had considerably increased his reputation at the criminal bar since Walker had first run across him two or three years ago, when he had prosecuted the Michael Dunn case. The two accused had separate defence barristers. For Warrington there was Rupert Halliday, an eloquent silk who often charmed juries into seeing things his way in spite of a mass of contrary evidence, while for Wilding Waugh had taken the (for him) daring step of briefing a top woman barrister, Norma O'Sullivan. Walker had not seen this lawyer strut her stuff but she had a reputation for striking good looks and a dramatic manner in court.

The judge, however, Mr Justice Geoffrey Winfield, was a familiar face, having tried cases of Walker's before. He was known to be fair and Walker had no quarrel with him.

In the well of the court, while waiting for Winfield, Halliday looked across at Fletcher. There was an enormous mound of evidence bundles and files in front of him and Fletcher was searching through one file while directing his junior, Matt Biggadike, to consult another.

'Dear boy,' whispered Halliday to his own junior, Laurence Camplin, 'do keep a full note of the opening for me. It looks as if Fletcher is up to his usual theatrics. I doubt we'll get a word in before lunch.'

Camplin nodded.

'Mr Warrington *is* taking his medicine, isn't he? We've made sure of that, I hope.'

Again Camplin nodded, with a characteristic and rather irritating exaggeration of the gesture.

'Absolutely, Rupert. But I think he's worried about his wife being in the public gallery.'

'And is she?'

'Yes – look. Second row, grey suit.'

Susan Warrington was indeed present, as was her powerful, controlling father, sitting close to members of the Booth family and not far from Rebecca Wilding.

Halliday, having spent considerable time with his client, thought her husband could cope with the presence of Mrs Warrington as long as he kept taking the pills and concentrated on winning over the jury. He looked across at Wilding's brief, O'Sullivan, who was meticulously sharpening a row of wooden pencils. She laid them out in a neat row on the desk in front of her and sat back with a toss of her flame-red hair. She at least was ready to do battle.

The two accused men were put up in the dock together, but their body language, leaning apart and never looking at each other, suggested anything but togetherness. Then the choosing and swearing-in of the jury was completed smoothly and, just before eleven thirty, Fletcher was invited by Judge Winfield to begin.

'This case,' said Fletcher, after introducing himself and his junior, and mentioning the names of the two defence teams, 'is about the abduction and murder of Cassie Booth, aged just fifteen at the time of her death. That fact alone may generate in you understandable feelings of horror as the details of the case emerge through the evidence. But you must do your best to put emotions aside so that you can look at the evidence coolly and calmly. You will hear that Cassie was an ordinary schoolgirl, living with her mother in Southfields. She had an early-morning paper round, which she had been doing five days a week for eleven months, delivering newspapers all across the Southfields area.'

He looked slowly around the court and then consulted a sheet of A4 paper.

'By all accounts she would follow the same route. From the newsagent's in the High Street, starting about seven a.m. and delivering the last papers to Warren Road about an hour later, before cycling back to her home in Southfields. On the morning of April the sixth 1999, she collected the papers as usual and set off on her round wearing a red bomber jacket, jeans, white ankle socks and training shoes . . .'

Fletcher went on to summarize the events of that tragic morning, from the delivery to Mrs Greenway to her sighting of a maroon Ford Mondeo, a car which she had seen in the area before, whose driver she would later pick out at an identification parade as being the defendant Karl Wilding. He told the jury how Cassie had disappeared, leaving her bike outside Mrs Greenway's, and how the other defendant, Stephen Warrington, had eventually led police to where her body was buried in a shallow grave close to his house. At this point Mrs Booth in the gallery audibly sobbed. Sitting alongside, her ex-husband took her hand and gently squeezed.

When he wasn't outside breathing the autumnal air and smoking, Walker paced the corridors of the courthouse. At one point, on impulse, he went down to the witnesses' waiting area. North was there, sitting across the room from Mrs Greenway and her friend, reading a novel. She seemed composed enough but, through the glass door, Walker noticed her suddenly brush her skirt with her hand. There was nothing there, but that sweeping-off movement, and the way she rubbed her fingers together afterwards, suggested she'd imagined something alive and disgusting on her clothing. He'd seen her perform this action dozens of times in the last six months, especially at moments of tiredness or stress.

He went in anxiously. North had just got up to collect a drink from the water-cooler.

'Hi, Pat. You all right?'

'Bit hot in here. You needn't have come down, you know.'

'I think Fletcher's still going strong.'

Mrs Greenway was looking at him now. She said in a quavering voice, 'Don't they want me yet? I've been here since the start. I could have stayed home for lunch.'

'They'll come and get you as soon as you're required, Mrs Greenway,' he answered. 'I'm sure you will be called first.'

He turned back to North.

'You sure you're OK?'

'Yes. No need to monitor my every move, Mike. You make me feel nervous.'

'Whatever for? You've got nothing to worry about.'

'It's not you that's been compromised, is it?'

Walker couldn't quite see the logic of this remark.

'What?'

'Forget it,' said North. 'Just forget it.'

In court, Fletcher was acquainting the jury with Wilding's statement.

'Interviewed by the police, Karl Wilding claimed that he was preparing to fly to France on a business trip that morning, when he received a call from Warrington. A call asking him to come to meet him at the swimming-pool car park in Barnes Lane. There, he claimed, he found Warrington, a man whom he had known for a number of years, in a highly distressed state, telling him some story about a girl in the boot of his car. Upon seeing the dead girl, he decided he wanted nothing to do with the business and calmly flew off to France, leaving Stephen Warrington in effect, as he put it, to sort out his own mess. On his own account he seems to have spared little thought, you may think, for the lifeless girl in the boot of the car. The Crown says that this account is quite simply absurd and is wholly unbelievable.'

Susan Warrington listened to this with a welling sense of grief and despair. Now she overflowed and scrabbled for a Kleenex. Her father patted her hand but his face was strained and disconcerted. This was far worse even than he had feared.

Fletcher reached for another file and began to give an equally sceptical account of Warrington's side of the story – that he was telephoned by Wilding and asked to borrow his car, and that when Wilding returned the car at the swimming-pool it had the girl's body in it. Wilding then supposedly bullied and blackmailed Warrington into agreeing to dispose of the body, which he eventually did after planting some of Cassie's clothing in Wilding's boathouse, in the hope of incriminating him.

'But, members of the jury, the Crown will argue that this story too is a tissue of lies and half-truths and that Stephen Warrington and Karl Wilding had in fact made

235

common cause in the murder of young Cassie Booth; that, in short, they are *both* guilty of this abominable crime.'

During the lunch break, Wilding's brief Norma O'Sullivan visited him in his cell, accompanied by Derek Waugh.

'Well, Fletcher's finished his opening speech, thank God,' she said. 'Bit long-winded but don't get disheartened, Mr Wilding. You can never tell very much from an opening.'

Wilding was sitting in front of a plate of untouched food.

'Do you still think,' he asked, 'that I shouldn't give evidence?'

O'Sullivan sat down and stared at her client for a good ten seconds.

'Let's see how we get on, shall we?' she said at last. 'The difficulty is in not being able to anticipate what stunts Mr Warrington might pull if he gives evidence. So you may have to go into the box, but let's see if we can avoid it. As I told you, this will likely turn into a bit of a cut-throat trial, you and Warrington attacking each other while the Crown sits there twiddling its thumbs.

'Don't communicate in the dock with Warrington. I know it's difficult being seated so near him, but keep as much distance as you can. You've done brilliantly so far. Always remember the jury will be watching you – they always do. So whatever you do don't eyeball them. Just look down at your shoes. By the end of the day I want a detailed description of your toe-caps, right?'

Wilding nodded obediently.

'But would you please get my wife to leave?' he asked. 'I don't think she's doing me any good at all. And she'll no doubt have a liquid lunch.'

He sighed as O'Sullivan rose to leave, rapping on the door of the holding cell to be let out.

'I'll see what I can do.'

After O'Sullivan had gone off to robe for the afternoon session, Waugh stayed behind with his friend, looking extraordinarily uncomfortable. This was not least because, at every opportunity, Wilding had felt it necessary to repeat to him assurances of his innocence. He did so again now.

'I am innocent, Derek. I swear before God, I never touched that girl. This has all been a terrible nightmare.'

Waugh shook his head in sympathy, and stared towards the window. Clouds, heavy with unfallen rain, filled the glazed aperture. He lifted his wrist and studied his watch.

'I'll talk to Rebecca, Karl, if you like. I doubt Miss O'Sullivan will have the time.'

'Thanks, Derek,' said Wilding sincerely. 'I really do appreciate your staunch support.'

In the robing-room, Halliday and O'Sullivan stood next to each other at the mirror, adjusting their gowns and wigs.

'My boy's a little aggrieved,' remarked Halliday airily, 'that his former friend has dragged him into this mess. Especially since he was kind enough to lend him his car.'

Norma O'Sullivan tweaked her wig to the left and fixed it neatly with a hair-grip.

'Your boy should learn,' she said, 'to keep his trap – and for that matter his flies – shut.'

Halliday raised his eyebrows.

'Oh, oh! We're not going to fall out with each other, are we?'

His colleague bared her teeth at him in a mock scowl.

'We are?' said Halliday. 'Oh deary me!'

Fletcher appeared behind them with a half-eaten sandwich in one hand and a cup of coffee in the other. He exuded confidence.

'Excuse me for intruding on your private grief, but I feel the very least I can do is buy you each a coffee – bearing in mind all the hard work you'll be doing for me, slicing each other into small pieces. Mind you, it couldn't happen to a nicer pair . . . Black, with sugar, times two, then?'

He swept away again towards the cafeteria, humming a cheerful snatch from the Eton Boating Song.

'And we'll all swing together . . .'

'Overgrown schoolboy,' commented O'Sullivan. 'Clearly never left Eton! By the way, Rupert, did you see their star eyewitness being led in? Let's hope she can find the witness-box.'

'Ah!' said Halliday. 'She might not see left or right, but hold up a solitaire diamond in front of her and she can tell at a glance how many carats.'

O'Sullivan stepped back for one last look, straightening her gown.

'Aren't carrots supposed to improve eyesight, Rupert?'

Halliday shut his eyes and groaned, just as the door opened and one of the court ushers put her head into the robing-room.

'His Lordship's ready to return to court!' she called out.

*

Mrs Greenway had made a good job of answering the simple questions Fletcher put to her, but life in the witness-box became more uncomfortable under O'Sullivan's cross-examination.

'I *know* what I saw,' protested the old lady in the face of the barrister's barely concealed scepticism. 'Don't you try to tell me I was wrong, with all your fancy words. You wasn't even there. I know what I saw and I picked him out. Number five, that's what it was, number five.'

'Mrs Greenway, I believe you suffer from a medical condition.'

'My arthritis?'

'No. You have a problem with your eyesight, don't you?'

'Yes,' admitted the old woman, taken aback. 'But it depends what I'm looking at. I only have a certain amount of vision.'

In the press benches a young reporter, whose accreditation said he was representing *UK News*, was scribbling furiously. But suddenly he stopped and turned back a page, tapping his lip with his pencil.

'A certain amount of vision,' repeated O'Sullivan, looking meaningfully at the jury. 'In both eyes?'

'Yes, but I can see directly in front of me.'

'So if somebody were to walk past you from left to right . . .'

O'Sullivan walked her fingers through the air to demonstrate.

'. . . they are very blurred up until about *here*, is that right? Then you can see them clearly at *this* point, but they become blurred again *here*?'

'That's right,' said the witness.

'So you'd really only get a fleeting glimpse of some-one going past you; say, the driver of a car?'

'Oh no, I was looking straight at him and I followed him round as he drove past.'

She showed how she moved her head to keep a moving object in vision. Interested, the judge leaned forward on the bench.

'So you wouldn't have been distracted by things happening to the left or the right?' he enquired.

'Or above or below,' added Mrs Greenway, grate-fully. 'I see straight through the middle.'

She pointed suddenly towards the dock.

'And there he was! Stood at number five!'

John Foster, the pathologist, was put up next, giving evidence of the state of Cassie's body and of the cause of death – asphyxia, without any evidence of sexual assault.

'It was as if a pad of material, or possibly a hand, had been held over the victim's nose and mouth,' said Foster, looking his usual, appropriately cadaverous self. 'However, she did bleed extensively from a blow to the nose.'

'Is it likely that her attacker's clothing would have been blood-stained, then?' asked O'Sullivan.

'It is very likely that it would have been contaminated in some way, yes.'

And, when Walker took the stand, immediately after-wards, he was forced to admit that, although he had seized clothing belonging to both defendants, similar to what they appeared to be wearing on the security video, he had found no trace of blood in either case. It was his opinion that the actual clothes worn that day had been burned or otherwise disposed of.

Walker felt that, on the whole, his evidence had gone well. He had told of the phone tip-off, the discovery of Cassie's clothes in Wilding's boathouse, Wilding's first lying statement, Warrington's equally mendacious statements, the second phone tip-off, the claims Warrington made about knowing the burial site and the way in which the police had finally been led to the body. Finally he showed the security video to the court, with its incontrovertible evidence that a meeting had taken place at the Barnes Lane car park, that both men knew that Cassie's body was in the car. When asked about the purpose of the meeting, Walker said he believed the men had killed Cassie Booth together and that they were arguing the toss over which of them should dispose of the body.

He had not let either O'Sullivan or Halliday rattle him and left the witness-box reasonably pleased with himself.

Mrs Greenway was free to go, but a journalist who had been in court was anxious to buttonhole her first. As she was helped down the court steps towards a waiting taxi, he rushed up.

'Excuse me, Mrs Greenway. Press. How did you feel at the identification suite when you picked out the man accused of murdering Cassie Booth?'

He was ignored by the old woman and shooed away by her helper. As Mrs Greenway's taxi pulled away, the young journalist flagged down a second cab which took off in pursuit of the first.

The journalist's editor always wanted colour, a human-interest angle. It had dawned on him that there was a story to write about the ID suite, and how the proceedings there would have struck an old dear like Mrs Greenway. The two taxis pulled up eventually at her house and, after waiting a few minutes for Mrs Greenway to reach her door, the journalist and photographer pushed through her garden gate.

'Oh, Mrs Greenway, I wonder if I could have a few words? *UK News*. It won't take a second. I just wanted to ask—'

'You were at the court,' pointed out the old lady sharply. 'Did you follow me here?'

'That's right. So tell me, what *did* you feel like when you picked out Karl Wilding?'

Mrs Greenway smiled, remembering the scene.

'Oh, I went straight for number five. That's my number, you see. I'm a five–five girl, born on the fifth of May. I always go for number five – it's my lucky number.'

He blinked, not quite able to grasp what he had just been told. It seemed to him that this vital Crown witness had been under the impression that the identification procedure had been some kind of guessing game.

'I got it right too!' she crowed. 'That police officer told me I'd got it right after I picked him out. That's what I told them in court.'

The journalist winked at her.

'Bet you play five at bingo, do you?'

Mrs Greenway sniffed.

'I don't play bingo! But I always have it on my lottery ticket – every week.'

'Mrs Greenway, thanks so much. I can't tell you how

fantastic this interview has been,' he said in perfect truth, experiencing a wave of elation. He had a hell of a story, and it had all been based on a hunch he'd felt during Mrs Greenway's evidence.

Derek Waugh was considerably less pleased than Walker at the day's events. When he reached his Wimbledon home that night his wife, herself no mean criminal lawyer, asked how it had gone for Wilding in court.

'Not so great. That security video is a killer, it's completely incontrovertible and it restricts one's options so much. But, as a matter of fact, I was more disturbed by something that happened outside the court.'

'Oh? What was that?'

'I met Rebecca on the stairs. Earlier Karl had said he found her presence in court upsetting – at least I think that was what he meant when he said it wasn't doing him any good at all having her up there in the public gallery. I promised to speak to her about this, so, when I met her like that, I told her Karl would prefer it if she didn't come to the trial.'

'Was she blotto?'

'Possibly. But you often can't tell with alcoholics, can you? Anyway, what disturbed me so much was her reply when I said I was sorry to upset her. She said, "The only thing that'll upset me is if he gets away with it." Now, what – on top of everything else – am I to make of that? I mean, he gave me his word he was innocent!'

'You poor darling! I think you deserve a large Scotch, yes?'

'Oh, that would be very heaven, my sweet!'

CHAPTER 22

THE PROSECUTION case continued into the second day and in the robing-room the defence barristers were anxious to know if Detective Inspector North was to be called. Both Halliday and O'Sullivan felt that the bizarre nature of her involvement with Warrington might help their clients, but both were also aware that, depending on the breaks, North could equally well hurt their cause.

'I'm quite happy to stick her in the witness-box,' said Fletcher, 'for you two to scrap over. I'll call her as the last witness and just give you to her to cross-examine. I do so enjoy a little cut-throat every now and then.'

Halliday did not so much relish the prospect. He well knew of Norma O'Sullivan's combination of what he called 'feminine wiles and a kick like a mule'. In situations when two defendants were implicating each other – the so-called 'cut-throat' defence – their respective barristers effectively became prosecutors of the other, although with the ability to raise past criminal history, which even official prosecutors could not do. O'Sullivan, then, would be a formidable opponent.

'It'll all end in tears, you know,' he said, shaking his head woefully.

'Kleenex at five paces, Rupert?' she replied caustically. 'I can hardly wait.'

When Fletcher called North to the stand it was merely to ask a few unsensational questions about Warrington's behaviour prior to the finding of the body, and then about that event itself. He did not press her for any of the details. Norma O'Sullivan, on the other hand, when she rose to cross-examine, was determined to press every drop of Gothic horror out of North's story. In her judgement, the more lurid and deranged Warrington's behaviour could be made to appear, the more the jury would see him, and not her client, as the murderer.

'Detective Inspector North, you're not yourself attached to the murder squad, are you?'

North had slept with the help of sleeping-pills and she had convinced Walker that morning that she was fine and ready for the witness-stand.

'No,' she said. 'I work for the Vice Squad at Embankment police station.'

'And your connection with this case arose out of matters which at first appeared quite unconnected with the murder inquiry, did it not?'

'That is correct.'

O'Sullivan reminded North that she had had a number of contacts with Warrington and that she had become 'something of a confidante of his – perhaps an unwilling confidante?'

North was slightly nonplussed and, before she could formulate her answer to this suggestion, the barrister had already added, 'Would it be fair to say that Stephen

Warrington seemed to have chosen you as an audience, while he unburdened his soul?'

North shook her head, still at a loss.

'I don't quite know what you mean,' she said.

'Well, he involved you at a personal level in what he saw as his problems. Would that be fair?'

'Yes, he did.'

O'Sullivan enlarged on the way Warrington had pursued North, so that his actions took on increasingly the character of a stalker, following North into her private life and forcing her to attend to his problems.

'Indeed, once, I think, when you were with your own children at a restaurant. Is that right?'

'My partner's children.'

'I'm sorry – your partner's children. Let's go back to the beginning, may we, Detective Inspector? Your very first involvement with him was after he had complained to his local police station that he suspected a house across the road was being used as a brothel.'

'That's correct.'

'And was it being used as a brothel?'

'We questioned the occupants and were satisfied that it was not, no.'

O'Sullivan turned a page of her notes.

'Did Stephen Warrington enlist your support in another matter, this time when he was accused of exposing himself to children in the Oxshott area, "flashing", in common parlance?'

The question immediately created a brief flurry of whispered comment in the court. No prosecutor would dare bring up such a matter – but then O'Sullivan was not officially a prosecutor but a defence barrister trying to establish her client's innocence.

'He had no need of my support. The charges were dropped.'

'But Stephen Warrington believed you were responsible for the case collapsing, and told you so, did he not?'

'Yes, but it had nothing to do with me whatsoever.'

'Then later, he had the misfortune to be arrested again for the same offence, this time to a different group of schoolchildren near the Embankment tube station in central London. And that, too, turned out to be an unfortunate misunderstanding?'

North had paused. Where had Wilding's team got all this from? Thinking, she groped for a response and had to be prompted by the judge to answer the question.

'I understand that, again, he was not charged, but again I was not the officer involved in that incident.'

'Not involved.' O'Sullivan nodded. 'And at the restaurant, with your partner's children, I suppose there was no question of him exposing himself on that occasion?'

In a trice, Halliday was on his feet.

'Really, my Lord, that is a wholly improper question to put and my friend knows it.'

O'Sullivan smiled her withdrawal of the question and North tensed, gripping the rail of the witness-stand until her knuckles whitened as she waited for the next one.

'Did it appear to you from what you observed that Stephen Warrington had an unhealthy interest in children and, in particular, in young girls?'

Halliday was up once again.

'My Lord, that question is hardly more proper than the last.'

Winfield looked down over his glasses at the attractive, but miscreant, lawyer.

'Miss O'Sullivan, shall we get on? Within the rules, if you will.'

O'Sullivan's face was a mask of total innocence.

'Certainly, my Lord. I apologize. I'll put it another way, and perhaps less contentiously. Did you feel at all uncomfortable with Stephen Warrington being around your partner's children at the restaurant?'

'Well, I, er . . .'

'The meeting was clearly not made by prior arrangement, it was achieved by him following you. Stalking you.'

Halliday tried to protest but Winfield cut him short, merely nodding at O'Sullivan, who promised to move on.

'Yes, I think you've made your point,' said the judge.

In the corridor, Satchell sought out Walker. He couldn't understand how his boss could be so oblivious when Pat North was being ruthlessly used by Norma O'Sullivan. Impatiently, Walker told him not to worry.

'Can't you see what that bitch of a barrister is doing?' he said. 'She represents Wilding.'

'I know!' retorted Satchell. 'That's what I mean. She's setting Warrington up, it's obvious. Two cases of exposing himself to kids—'

'In a straight trial they would never have been able to bring up past cases to the court. She's making it look like Warrington's the bad guy. And Wilding's pure as the driven snow.'

Suddenly something else struck Satchell.

248

'You never told me Warrington met your kids. You also never told me how long Pat was dealing with him. Sending cases of wine? You were slow off the mark.'

'You're getting right in my face, Satch.'

'Well, I think you'd better save hers. Your lady's in *trouble* – and you can't bloody see it!'

Satchell spun around and went back into court. Walker had not been able to produce an answer to his Detective Sergeant's sally. Now he was left thinking maybe his friend was right.

Back in court, O'Sullivan was still putting North through her emotional mangle.

'There was one other incident that happened to you in the course of this inquiry, I believe. In connection with a plastic bag?'

North stared straight ahead. It was the moment she had been dreading. A part of her had believed she would be spared it. But in another compartment of her mind she knew it was inevitable that she would be made to relive those horrors of last April.

After a moment's silence, O'Sullivan prompted her.

'Would you tell the jury about this incident?'

North forced herself to attention.

'Yes, ah, Mr Warrington arrived at the station insisting he speak to me. He had a plastic carrier bag with him and . . .'

'What did he tell you the plastic bag contained?'

She longed to close her eyes and make the whole trial disappear. Or alternatively leap from the witness-stand and run out of court. But she had no alternative other than to follow wherever Miss O'Sullivan was taking her

– just as, six months ago, in the gardens near his house, she had had to follow Warrington.

'It contained the rotting body of a small dog,' she said.

'That was not my question. What did he *tell* you it contained?'

'He said it contained the head of Cassie Booth.'

From the public gallery there was a gasp followed immediately by a string of half-suppressed sobs from the distraught Mrs Booth.

'Did Mr Warrington say anything else about her?'

'Yes, he went on to say that he would admit to killing Cassie Booth if I agreed to help him stop his wife from beginning divorce proceedings. If I agreed, he would show me the rest of her. If I was nice to him.'

The crying and buzz of comment in the gallery increased and Winfield had to call for order. He then told O'Sullivan to continue.

'He said the bag contained Cassie Booth's head, and he'd tell you where the rest of her body was *if* you were nice to him? *If* you persuaded his wife to stop divorce proceedings, he would also admit to the murder of Cassie Booth?'

'That's right,' said North bleakly.

'But in fact the bag contained a dead dog?'

'Yes.'

'Could you describe it to the jury?'

North's mouth worked for a moment as her imagination pictured the revolting scene. She gave her answer in a feather-light voice, almost a whisper.

'It was in an advanced state . . . of putrefaction.'

'You mean it was crawling with maggots?'

'Yes.'

It was almost a whisper. She cleared her throat and tried again.

'Yes.'

'I'm sorry if this distresses you, but we do need to have the full picture, Detective Inspector. Stephen Warrington slammed this bag down on your desk and you ended up with maggots crawling all over you, in your hair, on your clothes?'

'Yes.'

'Like something from a horror film. And during this incident he called you a two-faced bitch?'

'Yes, he did.'

'Did he tell you how he came by a dog in this condition?'

'No, he didn't.'

'Did you know that the Warrington family pet had gone missing – a Jack Russell terrier called Peggy?'

At this point Warrington, who had been sitting in the dock continually biting his knuckles, could stand no more. He leapt to his feet.

'The dog got run over! It was a complete accident!'

Next to Warrington, as he listened to the judge's reproof of his co-defendant, Wilding sat impassively. He remembered that he must show the jury nothing which might prejudice them against him. Pretending to ignore Warrington's scene, he concentrated on the contemplation of his shoes.

'Detective Inspector,' went on the remorseless barrister, 'were you not ever concerned about Stephen Warrington's mental state?'

'It was not something for me to judge. But I

considered I was dealing with someone who was behaving in . . . who was behaving in a somewhat unstable manner.'

O'Sullivan paused now. She consulted her notes, and drew breath to launch another assault. But then, quite suddenly, she seemed to think better of it. She said only, 'Thank you very much, Detective Inspector.' And sat down.

North heaved a deep, almost sobbing breath and prepared to leave the stand. But then she saw Halliday rising and realized she had yet to face his cross-questioning.

In fact it was nothing like as difficult. Halliday was anxious mainly to dispel the impression that Warrington was a dangerous psycho. Instead he tried to paint a portrait of a loving husband who had got caught up in something beyond his control, and who took steps to help the police anonymously, such as making those two phone calls, to help the police track Cassie Booth's killer. It was only at the end of his questioning that he asked about Warrington's co-defendant.

'Did Mr Warrington ever mention Karl Wilding to you?'

'No, he did not.'

'He did not tell you of the meeting in the Barnes Lane swimming-pool car park?'

'No, he did not.'

'Do you know of any hold that Wilding had over him, something that might prevent him from openly—'

'My Lord!'

O'Sullivan was on her feet. Halliday, desperate to insert some few small shreds of credit into the jury's impression of his client, had gone far beyond what the witness could properly answer.

'Mr Halliday,' said Winfield sonorously, 'I cannot see how this witness can help you.'

Halliday bowed to the inevitable.

'No, my Lord. That is all I ask.'

And he sat down.

'Ten thirty in the morning, please, members of the jury,' ordained Winfield briskly, gathering up his papers and sweeping out of the court.

It was after one o'clock when Walker awoke, and the bed beside him was warm but empty. He rolled out of bed and wandered into the sitting-room.

North was sitting in the dark with a glass of brandy.

'I didn't hear you get up. You all right?'

'Stop asking me that. I just couldn't sleep.'

'Don't go to court tomorrow. Not if you don't feel up to it.'

'Stop telling me what to do.'

Walker stood in front of her and stretched out his arms.

'Stop making me feel so useless.'

She jerked her head up, as if suddenly brought to attention.

'Oh! I *am* sorry! Sorry for making *you* feel in any way useless!'

'Pat! I didn't mean it to sound like that. Hey, let me get you some hot chocolate, or . . .'

Realizing there was no hot chocolate, he searched his memory for something else the flat might have to offer in the middle of the night. He had no idea what he could do or say to make her feel better. In the end he asked, lamely, 'What *can* I get you?'

'Nothing. I don't want anything. Just leave me alone.'

Walker crossed back towards the door, but hesitated. He didn't want to leave her and it also felt important that he shouldn't. In the end he said simply, 'I'd like you to come back to bed.'

'No, I'll stay down here.'

Walker returned to her across the room. She was depressed, obviously. He couldn't leave her like this.

'You did nothing wrong, Pat. You held up like a Trojan in that box.'

North was shaking her head.

'We both did wrong, Mike. You should have arrested Wilding sooner.'

'It wasn't just Wilding. It was Warrington too. They both killed her!'

She lay back on the sofa, shutting her eyes.

'Oh, just leave me alone, Mike. Go back to bed.'

Anger sparked in him. She was pushing him away. Why? He couldn't fathom her mood. Well to hell with it.

'Good-night,' he said grimly, and left her alone.

CHAPTER 23

NORTH WAS not quite sure why she went to the court next day. Her evidence was finished but she felt her business with the trial was not, and she gravitated towards the Crown Court building as if in search of that ending.

As soon as she got there, at about ten o'clock, she knew it was a waste of time. She had plenty of things to do at the office and nothing to do here. The trial wasn't suddenly going to finish, and Walker would keep her informed of events each evening. Deciding to go to the office, she was just crossing the entrance hall when the office came to her, in the shape of Hutchens.

'Thought I'd find you here. Still giving evidence?'

She felt peculiarly glad to see him.

'No,' she said. 'Finished now. What's been going down at the Factory?'

He gave her a quick rundown of the previous day's developments in two or three ongoing cases, then suggested a coffee. As he brought it back, he noticed Walker approaching from the other direction.

'Hi,' he said to the Detective Superintendent, noddng his head towards North. 'Just came by to give the boss some developments.'

'Right!' said Walker.

He approached North and they exchanged a look, grimly, it seemed to Hutchens.

'See you later,' growled Walker, and headed off for the court.

Hutchens handed over the coffee.

'Suppose all this is putting quite a strain on you and— Sorry! None of my business.'

But North nodded, sadly.

'Yes, as a matter of fact it is a strain.'

Hutchens grinned.

'Well, you know what they say. Never mix work and pleasure.'

'Oh, please! You're a fine one to talk. How's your Nurse Emily, by the way?'

Hutchens looked around before answering, as if this was for her ears only.

'The good news is I finally got the leg over. But you're not going to believe this, though I thought you should know about it—'

'What? She asked for fifty quid?'

Hutchens sniggered briefly.

'No, but Warrington wasn't too far off the mark about her place being run as a brothel.'

'What? You serious?'

'Yeah – but it's for gay men! Alex, the mechanic. He swings both ways. Advertises for punters in local telephone booths. Does a roaring trade. So your pal Warrington wasn't lying. I put Jones on surveillance one night just to check it out: counted five punters, in and out, so to speak.'

North shook her head, musing.

'I'd sort of thought Warrington had been making all

those complaints to force us to look over the house. You know, find Cassie's body in the garden.'

Hutchens shrugged.

'Who knows?'

North tossed her empty coffee-cup into a bin and hitched her bag up her shoulder.

'Well, it sounds like I'd better get back to the station. I'm not really needed here. You coming?'

This was to be Stephen Warrington's day in court. In putting him in the witness-box, Halliday was adopting a high-risk strategy. He knew his client had charm. The man was, after all, a brilliant salesman. The question was, would he sell himself to the jury as someone perhaps misguided but essentially innocent, or as a dangerous lunatic?

Warrington remained calm at first, as Halliday led him through his version of events on the morning Cassie Booth died. But when it came to Halliday's questions about why he'd agreed to dispose of the body, he became riled and defensive.

'So whose idea was it that you should take the body and dispose of it. Was it yours?'

'No, I'm telling you, it was Karl. I just did what he told me to do.'

His voice was on the edge of shrillness by now and Halliday, sensing it, tried to slow things down.

'You just did what he told you to do . . . But we are not talking here about collecting groceries, or posting a letter. We are talking about something tragic, horrific.'

'Yes,' said Warrington in a lower voice. 'That is correct.'

'What did Wilding tell you he wanted to borrow your car for?'

'I didn't ask. I had some notion, obviously . . . I knew about his perversion.'

Halliday looked up from his notes.

'Oh? What perversion is that?'

But now, as if stung, Norma O'Sullivan was on her feet.

'My Lord!'

Winfield nodded and the question would have gone unpursued, had it not been for Stephen Warrington's sudden call from the dock, pointing directly at Wilding.

'Just ask him about his penchant for young girls.'

'I will,' said Halliday, looking round at O'Sullivan meaningfully. 'If I get the opportunity.'

Winfield was frowning deeply, moving his lips. He would have to put a stop to these outbursts. But he gave Halliday the chance to pick up the threads of his examination.

'You told us, did you not, that Karl Wilding called you on your mobile phone at the swimming-pool and asked you to meet him outside in the car park?'

'Yes, that's exactly it. I had driven my daughters to the swimming-pool, parked my car and left the keys in the ignition for him.'

'And when you met Wilding outside in the car park about forty minutes later, he did what?'

'He opened the boot of the car – my car – and showed me the body . . . Cassie Booth.'

'Showed you the body. Until that moment, had you ever seen Cassie Booth before?'

'Of course I hadn't!' said Warrington, growing testy again despite Halliday's stealthiness. 'Why don't you listen to me! I have said this repeatedly. He showed it me and ordered me to get rid of it.'

'Just like that? As if it was rubbish just to be got rid of? What did you think when you saw the body?'

'Well, I was in a terrible state of shock. I know I should have phoned the police, but he was very threatening.'

'Threatening?'

'Yes. He knew I had the girls with me.'

Halliday nodded, to show his complete understanding. But then he adopted a slightly puzzled frown.

'But I still want you to tell the jury what precisely made you agree to help Karl Wilding get rid of this body.'

Warrington looked down at his hands, tightly grasping the bar of the witness-box.

'I was scared,' he said simply. 'He said he would tell my father-in-law about . . . about something from my past.'

'So, in effect, he was blackmailing you?'

'To force me to get rid of the body for him – yes.'

'And the most important thing in your life is your family and your deep love for your wife?'

'Yes. I was terrified. I knew Susan would leave me if she ever found out about my past.'

'And you would have done anything to avoid your wife, your children and your father-in-law knowing. Even if it involved disposing of this body?'

Warrington let go of the bar and opened his hands wide.

'There was nothing I could do to bring her back to life.'

He pointed at Wilding.

'Not after what *he'd* done to her.'

Halliday collected his notes and took off his glasses.

'That's all I ask – could you wait there, please?'

'Mr Warrington!'

Norma O'Sullivan was on her feet.

'That is your name, isn't it?'

'Yes.'

'Not Mr McClaren?'

Warrington's eyes widened and, suddenly frightened, he looked round the court, at the police benches, the press, the public gallery. There was no sign of Susan or her father. He opened his mouth to speak but could make no sound.

'I think the jury might like to know,' went on the barrister, 'why you are now calling yourself Stephen Warrington, when you were christened Stephen McClaren.'

Warrington was clasping and unclasping his hands.

'If you must know, changing my name was *his* idea.'

Again he pointed to Wilding.

'He said it was easy to do and that I'd never be traced. He knew what he was saying, of course, because he did it himself.'

'I'm sorry, I don't follow you,' said O'Sullivan. 'Are you saying that Mr Wilding got your name changed for you?'

'No, that is not what I am saying at all. You are trying to put words in my mouth. Ask your client. He wasn't always Karl Wilding. He told me that he lived in South Africa for a while, way before we met, under the name of . . . Westerhouse, I think.'

Wilding looked shocked. He had long since lost interest in his toe-caps and had clapped his hands on to the dock hand-rail, leaning forward to stare intently at Warrington. Walker, on the police benches, jotted down the name Westerhouse on the back of an envelope. O'Sullivan was, for a moment, left speechless.

Warrington was pleased with the effect he was having. He looked around the court, with a sudden sense that he was in charge here, commanding the room.

'Didn't you know? I don't think the police know what they're doing half the time. How many times did I try to direct them to the body – the boathouse and the place where I'd buried the body?'

If his remarks had been calculated to annoy Walker, they had no effect. He had already left the court, armed with this new piece of dramatic information.

CHAPTER 24

WALKER WAS back at Southfields twenty minutes later. He had one name on his mind – Karl Westerhouse. And he had three questions he told his team to answer.

'One, I want to know when he changed his name. Two, why did he change it? And three, does he have a criminal record? Get on to it, everybody.'

Half an hour later, Walker finished a fruitless telephone call to the South African High Commission. The guy in charge of legal affairs was out. Then Barrow came up.

'Nothing come in yet from sunny Springbokland.'

Walker sat back in his chair.

'He just bloody came out with it. And, by the look on Wilding's face, it's got to mean something.'

'Maybe he just didn't like the name Westerhouse.'

'No, there's more to it than that. He's hiding something, or *from* something. Are we on to Interpol?'

'I'll check,' said Barrow.

He headed out but, turning round at the door, stopped to ask, 'Is Wilding going in the box?'

Walker shook his head.

'I don't know. But it looks like Warrington's going to be there for a while yet.'

Walker sighed deeply.

'He's really nuts, you know. Sometimes he acts like he's enjoying himself – at least when his wife's not in court. When she's there, he shrivels up, gets like a schoolkid.'

As Barrow chased off after the Interpol connection, Walker went to find Satchell.

'What you got, Satch?'

Satchell looked up gravely from his computer screen.

'There's a guy here on the Net from the African Wildlife Trust – he's accused of having sex with a mongoose. Could it be our man?'

'Shut up, fool. Ross, have you come up with anything?'

Ross was hanging on the phone.

'Not yet, Guv. How's Pat? She had quite a grilling yesterday, I hear.'

Walker waved his hand in a not-to-worry gesture.

'She's fine. Handled it well, but – well, she's still a bit jumpy . . .'

There was a loud bang as the door was flung open.

'Hey get this!'

It was Holgate, running in with a freshly received fax.

'There's an extradition request for a Karl Westerhuis – that's h-u-i-s. It was issued in Capetown and the charge is kidnapping!'

Walker snatched the fax and studied it.

'Right, it must be him. Somebody see if the prints check out. We don't want any more cock-ups.'

Walker had been too busy pursuing the Cape Town connection to find out what had happened in court. But there would be time enough, he felt sure. There was the fingerprint identification to settle and then he'd see Fletcher in the morning with the new evidence. In the meantime he went home hungry, in hope of his first square meal since the opening of the trial.

It was still only just after eight, but North was sitting in her bathrobe with a cup of tea, staring into space. She jumped when Walker banged into the flat.

'Pat! PAT! Oh, there you are!'

He tossed his coat savagely into a corner.

'Bloody Karl Wilding, a.k.a. Westerhuis. There's a warrant out for his arrest, Pat! Guess what for?'

North shook her head, looking blank.

'Attempted kidnapping and absconding, Cape Town, 1981. He tried to force a fourteen-year-old – listen to this, Pat – a fourteen-year-old newspaper delivery girl into his car!'

She looked up.

'What?'

'Can you believe it? Apprehended at the scene, but they reckon he left the country using a false name a few weeks later, before anything came to trial.'

He fell back into a chair.

'We're just dotting the 'i's now. First thing in the morning I'll show what we've got to the prosecuting counsel.'

'Is it admissible in court?'

'Well, if it isn't a "similar fact", I don't know what is. Bull's-eye! So, how come you weren't in court today?'

'Something came up at the station.'

'Well, I'm starving. What's for dinner?'

North shook her head, her face wan.

'Oh, I'm not hungry. Thought I'd have an early night.'

Walker looked concerned.

'You want me to make you something? Or I could go out – get in some Chinese.'

She looked at him, tired.

'I just said, I'm not hungry, Mike.'

'I just thought maybe you didn't feel like cooking.'

'No. I meant I'm not hungry.'

Walker jumped up and collected his coat.

'Fine. I'll get something at the pub.'

North sipped her tea, then said, almost in a whisper, 'If you're going to be late, don't wake me.'

Walker stood by the door, staring at her, his eyes narrowing as he tried to work this out. Then he walked out. North sighed deeply and laid her head back.

Five seconds later, with his hand on the front door latch, Walker knew he was doing the wrong thing. He turned and went back to her. He chucked his coat back into its usual corner.

'How long is this going to go on for?' he asked.

North still had her eyes shut.

'Mike, I'm just worn out.'

'Yes, well, I'm not exactly bright-eyed and bushy-tailed myself. But that's not what I'm talking about, and you know it.'

He sat down next to her, struggling to find the right words.

'There's this big . . . barrier between us. You think I can't feel it? I just don't know if I should put my arms around you, or have a bloody good row with you.'

She sighed again. She wanted out of this conversation.

'Try putting yourself in my shoes, just for one brief

moment. I was in that box for *hours*. I've had to go over every detail of what that sick bastard put me through.'

'You saying you're not used to it? How come *this* has got to you? Those other two cases we worked on, especially the last, were much worse.'

'Maybe I just haven't been a bloody victim before! Stephen Warrington frightened me. Understand what I'm saying? He frightened me, and all my training and everything's gone haywire. He *really* frightened me and this trial's bringing it all back. It just . . . won't go away.'

Walker turned and reached for her.

'Ah, sweetheart . . .'

She flinched away.

'*Don't* do that. Don't treat me like that wretched daughter of yours.'

Walker looked shocked.

'Hey, leave my kids out of this!'

'I've got to take responsibility for myself. I just feel . . . violated.'

'Ah, come on! It's not as if he raped you . . .'

No sooner had he said it than he saw her look of astonishment and hurt. Frantically, he backtracked.

'Sorry, Pat, I didn't mean that the way it came out. What I meant was—'

'He raped my mind – how's that?'

Her voice had gone very quiet. Walker answered in the same tone.

'That's very theatrical.'

She hunched her shoulders, then stood up and turned on him.

'And you are an egotistical son-of-a-BITCH!'

She had shouted the final word with all her strength.

'Oh, yeah?' said Walker, bristling. 'Why don't you

throw in uncaring? Better still, throw a punch at me. It'd maybe make you feel a whole lot better.'

Was he mocking her? Goading her? In responding as she did, she couldn't help herself.

'You think this is funny?'

'I don't think it's funny seeing you – of all people – like this.'

'Oh, I am so sorry. Maybe you should go back to your wife.'

He raised a finger. He didn't think *that* was funny.

'Don't push me too far.'

'Don't push *you*? You're unbelievable. Who's doing all the pushing here?'

She suddenly lunged at him with doubled fists, trying to throw a punch. He dodged out of the way but she grabbed a cushion and attacked him again, landing some blows on his head and shoulders. Walker, alarmed, pushed her aside, got up and bolted for the stairs. She chased him up them to the door of their bedroom, still trying to land blows with the cushion and shouting, 'You bastard! You selfish brute! You haven't the faintest fucking idea!'

Walker burst into their bedroom and landed on the bed, like a rugby player scoring a try. He rolled over and caught her as she launched herself on top of him, still trying to swing the cushion. She struggled to land another blow then, quite suddenly, the anger left her as quickly as it had come. She looked at Walker and he at her, both of them panting from the chase. He smiled. She felt the laughter reflex rising unstoppably inside her. Then they were both laughing, not exactly from joy but from relief that their anger had been purged. It was a moment to be enjoyed, anyway. They had not laughed

267

together for many months. She rolled on to her back and they lay side by side, abandoning themselves to it.

'Gotcha,' he said at last, reaching out his arms. 'Now come here, right here. Let me hold you. Come on.'

She slid across the bed to him and let herself be held.

'Let's talk it all out. I want to get every single one of those maggots that you still feel crawling all over you. We'll get them and stamp on the bastards.'

He stroked her hair.

'Nobody's ever going to frighten my girl again.'

She sniffed, her eyes watery.

'You big jessie,' she said.

'Yeah – but I love you!'

CHAPTER 25

H E COULDN'T remember how long it had been since he'd felt so happy and buoyant first thing in the morning. The reconciliation with Pat, when he'd begun to sense their relationship was coming unpeeled around the edges, had a sense of wonder and new discovery about it. And a full night's sleep had put a cap on it.

Walker called in at Southfields, picked up his copy of a fax that had come in overnight, and joined Satchell for the drive over to the Crown Court. He was whistling as he read it.

'You sound like a happy man,' Satchell told him.

'I am, Satch. And this fax makes me even happier. We've got the son-of-a-bitch now. Did you send prosecuting counsel a copy?'

'Yes, this morning. He should have it by now.'

Walker found Fletcher hurrying through the courthouse hall, on his way to the bar mess. He showed him the fax.

'If this isn't "similar facts", Mr Fletcher, I don't know what is.'

Fletcher smiled, but it was half-hearted.

'Oh yes, absolutely. But, as they say in the casino, *rien ne va plus.*'

What the hell was Fletcher on about?

'I don't follow,' said Walker.

'No more evidence after the jury have retired.'

He made a throat-slitting gesture.

'Schluss! Keep it for the retrial, if we get one. I'll be in the bar mess if you need me.'

Walker, who had had no idea the judge had even finished his summing up, was flabbergasted.

'Shit! Shit! Shit!' he said to Satchell. 'The only time you want a trial to drag on and it finishes behind your back in three days flat.'

There was noise on the stairs and they watched a group of barristers coming towards them, led by Halliday and O'Sullivan, with their juniors dancing attendance. Halliday was telling a profane joke involving a parrot and a crucifix, at which he laughed uproariously. O'Sullivan, an Irish Catholic, gave merely a polite smile as she led the group into the bar mess.

While a jury deliberates the court remains in session, but the actual courtroom is empty of all officials. Only the public are likely to remain in their places, for fear of losing them at the very climax of the drama, the announcement of the verdict.

Meanwhile, the judge waits in his chambers, amusing himself in whatever way he can, and the barristers relax in their mess. Sometimes there is a bridge four or even a poker school. Always there is loud talk and schoolboy humour: exactly what you would expect from a roomful of clever men and women whose substantial egos are jostling for breathing space.

Halliday was studying the day's racing card, with a view to having a substantial bet on one of the races at Newmarket.

'Biggadike passed on a good tip for the one thirty,' he told the room in a booming voice. 'Kieren Fallon on board, low in the weights and first time in blinkers. The name of the horse catches the imagination too: Head Case. Good description of your client, Norma.'

'And yours,' O'Sullivan retorted. 'I'll have ten each way. You think we'll still be here at one thirty?'

Halliday shook his head.

'I doubt it.'

Willis Fletcher came over to Halliday and O'Sullivan with a tabloid paper in his hands: *UK News*.

'We have major problems,' he announced, shaking the paper at them. 'Take a look at this, as given to me by Biggadike two minutes ago.'

Halliday pursed his lips.

'Don't tell me the horse has been scratched. We're all backing it.'

Instead of showing it to them, Fletcher opened the paper and read: '"*BLIND WITNESS IN IDENTITY PARADE BLUNDER* – quote: 'I always go for number five, it's my lucky number,' said Mrs Greenway."'

'What?' said O'Sullivan. 'Is that today's?'

'It is.'

Halliday waved a hand.

'The jury won't have read that. They looked like *Guardian* readers to a man at the beginning of the trial. A very high-minded lot.'

'Yes. But don't forget they've been listening to one of your closing speeches,' she teased. 'That's enough to rot anyone's soul. But this is trouble.'

O'Sullivan laughed, relishing the idea.

'Of course it is,' said Fletcher, more gravely. 'We have a problem. If this is actually what the old dear said, and meant, what price her ID? And spare a thought for poor Karl Wilding, who was quite randomly assigned place number five.'

'Good God,' said O'Sullivan. 'Does the stupid woman mean she'd have said number five whoever was standing in front of it?'

'It certainly reads like that,' admitted Fletcher.

'Oh my God, we'd better tell Winfield. He'll not be hugely impressed.'

O'Sullivan laughed.

'Assuming he didn't read the offending rag in his bath this morning. What'll he say? "Wouldn't have happened in my day, when we locked up juries in hotel rooms without access even to the *Times*." '

Halliday shook his head in mock-prophecy.

'This is going to be lashings of contempt of court and swingeing fines all round.'

'Not to mention huge fees for people other than us lot for defending the newspaper,' said O'Sullivan.

'We'd better let Winfield in on it, eh? What a stupid woman!'

'Good God!' exclaimed Halliday, clapping his palm to his forehead. 'I won't have time to get our bets on, unless I catch my clerk. Longer I leave it, the more the odds will shrink. It was twenty to one in the paper.'

But their progress up to Winfield's chambers was interrupted by the tannoy.

'ALL PARTIES IN WILDING AND WARRINGTON RETURN TO COURT ONE, PLEASE. ALL PARTIES TO COURT ONE.'

The jury was ready to come back.

'Why don't you have a Ladbroke's phone account?' asked O'Sullivan of Halliday, as they began to file out.

'Good God, no. Wife wouldn't allow it!'

Meanwhile, in Winfield's room, the judge was settling down to watch the first race from Newmarket on Channel 4. His clerk interrupted him.

'Counsel's in court, my Lord.'

'Already? Surprising how fast they move when you don't want them to, eh? Let me know when the defendants are up.'

In his holding cell, Stephen Warrington carefully combed his hair.

'God, I miss my home-cooked breakfasts. Always used to have them, you know. Bacon, eggs, sausage.'

He suddenly, spasmodically, shut his eyes.

'Oh please God! I didn't do it. I didn't do it.'

'Ready now, Mr Warrington?' called the security officer, waiting beside the door.

'I'm ready,' he said.

As, in a neighbouring cell, was Karl Westerhuis, alias Wilding. He had adjusted his tie, polished his wire-rimmed glasses and rubbed his shoes. Now he straightened his back, pushed his hair behind his ears and said, 'OK, Officer, let's get it over with.'

*

All murder trials build towards this moment, like a drama accelerating to its denouement. This is when the tension is greatest, when there is the most at stake, when extreme emotions of anger, terror, weeping and joy are released. No wonder the place is always packed: press benches jammed, public gallery filled. There is even sometimes pressure for space on the police benches, as officers connected with the case compete for the chance to be in at the kill.

Coming in to claim his place, Walker was surprised to see North already there. He slid along the bench, bumping up beside her. He said, out of the side of his mouth, 'You free for dinner tonight?'

'Might be,' she said.

She looked as he felt, refreshed and relieved. And, he thought, looking through newly smitten eyes, outstandingly attractive. She nudged him.

'Here he comes now.'

'Be upstanding,' ordered the usher, and Winfield made his entrance. Barristers and court officials bowed and he settled himself. Now Warrington and Wilding were put up, the former looking wild-eyed, the latter's face impossible to read. Nevertheless, every eye followed their arrival with a critical or at least assessing gaze. Only when Warrington looked up to catch her eye in the public gallery did Susan look sharply away.

'Counsel may have already been informed,' said Winfield, 'that the jury have indicated they have reached a verdict.'

The court usher slipped out to fetch the jury, who then filed in, looking down at their feet for the most part, as if feeling their exposure to public view after several hours of sequestration. When they were seated the clerk directed the defendants to stand before turning to the jury.

'Would the foreman of the jury please stand?'

Awkwardly, aware of every eye in the room boring into him, the jury foreman rose to his feet.

'Mr Foreman, please answer this question, yes or no. Have you reached verdicts in respect of both defendants, on which you all agree?'

'Yes,' said the foreman, nodding his head for emphasis.

'Do you find the defendant Karl Wilding guilty or not guilty of murder?'

'Not guilty.'

There was a mixture of gasps and murmurings around the court. Wilding closed his eyes, savouring the moment. Walker gritted his teeth: knowing what he knew, he was now certain that Wilding was the real killer.

'Do you find the defendant Stephen Warrington guilty or not guilty of murder?'

The foreman had been clearly aware of the drama which flowed into and from his pronouncement. He paused for one, two seconds, drew breath and said, 'Guilty.'

'Are those the verdicts of you all?'

'They are.'

The effect on Warrington was palpable, but he did not try to speak. He threw his head up and swayed forwards and backwards. Fearing he might faint, a security guard placed himself in a precautionary position behind him.

Walker scanned the court. Norma O'Sullivan was exultant, Halliday despondent. Fletcher seemed to strike a mood half-way between the two. The jurors were generally cheerful, perhaps relieved that it was over and thinking of the jobs and homes they could go back to, no longer having to think about the two men's lives and futures that were in their hands. The foreman was chatting to another juror. They were laughing together. The other juror's arms moved and the paper he had held clamped under his armpit fell to the ground. As he retrieved it, Walker saw that it was *UK News*, and it had fallen open at a story about a cock-up at a police identification suite. Walker would not know the meaning of this little scene until he got back to Southfields.

O'Sullivan saw the same thing, but she knew its significance already. She nudged Halliday.

'You see what I see – that juror's favourite reading matter?'

Fletcher, standing by, merely said, 'No, I'm far too short-sighted. By the way, that was a good tip of Biggadike's. Horse came in at twenty to one.'

Halliday shrugged philosophically.

'I didn't get the money on. Bugger it – lost all round today! Well, tomorrow's another one. Thank God.'

Outside the court, Walker and Satchell stood together, the former dragging sharply on a cigarette. They watched as Wilding came striding out, with his barrister. He warmly shook O'Sullivan's hand, sidestepped the corps of shouting journalists, and stepped into the chauffeur-driven Rolls-Royce which had drawn up on cue right in front of him.

'There he goes,' said Satchell.

'They got the wrong one,' said Walker blankly.

Going towards their car, they were joined by North. She looked shy and depressed. Walker put his arm around her shoulder.

'It's over, sweetheart. All over.'

She looked into his face, trying to summon all her reserves of brightness and optimism.

'Yeah, Mike. Let's hope so.'

POSTSCRIPT

AFTER THE trial, Karl Wilding sold his house in Barnes and moved to a larger home in Surrey. Wilding never made any statement to the press but always privately maintained that he was totally innocent of the death of Cassie Booth and pointed to the court's verdict as proof of this. He would say that he had misguidedly protected Stephen Warrington because, at one time, he had looked on him as a son.

Sentenced to life imprisonment, Stephen Warrington had high hopes of having his conviction overturned. He provided statements to his solicitor with certain details that had not emerged in the trial, saying that he knew Karl Wilding had been stalking Cassie Booth for many months as she did her newspaper round. Wilding had begun to befriend the girl, buying her small gifts such as the beanbag animals and using his wife's car. Then, after mistakenly approaching and frightening a fair-haired boy whom he thought was Cassie, Wilding asked to borrow Warrington's car. He threatened that if Warrington did not comply he would inform Susan Warrington, and her father George Ashby, of Stephen's criminal past. Warrington allowed Wilding to use his maroon Mondeo on certain mornings, usually during

Warrington's children's swimming lesson. Warrington accepted that he should have refused to cooperate but he was frightened of the threatened exposure, which might lead to the break-up of his marriage.

Warrington also detailed what Wilding had told him about Cassie. He had had no intention of harming her, he said, and her death had been an accident. She had screamed when touched and in trying to shut her up Wilding had made her nose bleed. He had tried then to cover her face and, in doing so, had clumsily suffocated the girl. As at his trial, Warrington admitted that, under the influence of Wilding's threats, he had driven the victim around in the boot of his car, seeking to dispose of the body for Wilding. Warrington insisted that he had played no part in the abduction and murder of Cassie and that his only crime was in disposing of the body. He admitted that he had tried to conceal the part he had played in the offence, though he had twice anonymously tried to direct the police to the body. It had been a time when his illness made him frantic, desperate and irrational. He had failed to drop the body in the river because of a low tide, so he had buried her in the garden of the house about which he had previously complained to the police. There was no logic in this decision but his mental state was precarious, as he had not been taking his medication. The High Court listened to Warrington's statements but was unimpressed. Leave to appeal was refused.

Susan Warrington divorced her husband and, three days later, he committed suicide in his cell. Warrington defended his innocence to the end, leaving a scrawled note addressed to his daughters, asking them to believe that his only crimes came from his fear of losing the family that he held so dear. The note ended: *This fear made me weak and foolish. What I did was unforgivable. I beg you to forgive me. Your loving father to the bitter end, Stephen Warrington.*

Although the Metropolitan Police acted on the Republic of South Africa's request to extradite Karl Westerhuis, alias Wilding, the extradition ultimately failed through lack of evidence.